2a

Guilty Pleasures

Lawrence Sanders

Guilty Pleasures

WHEELER
PUBLISHING, INC.
ROCKLAND, MA

★ AN AMERICAN COMPANY ★

Published in Large Print by arrangement with G.P. Putnam's Sons,
a member of Penguin Putnam Inc. in the United States and Canada.

Wheeler Large Print Book Series.

Set in 16 pt Plantin.

Library of Congress Cataloging-in-Publication Data

Sanders, Lawrence, 1920-
    Guilty pleasures / Lawrence Sanders.
        p. (large print) cm.(Wheeler large print book series)
    ISBN 1-56895-634-7 (hardcover)
    1. Publishers and publishing—Florida—Fiction. 2. Family—Florida—
Fiction. 3. Florida—Fiction 4. Detective and mystery stories. gsafd
5. Large type books.
I. Title. II. Series
[PS3569.A5125G85 1999]
813'.54—dc21
                                                                99-010599
                                                                CIP

FICTION
5/99

BOOK
1

1

THE DOUBLE TRAP

Orange clays whirled up against a sky as dead as pavement. Emmet Richard Folsby aimed, fired. A disk shattered. He swung, leading the second, fired again. The clay, unhit, sailed on and then curved to earth.

Folsby stood a moment, staring at his defeat. He turned to his daughter, trying a wry smile. Barbara Ann rose from the scorer's bench, snapped her shotgun closed. They traded places.

He watched her on the firing line. He was blighted by her beauty. Her posture and poise were regal. Her long blond hair was plaited in a French braid. Elegant. Then she assumed an idiosyncratic shooter's crouch: knees bent, shoulders hunched, torso thrust forward. Predatory.

"Pull," she said clearly.

He pressed the button. Twenty yards out on the range two orange disks soared aloft. Barbara aimed, fired, smashed the first, swiveled, fired, demolished the second. She straightened, turned to her father, held out a hand.

"Pay up," she demanded.

He took out his wallet, gave her a ten-dollar bill.

"I think I need a new gun," he said.

"I think you need new eyes," she said, then laughed and squeezed his arm.

He was aware she did it habitually: said something sharp (and sometimes hurtful) and immediately compensated with a laugh, a touch. First the bite, then the lick.

The pro came from the gun shop and took their Remingtons. "Congratulations on your graduation, Miss Barbara," he said.

She gave him a radiant smile, saw his eyes change, knew what he was thinking. "Thank you, Scotty," she said. "My four-year vacation from the realities of life is over. Now I've got to go to work."

"There's always a job here for you," he said and was bewildered by the Folsbys' laughter.

Barbara and her father walked out to his white Cadillac convertible.

"Scotty is an old goat," she said.

"Not so old," Emmet said. "Would you like to stop at the club for a drink?"

"No, thanks. I want to get home and work on my speech."

"Will I like it?"

"Do you have a choice?"

He lighted a cigarette before they left the range and headed for Copans Road. The air was sultry. There was a faint paradiddle of thunder coming from the Everglades.

"What are your plans for the evening?" her father asked.

"Dinner with Oliver Pendragon."

"I think he's in love with you, Barb."

"I know he is."

"You could do worse."

4

"Who?" she said. "Em, did you hear from Brett?"

"Around noon. He's flying to New York tomorrow morning. He'll meet us on campus."

"Sober, I hope."

"Barb, your brother doesn't drink that much."

"No? If he calls me Barbie one more time I'll cut his balls off."

"I've asked you not to talk like that."

"I know you have. When is he going back to Chicago?"

"Saturday night. We'll be able to have dinner before he leaves. The trade show ends on Tuesday."

They were heading eastward toward the sea. Traffic was light; tourists were gone; South Florida was slowing to a summer lethargy.

"The reason I asked about your plans," her father said, "is because the Judge asked to see you before we leave. Can you make it?"

"No problem. I'm going to dump Ollie by ten o'clock. Then I'll go over to see the Judge. He'll be awake, won't he?"

"Of course. He never goes to bed before midnight. I think he has a present for you."

"That's nice."

"He was delighted to hear you're summa cum laude."

"Brett got only a magna when he was graduated," she said, and he heard the gloat in her voice.

"Only?" Emmet said and laughed. "That

more rightly applies to me. I received only a gentleman's C and was lucky to get it."

They turned north on A1A, crossed the inlet, and were on the Hillsboro Mile. A short side road to the Folsby mansion cut through heavy foliage and then became a bricked driveway bordered with royal palms. Emmet drove into the four-car garage and they exited to inspect again his graduation gift to her: a brand-new pearlescent blue Corvette.

"I wish you had selected something more sedate," her father said. "This brute has too much power."

"Not for me," Barbara said, caressing the hood. "Not enough. Never enough."

"At least you could have waited a few months until the seventy-nines come out. But you have no patience."

"I wonder who I inherited that from," she said.

They paused on the porch before entering the house. They agreed Emmet would visit with Constance first. Then Barbara would take his place.

"Too many visitors at once confuse her," he said. "Your mother is suffering, Barbara."

The daughter cast down her eyes. "I can't endure it," she said in a low voice.

"She can," the father said.

2

GAMES AFOOT...

A ground floor chamber originally designed as Emmet's study had been converted to a sick-room when Constance Louise Folsby became seriously ill. A hospital bed was brought in, and a TV set, radio, and whatever personal belongings she needed to make her disability more bearable. A window air conditioner was installed to supplement the central system since coolness seemed to relieve her symptoms.

Emmet had hoped to find his wife alert and perhaps reading in her motorized wheel-chair. But when he entered, he saw she was in bed, eyes closed, a silk sheet drawn up to her chin. It was so chilly the daytime nurse's aide, seated in a corner armchair with a fashion magazine, was wearing a wool cardigan.

He stood at the bedside, relieved to see her breast rising and falling regularly. His golden hair had silvered with age; hers had become flaxen and thinner as the disease pro-gressed. He was glad she apparently slept; her doctor had emphasized the need for sleep, including naps.

Her skin had become almost translucent; he fancied he could see a veined network and the slow course of blood. Sometimes her eyes had a wet gloss as if she continually wept. Her vision had dimmed. On the night stand were two current bestsellers, unread: *The Women's Room* and *Looking Out for Number One*.

Constance's eyes opened, focused on him, recognized him. She smiled faintly. He pulled a straight chair to the bed, took up one of her hands lightly. It felt like crinkled parchment.

"How are you today, dear?" he asked.

She nodded. "Much better. Tip-top."

Same question, same answer. For how many yesterdays and how many tomorrows?

"What did you have for lunch?"

She thought a long moment. Then: "Chicken. White meat. And a fresh peach. Sliced."

"Sounds good. I heard from Brett this morning. He sends his love."

She brightened. "Is he enjoying Mexico?"

Emmet hesitated. He had asked her physician about her frequent memory lapses and occasional hallucinations. Should he correct her or accept her delusions without comment? Dr. Jacob Steiner was an excellent neurologist and a tough bastard. He had shrugged and said, "It's your call."

"Brett will be home next week," Folsby told his wife. "Probably by Wednesday."

"Mexico," she repeated. "Remember Acapulco?"

That at least was accurate. "Do I ever!" he said enthusiastically. "One of our most wonderful weeks."

"I think Barbara was conceived in Acapulco," she said, and the memory lived.

"Constance," he said, speaking slowly and hoping she understood, "Barbara and I are

8

flying to New York tomorrow morning and then going on to her college. Commencement starts at one o'clock. Barbara is to deliver the valedictory address. We're so sorry you won't be able to be there, but a video tape will be made of the entire ceremony so you'll be able to see the whole thing in about a week."

"That's nice," she said, obviously not recalling he had told her the same thing twice before. "Will Brett be there?"

"Naturally. He wouldn't miss an occasion like that."

She looked at him directly. "They love each other, don't they, Em? Barbara and Brett?"

"Of course they do," he said heartily and hoped she was convinced.

Barbara Ann came into the room. She had unbraided her hair; it cascaded to her waist. Her smile was a sunrise.

"Here's Barb!" Emmet said loudly. "And I have some phone calls to make. Darling, I'll stop by again before we leave tomorrow."

"Where are you going tomorrow?" she asked. He stifled a cry of dismay, kissed her soft cheek, and fled.

His desk, swivel chair, file cabinets, and bound copies of Folsby magazines had all been moved to the second floor and into what had formerly been his wife's bedroom. The pastel wallpaper and flowered drapes she had selected remained. Sometimes he imagined he caught a slight scent of her Chanel No. 5.

He sat at his desk and phoned the Folsby Press Building on Corporate Boulevard in

Boca Raton. He was put through to Mrs. Blanche Singer, his executive assistant. They spoke for almost thirty minutes. Emmet jotted notes on a scratch pad as she detailed his schedule.

"Blanche," he said when she concluded, "you've done a marvelous job and I thank you. I'm sure everything will go without a hitch. And by the way, there's no need for you to be at the airport tomorrow morning. I'm sure you have plans for the weekend."

"Oh, no, Mr. Folsby," she said. "I want to be there to congratulate Miss Barbara. What a gifted young woman she is!"

He laughed. "Thank you, but at the moment she has more gifts than she can use. See you tomorrow morning, then. And thank you again."

He was reviewing his scrawled notes when Barbara Ann entered without knocking. She sprawled in a leather armchair alongside his desk and let her hair hang down the back of the chair.

"Well?" her father asked. "What do you think of her condition?"

"Spacey."

"What did you talk about?"

"Mostly I thanked her for the European trip. Gracie McCall wanted to phone her thanks, but I told her a letter would be better."

"Of course it would. When are you and Gracie leaving?"

"After July Fourth. For about three weeks. England, France, and Italy. We'll be back late July. Europe is dead in August. Em, I've got to work on my speech." She rose, moved to the door, paused, and turned. "Where are we staying in New York?"

"Blanche Singer got us a two-bedroom suite at The Plaza."

"Two bedrooms?" She looked at him with cool, appraisive eyes. "We must remember to muss the other bed."

Sometimes he was amused by her brazenness. Sometimes it alarmed him.

"You think of everything," he said.

"Yes," she said, "I do."

3

AT FIRST SIGHT...

"Did anyone ever tell you how beautiful you are?" Oliver Pendragon asked Barbara Folsby.

He was, she decided, the most socially inept man she had ever met. E.g.: his silly touchiness about his surname. Acquaintances persisted in calling him "Pen-dragon" despite his pedantic insistence it be pronounced "Pendragon."

And if he thought his given name made people recall Oliver Wendell Holmes he was mistaken; they recalled Oliver Hardy. The diminutive was even worse; Barbara had once told him "Ollie" sounded like a sandwich spread.

She had additional carps she had no hesitation in voicing. He dressed like a mortician—but what self-respecting undertaker would wear a plastic pocket protector jammed with ballpoint pens? Then there was his mustache which, on his round, fleshy face, looked like a toothbrush glued to a large honeydew melon.

But Barbara found his manner more offputting than his appearance. He was so solemn, so mirthless and pontifical, she could not believe he was a dynamite microbiologist with a brilliant career predicted. Ollie a genius? That quintessence of dullness?

"How do you *stand* him?" Gracie McCall had demanded. "The man is a *yuck*. A roly-poly yuck."

Barbara explained Oliver's love for her was like an untouched savings account squirreled away. You might invest in stocks, bonds, and all sorts of speculative ventures. But you knew in case of bad luck, a disappointing return, or even a financial calamity, there was always your passbook to fall back on.

His question about her beauty was asked as they sipped kir aperitifs at dinner. The restaurant was on the Intracoastal Waterway in Fort Lauderdale. They sat at wide windows and could watch yachts moving northward for the summer.

Had anyone told her how beautiful she was? She was tempted to reply, "Why no, Ollie; no one has ever mentioned it." But irony would be wasted on him. Or she could tell the truth: There had been scads of admirers—including all those sappy youths from Harvard, Yale, and Princeton, the randy studs she and Gracie called Bone Jumpers.

And there were the hundreds of strangers she had encountered who looked at her longingly, eyeballs awash in lust. Susan Rudnick, a classmate and premed major, termed it the Testosterone Stare. Barbara had learned as a Girl Scout to avoid direct eye contact with passersby. Male passersby.

She merely murmured, "Thank you, Ollie. You're very kind."

She was saved from spluttered compliments on her hair, lips, complexion, bosom, and bare legs by the arrival of their escargots swimming in butter and garlic. But he returned to the subject of their relationship when the salad was served.

"Do you remember when we met?" he said eagerly. "I do. At the McCalls' Christmas party. It was love at first sight."

She remembered very well. He had dropped a wedge of pizza on her white silk slacks.

The chateaubriand was brought and sliced at their table. Bordeaux was served. Barbara had selected the vintage since Ollie was more familiar with Diet Coke and Gatorade.

"I realize I'm thirty-four and you're only twenty-two," he said, his mouth full. "But there's not all that much difference between us, is there?"

"Not in years," she said, and he missed it completely as she knew he would.

"Do I have a chance?" he pleaded.

"Ollie, I'm not ready to make a commitment," she said, a line she had used so often with so many men it had become a mantra.

"You're not against marriage, are you?"

She wanted to say, "Only to you," but she said, "At the moment, all I want is to get a job and go to work. Tell me about your work, Ollie. What are you doing now?"

"Investigating the genetic origins of breast cancer."

"You mean it can be inherited?"

"Possibly. Or a predisposition can. Other causative factors such as diet, environment, and so forth may be involved."

"My mother has multiple sclerosis. Could I inherit it?"

"I know little about MS. What do her doctors say?"

"Everything is being done that can be done. And there is no known cure."

"Well then?" he said, uninterested in her mother's illness or her concern. "Let's have dessert. You pick out something nice."

She ordered plums in brandy.

"Yum," he said after tasting. "I hired a new girl this week and her name is Plummer. Isn't that a coincidence?"

"She's six years old?" Barbara asked.

He didn't get it. "Six? Why no, she's twenty-five."

"Then she's a woman, not a girl, isn't she?"

"Oh," he said. "Well. Sure. Zoe's a whiz in the lab. Her slides are even better than mine."

They finished. Oliver paid the bill with

14

cash and left a mingy tip. When he went to the men's room Barbara slipped back to their table and gave the old waiter an additional ten.

"Thank you, miss," he said gratefully. "May I say you look beautiful tonight."

She was pleased. She was wearing a loose sheath of creamy gray cashmere with a cloche of pale blue velvet. She knew bright colors and frippery made her appear tarty. She wore Halston for his pure elegance of line, more art than fashion. And cloches accentuated her high cheekbones, full lips, assertive chin.

They waited outside while Pendragon's black 1967 Volkswagen Beetle was brought around. "Don't see many cars like this," the parking valet said.

"Only in museums," Barbara said, and when she saw Oliver's wounded look she gave him a dazzling smile and patted his fat cheek.

They drove home and stopped in front of the Folsby manse. She let him kiss her. He didn't do it well.

"Thank you for a super dinner, Ollie."

"I have something for you," he said. "A graduation present."

He fished in his jacket pocket, handed her a small tissue-wrapped packet. She opened it slowly, hoping it wasn't an engagement ring. It wasn't. It was a loose chain bracelet with two interlocking hearts of gold in the center.

"It's lovely," Barbara said and started to loop the fine chain around her wrist.

"No, no," Oliver said. "It goes on your ankle."

"A slave bracelet," Barbara said. "Just what I've always wanted. Thank you, Ollie. I'll think of you every time I wear it."

"Oh, Barbara," he said soulfully. "I love you so very, very much. I'll wait for you no matter how long it takes."

She watched his Volkswagen dwindle down the driveway. She had known beauty was power just as money was. Now she understood a difference: Money buys things; beauty buys people.

She unlocked the front door, walked along the tiled hallway toward the terrace facing the Atlantic Ocean. She passed the open kitchen door, looked in, and saw the cook and houseman seated at the butcher-block table playing checkers. They returned her wave.

She descended the terrace stairway to the sand and paused to remove her satin pumps. She could have gone out to the highway and headed north to the Judge's home, but it was easier and quicker to stroll along the beach.

But first she ran down to the water's edge, carrying her shoes in one hand. She halted and threw Oliver Pendragon's slave bracelet into the sea as far as she could fling it.

Ripples lapped gently, a perfumed breeze caressed, stars winked in a cloudless sky, the Man in the Moon smirked shamelessly: a scene that would have enchanted a poet or a romantic. Barbara Ann Folsby was neither.

4

JUDGE NOT...

Judge Seth Parnell Hampton, formerly associate judge of the U.S. Court of Appeal, First Circuit, owned one of the larger and more lush mansions on the Hillsboro Mile: three stories high, six bedrooms, library, billiard room, indoor swimming pool, exercise room, and wet and dry saunas.

Judge Hampton was seventy-two and divorced. His ex-wife Matilda was currently living in Honolulu with a young man who made paper leis for sale to tourists. The housekeeper and factotum of Hampton's residence was Sarah Demijohn, forty-eight. Her father had been black and her mother a full-blooded Chickasaw. Her husband—knifed to death in a Baltimore alley—had been Jamaican. Her son Noah, now fourteen, also lived in the Judge's house.

It was Sarah who answered Barbara's ring at the front door. She was wearing one of the Judge's old dress shirts, sleeves rolled up to her elbows, tails flapping over denim jeans. The two women embraced with cries of joy.

"Don't you look *choice*, honey!" Sarah said. "My oh my oh my! Pretty as a picture!"

"How *are* you, sweetie?" Barbara asked.

"So healthy and happy it scares me."

They stood with arms about each other's waist.

"How is the Judge?"

"Younger every day. And your folks?"

"Father is as bouncy as ever. Mother's not so good."

"Oh lordy, the poor woman. Pain?"

"Some. But mostly just weakness."

"I pray for her. And Brett?"

"He's okay, I guess. How's Noah?"

"Wonderful. He starts high school in the fall. Can you believe it? Time does fly. Right now he's asleep because he's starting a summer job tomorrow morning, caddying at the Boca club. The Judge arranged it. Let's go up now. He'll be so happy to see you."

But they paused a moment grinning at one another. Sarah had two extreme expressions: ecstatic happiness and doomful melancholy. She seemed to feel no other shades or gradations of emotion. Between glee and grief, impassivity set her broad, carved features.

They walked slowly up the wide staircase to the Judge's library and entered. He was seated at his desk reading a new translation of the *Odyssey* through half-moon glasses. When he saw Barbara his craggy face creased into a welcoming smile and he rose to his feet with the aid of a stout cane. The handle was an arched silver dolphin.

Barbara went forward to give him a soft hug and kiss his washboard cheek. He motioned both women to a green leather chesterfield and didn't sit down again until they were seated. He inquired about the well-being of the Folsby family and assured Barbara he was feeling uncommonly fit.

His face showed both ravagement and repair. He had previously worn his white hair cut *en brosse.* But when he was released from the hospital he had found it necessary to hire a barber to come to the house. The *peluquero,* a young Cuban, persuaded the Judge to have his hair "styled" rather than cut.

After almost three years of monthly stylings Hampton now had a head of thick white hair artfully coifed into heavy waves. Women said it made him look distinguished. Men didn't say anything.

"By this time tomorrow night you'll be an old grad," he said, still smiling at Barbara.

"That's right. I'll be happy when it's over."

"And I understand you're to deliver the valedictory address. Congratulations!"

"Condolences would be more suitable."

"Oh-oh, that sounds like trouble. With the speech?"

She nodded. "I wanted it to be something special. But it's just pedestrian."

"How much time do you have?"

"They've given me fifteen minutes."

"Plenty. Remember, Lincoln needed only two minutes at Gettysburg. My professor of rhetoric at Harvard said anything over twenty minutes is wasted. People stop listening. What is the subject of your address?"

"The first half is the usual boilerplate: alma mater forever, new friends everlasting, courage and ambition, remake the world, blah, blah, blah. But I wanted the second half to be directed to the women in the graduating class. I am not a radical feminist, but I do think women are still enchained by a rusty patriarchy."

"If that means what I think it means," Sarah said, "right on, sister!"

"I wanted to tell my female classmates to stand up to prejudice and harassment, to assert their rights, and never, never surrender control of their bodies, minds, or future to male hegemony."

"I see nothing objectionable there," the Judge said. "What is the problem?"

"The tone," Barbara said almost desperately. "I have no desire to start a revolution. I mean, I don't want to scream, 'To the barricades!' "

"But you want to galvanize your listeners?"

"Even that is too strong a word. But I do want to inspire them. Instead, the speech sounds strident and shrill. I just can't seem to capture the style and mood I want."

The Judge stared at her a long time in silence. Both women watched him, awaiting his judicial comments.

"You have not asked for my advice," he said finally to Barbara, "but please allow me to offer it. I suggest you reread the Declaration of Independence before you finalize your address. For what you have described is exactly that—a declaration of independence. I recommend you analyze how Jefferson organized his thoughts: first a recitation of universal rights, then a listing of violations of those rights, and ending with a statement of a future course of action. Throughout, the tone is temperate, rational, even respectful. But it is all the more impressive for the absence of rabble-rousing. I think you would do well to emulate Jefferson. Why, you might even use some of his phrases to convince your audience you are indeed declaring independence. Don't use 'When in the course of human events...' That would be too obvious a plagiarism. But I think you might find 'We hold these truths to be self-evident...' would give your address the stature and seriousness your theme demands."

Barbara's reaction was immediate. "Judge, that's an absolutely marvelous idea! It's exactly what the speech needs: an intellectual spine. I'm sure Father has a copy of the Declaration in one of his reference books. I'll reread it tonight and rework my speech just as you said."

She rose to her feet, excited and impatient, but Judge Hampton held out a restraining palm. "Whoa!" he said. "We can't let you go without giving you a small token of our love and our best wishes for your future." He opened a desk drawer, withdrew a small blue Tiffany box tied with a white ribbon. He handed it to Barbara. "No gushy card," he said, "but it's from Sarah and me on your graduation. We're so proud of you!"

She opened the box hastily. Within was a jeweled brooch: a platinum bird set with diamonds and rubies perched on a large cabochon amethyst. It was at once amusing, splendid, fantastic: an extravagant objet d'art. Barbara uttered a yelp of delight and immediately pinned it to the neckline of her cashmere sheath. The scintillant bird seemed to preen.

Her thanks to the Judge and Sarah were almost tearful. She kissed both and promised to give them a report on how her commencement address was received. The housekeeper accompanied her downstairs.

"Wait a minute, honey," Sarah said. "I've got something for you."

"Not another gift," Barbara protested.

"Something personal. From me to you. The Judge has never seen it."

She ducked into a small anteroom she used as an office. She came out bearing a small object, unwrapped, and thrust it into Barbara's hands.

It was a statuette, perhaps eight or nine inches high, of a man standing on what appeared to be a sea turtle. It had been primitively carved from a hard, dark wood, which seemed smoothed and glossed by handling. The little man was naked except for a curious conical hat with a narrow brim. His legs were pressed together and his arms hung straight down, joined to his body. The work was obviously ancient, crudely fashioned but with an enigmatic appeal.

"What on earth *is* it?" Barbara asked.

"Juju," she whispered. "An old Haitian woman gave it to me before she died. If you want to hurt a man, you think of him whilst you stick a pin or needle in the part of the doll you want to hurt."

"Oh, Sarah, do you believe that?"

"Well, I don't believe and I don't not believe."

Barbara was convinced she believed. "What if you want to hurt a woman?"

"I guess it would work if you think of her whilst you're sticking in a pin. Anyway, I wanted to give you something secret, just between us."

And something she treasured, Barbara reckoned. She thanked Sarah again, the two embraced, shared a cheek rub. The housekeeper offered to walk back home with her, but Barbara refused. She said if anyone mugged her she'd put a juju curse on him. The other woman didn't laugh.

After Barbara departed Sarah locked the front door and went back upstairs to the Judge's library. Noah, the two maids, the cook, and the houseman were in their rooms. The big house was quiet except for an occasional rattle of the hurricane shutters when the ocean breeze gusted.

"I think she liked our gift, don't you?" the Judge asked, removing his reading specs.

"Of course she did," Sarah said. "You could see her eyes just light up. Do you want your brandy now?"

"Please."

She went to the oak sideboard and carefully poured exactly one ounce of cognac into a crystal shot glass.

"You, too," he said, and she poured herself more than an ounce. She sat on the couch and they lifted their drinks to each other.

"One drink a day," the Judge said sadly. "How have the mighty fallen! I never expected to become a one-a-day man."

"Not completely," she said with the ecstatic smile and he laughed.

"I thought Barbara looked lovely tonight," he mentioned.

"Judge, she's a beautiful young woman."

"Yes. A blessing and a curse. I'm sure you're aware of the popular prejudice; people simply cannot believe a beautiful woman can be intelligent. They think a woman can have either looks or a brain but not both."

"What about handsome men?"

"The same holds true," he said, moving his palm lightly over the waves of his thick white hair. "But the prejudice about females is more prevalent. Barbara is a beautiful woman and she is also an intelligent woman. I fear she is going to spend her life proving it."

"Judge, do you think I'm beautiful?"

"I do, Sarah. You know I do."

"And intelligent?"

"You have an innate intelligence that doesn't come from reading. And believe me, it's superior to bookishness."

They finished their drinks. The Judge straightened up, sitting erect in his heavy wing chair. He beckoned with both hands. She stood and went to him. She unbuttoned her shirt. Her brassiere had a front closure and she opened it. She stepped close and offered her long, taut breasts. He leaned forward with eager lips.

She put a hand to his wavy white hair. "Sweet Daddy," she said.

5

FLIGHT OF FANCY...

The corporate jet, washed and fueled, sat on the apron in front of a private hangar. The aircraft was painted a dove gray with a longitudinal purple stripe. THE FOLSBY PRESS was printed on the side in heavy block letters. Under the cockpit windows was the plane's name, *Constance,* in a graceful script.

The crew, two men and a woman, stood at the folding stairs. They wore Folsby uniforms of gray with purple piping. Emmet and Barbara, both carrying raincoats, stopped to chat with them while Mrs. Blanche Singer directed the handler stowing their luggage: one suitcase for each plus Barbara's square makeup kit.

"What's the weather like in New York, Jean?" Folsby asked the pilot.

"Overcast with a light drizzle, sir," she said. "No problem."

"Fine. I hope you have some food aboard. We didn't have time for a decent breakfast."

"We're loaded, Mr. Folsby," the steward said, grinning. "Juice, coffee, those mini-croissants you like, and honey. Bacon and eggs if you want."

"Good planning, Marco," Emmet said. "How're the twins, Rudy?"

"Full of the dickens, Mr. Folsby," the copilot said. "And big! Try to lift them and it's instant hernia."

They all laughed and Barbara marveled again at her father's ease with his employees. There were now more than a thousand men and women working for the Folsby Press and Emmet apparently remembered the names of all and knew details of their private lives.

"Well," he said, "what say we get this show on the road."

Mrs. Singer came up to Barbara and clasped her hand. "Have a wonderful, wonderful day. I just know your speech is going to be a big success."

"Keep your fingers crossed. Mine are. And thank you for all your help in arranging the flight."

An hour later they were somewhere over the east coast flying northward through a clotted sky. The Folsbys had finished their second cups of coffee and Marco was cleaning the round table.

A professional decorator had designed the cabin interior of the nine-passenger jet, using the Folsby colors in the carpeting, padded walls, and ceiling. Chairs, tables, cellarette, and a six-foot couch were done in bleached wood and mellow cowhide. Lampshades were faux antique maps. A Remington bronze was bolted to a fluted pedestal and on the cockpit partition was fixed a small framed Winslow Homer seascape.

Barbara thought the cabin verged on the garish—a little too much commercial flash. But she had to admit this upholstered cocoon conveyed an impression of moneyed comfort. Affluence bought security and service. It also, she was aware, grew confidence, if not a casual arrogance.

They lighted cigarettes. "Nervous?" her father asked. "About the speech?"

"Nope."

"If you'd like a drink before we land, just say so."

"No, thank you," she said, then added, "I'm not Brett," and he frowned.

She moved her chair so she was facing him directly.

"Em, I've thought over what we talked about. I still want a job with the company."

"No graduate school? No MBA?"

"Maybe in a few years. Right now I want a job working for you."

"I explained you wouldn't be working for me. Not directly. We do have a chain of command, you know. You'd probably begin as an assistant to an assistant to an assistant."

"I don't expect to start at the top. I'll do what I have to do for as long as it takes."

"You'll have to file an application like every other wannabe. Then there are written tests and personal interviews, all evaluated by an independent agency. If you get through all that—and only about one in twenty applicants is hired—there's a year of orientation and training. And even after that you can't select the city where you'll be working. It may not be our Florida headquarters. Don't expect any favors because you're a Folsby. No nepotism. You'll be on your own."

She lifted her chin. "If Brett did it I can do it."

He turned his head to look out the square window at the heavy clouds scudding by. She saw him in profile.

Age had given him a dignity he had lacked as a young man. His energy had not diminished, but he had become more contemplative, less voluble. His face had hardened, not grown slack as it so often did in middle-aged men. If young forcefulness had quieted, he had achieved assurance and steady purpose. He was fifty-two.

He turned back to his daughter. "Very well," he said. "File your application after Labor Day. That's when we hire a new crop of hopefuls."

"Thank you, Father," she said.

The *Constance* arrived in New York only twenty minutes late, landing in a light but steady drizzle. Barbara and Emmet donned raincoats before they disembarked and found the people awaiting them similarly clad and carrying black umbrellas.

They were Tom Jessup, manager of the New York office; Judith Kopp, his executive assistant (the job title of secretary had been abolished at the Folsby Press); and the chauffeur of the Lincoln limousine parked nearby. The limo was a company car providing transportation for Folsby execs and visiting VIPs, mostly advertisers.

Greetings were exchanged and Judith Kopp presented Barbara with a bouquet of tiger lilies, mums, and wild daisies. "We wish you a happy, happy day," she said shyly. "And congratulations on your graduation."

"Ben," Emmet said to the chauffeur, shaking his hand, "you're looking well. Yankees going to take it again?"

"Sure they are," Ben said. "They'll go all the way."

"Wait till Florida gets a major league team," Em said. "Then you'll have some real competition."

"From Florida, Mr. Folsby? What are they going to pitch—oranges?"

Emmet laughed and drew plump Tom Jessup aside for a moment to talk business. Ben left to transfer luggage to the Lincoln. Barbara and Judith Kopp walked a few steps away.

"Is old lard-ass still chasing you around the desk, Judy?" Barbara asked in a low voice.

The other woman nodded. "Hasn't caught me yet," she said with a nervous laugh.

"File a complaint," Barbara advised. "You know my father won't stand for that kind of nonsense."

"I don't want to cause trouble," Judith said. "I like my job and Mr. Jessup needs his. He's got a wife and two kids."

"Screw him!" Barbara said fiercely. "He's got no right to paw you. Listen, Judy, I'm joining the company after Labor Day. Hang in there and maybe I'll be able to do something about it."

"That would be great."

"Meanwhile, keep a record of everything he does and says to you. Has he written you any notes or letters?"

Judith nodded. "I've kept them."

"Juicy?"

"Very."

Barbara smiled with great satisfaction. "He's dead," she said.

The Folsbys waved goodbye from the Lincoln and Ben drove west to the Parkway, switched to the Expressway, and eventually turned north on the Thruway.

"Folks," he called, "there are chicken sandwiches and Cokes in the cooler back there. Also ice cubes. And the decanters in the bar are filled, Mr. Folsby."

"Thank you, Ben," Emmet said.

"Looks like an all-day wet," the chauffeur went on. "Sorry about that. There's an umbrella in the trunk if you need it when we get there."

They drove steadily through light traffic. Emmet read the *Barron's* Tom Jessup had given him and Barbara studied notes of her speech jotted on index cards. It took almost two hours to arrive at the college town. Barbara directed Ben to the campus.

"If the rain gets worse," she said, "they'll move everything into the chapel."

"Doesn't look so bad right now," her father said. "More mist than drizzle."

They found the guests' parking area, and a freshman in a green beanie directed them to a vacant slot.

"I have to go over to the gym for my cap and gown," Barbara said. "You take the umbrella and see if you can find Brett. Try to sit down front; the PA system isn't the greatest."

She hurried away. Ben took the umbrella from the trunk and passed it to Emmet. It turned out to be a big, thick-shafted golf bumbershoot with alternating panels of bright yellow and red. Emmet carried it unopened as he went looking for his son on the quadrangle, where rows of folding chairs had been set up.

Brett Sherwood Folsby was not hard to find. He was the center of a circle of young women, two of whom were wearing black mortarboards and gowns. All were laughing and one was clutching Brett's arm possessively. Emmet recognized her as Gracie McCall, his daughter's best friend. He stood apart a few moments, observing his son's talent for charming women. He was amused and, yes, he admitted, a mite envious.

Brett was tall, even taller than his father, and slouched lazily. He did well at projecting what he considered the Holy Grail of men's fashion: careless elegance. A trench coat was thrown over his shoulders like a cape. Beneath was a two-piece suit of chalk-striped charcoal flannel. His Turnbull & Asser shirt was enlivened by a Sulka tie. The shoes were Italian, hand-stitched, and his pearl gray trilby was worn with the brim rakishly slanted. Set on the ground was his black alligator attaché case.

As Brett listened to the chatter of the women surrounding him his head was tilted slightly to one side as if he were paying close attention to their gossip. But his thoughts were elsewhere. One of Barbara's classmates had been introduced to him as Bertha Tolliver, and her first name had stirred a fond memory.

When he was sixteen, a sophomore in high school, he had been caught hugging and kissing a girl in an empty classroom. The intruder had been Mrs. Bertha Mulrooney, who taught English literature. She had separated the amorous couple, reprimanded both, and sent them on their separate ways.

"Brett Folsby," he thought she said to him, "I do declare you are a fawn. Definitely."

The remark puzzled him a long time. About four months later he lost his virginity one dark night to Mrs. Bertha Mulrooney under the bleachers of the football field. After he had been thoroughly deflowered, he had leaned close to peer into her eyes. He asked why she had compared him to a baby deer.

She laughed. "I didn't say you were a fawn, f-a-w-n. I said faun, f-a-u-n."

"What is a faun, f-a-u-n?"

"Go home and look it up," she advised.

He did and was pleased.

Now, at twenty-six, standing in a thicket of attractive fans at his sister's graduation, he remembered Mrs. Bertha Mulrooney and laughed.

"Why are you laughing, Brett?" Gracie McCall demanded.

"Because I'm happy," he replied, and his roguish smile made them all happy.

6

WE HOLD THESE TRUTHS...

The invocation was delivered by the college chaplain.

The college choir sang "Amazing Grace."

The college president welcomed families and guests. He spoke of the academic benefits of a small liberal arts college.

The dean of students welcomed families and guests. He spoke of the social benefits of a small liberal arts college.

The college choir sang a sea chantey.

The salutatorian, an earnest young man, spoke of a glorious world when every man, woman, and child would own a personal computer.

The valedictory address was delivered by Barbara Ann Folsby.

The keynote speaker, Senator R. Jack Brimbrigge, assured the audience the United States was the greatest nation on earth and possibly the greatest in the history of mankind.

The college choir sang "America, the Beautiful."

Diplomas, rolled and tied with a ribbon in the school colors, were awarded to the graduating students.

The college chaplain delivered the benediction.

Everyone—faculty, graduates, students, families, and guests—rose and joined in singing the college song in which the phrase "hallowed halls" was rhymed with "twilight falls."

The commencement took two hours and three minutes. The drizzle had lessened, but a heavy mist had persisted throughout the ceremony. Despite this inconvenience, everyone present considered the occasion a success. When it ended, there was an excited mingling of graduates and guests. Kisses and handshakes were exchanged. Tears were shed, farewells made, vows sworn to keep four-year friendships alive forever and ever.

Brett and Emmet Folsby had managed to snag chairs only five rows from the speakers' platform. They had listened attentively to the speeches preceding the valedictory address. Occasionally they had traded ironic glances and twice Brett had rolled his eyes incredulously. When Barbara stepped to the lectern both men leaned forward intently.

She had removed her mortarboard; long

blond tresses hung damply about her shoulders. She greeted the audience with a somewhat cramped smile, began speaking in a rather wispy voice. She halted, drew a deep breath, began again in strong, resonant tones.

The first part of her speech had been described to Judge Hampton as boilerplate. But it was not totally blah, blah, blah since it dealt with her memories of the beauty of the campus as the seasons changed. She spoke movingly of the spring sun shimmering off the tiled roof of the chapel; the colorful spectacle of fall football games in the stadium; the quiet of winter when the quadrangle was buried under a tide of unsoiled snow.

"Now," she said, "I would like to conclude by directing my remarks to the women of my graduating class, undergraduate women, and women everywhere."

She began with a brief recital of those natural rights to which every individual is entitled, regardless of gender, color, or creed. She then listed the prejudices to which women were subjected: discrimination and sexual harassment in the workplace; limits to what they might hope to achieve in the worlds of business, politics, and the arts; belittling of those who chose to devote their lives to home, children, family.

She ended with a plea to her "sisters" to demand equal partnership with men in all spheres, to maintain control of their bodies and minds, to have the confidence to strive, to be willing to succeed or fail providing it was their abilities put to the test and not the sometimes irrational or selfish dictates of male autocrats.

None of the ideas Barbara expressed was new or unique. But she imbued them with such conviction and fervor the audience was forced to listen, some against their will since she was not preaching solely to the converted. When she finished and moved away from the lectern there was a spatter of applause, more than mere politeness but less than an enthusiastic accolade.

When the commencement had ended and the crowd was engaged in confused and noisy celebration, Emmet and Brett stood and looked at each other.

"Barb's address was excellent," Em said. "Don't you think so?"

"Mmm," his son said. "But—"

He was interrupted when Gracie McCall came dancing up to them and grabbed Brett's arm. Her cap was pushed to the back of her mop of red curls. "Hi, Mr. Folsby," she said brightly. "Barb was a smash—right? Listen, I want to borrow Brett for a few minutes. I've got a friend who's dying to meet him. I promise to return him in good condition."

She tugged Brett away. Emmet looked at the speakers' platform. Barbara was speaking to the dean of students. She turned, searched, saw her father, and held up a hand with fingers splayed. He presumed it signified a wait of five minutes.

But it was almost ten before she joined him. She had left her cap and gown somewhere and was wearing her pinkish Burberry raincoat and a knitted wool cloche. She clutched her rolled diploma tightly. He had expected her to be ebullient but she seemed subdued, not exactly dejected but certainly unsmiling.

He kissed her cheek. "Congratulations, Barb," he said. "A wonderful speech."

She shook her head. "No, it wasn't. Okay, but not wonderful. You know, Em, I wanted it to be something dramatic, either a howling success or a completely awful dud. It was neither. It was just a middling speech, not first-rate and not third-rate. An in-between effort. And I hate being in between. In anything."

He didn't know what to reply so he said, "Brett is here. He arrived before we did."

"I know," she said shortly. "I saw him. He already had a harem. Didn't take him long." But she wouldn't change the subject. "The dean spoke to me about my address. He said, 'It exceeded my expectations.' Was that a compliment or a slam? I don't know. It sure didn't exceed *my* expectations."

"It was a good speech," he told her quietly. "Don't be discouraged."

"Discouraged? Not me! It's over and done with. On to a new life! Never look back."

He laughed. "You're quoting Satchel Paige. He said, 'Don't look back; something may be gaining on you.' "

"And here it comes," she said as Brett

joined them, grinning. "Well?" she asked him. "How many telephone numbers did you collect from your groupies?"

"None," he said. "Except for Gracie McCall they all seemed to be from places like Oshkosh and Red Wing."

"They're too old for you anyway, Brett. They're all over twenty."

This kind of brittle chitchat made Emmet uncomfortable. "Let's go back to the car," he suggested. "I think a drink is in order to celebrate Barb's diploma."

There were several tailgate parties going on in the parking area. They sat in the back of the limousine and each had a chicken sandwich and a gin-and-tonic. Ben, supplied with sandwich and cola, wandered off to give the Folsby family privacy.

"Brett," Barbara said, "you didn't say what you thought of my speech."

"Very nice," he said.

"*Nice?* Oh my God! The kiss of death."

"Well, if you want the truth, I thought it was wrong."

"Wrong? You mean my ideas are mistaken?"

"Oh Lord no. I agree with everything you said. The speech was well organized and well delivered. But it was the wrong speech for that time and place. It's a matter of context."

"What's that supposed to mean?"

"Look, if we had a marvelous article on new meat-processing equipment and published it in a magazine devoted to earth-moving machinery, the article would be out of context and no one would read it. The senator who spoke today came across as a windbag. His address was a paean of platitudes. But he happens to be an intelligent man who's a heavyweight on the Foreign Relations Committee. He probably knows more about our international friends and foes than anyone else in the Senate. But he didn't speak on his area of expertise because he's a street-smart politician and knew his audience was in a celebratory mood. It was a festive occasion. Everyone wanted to be happy, hear happy speeches, think happy thoughts. It wasn't the time or place for a deep, troubling account of our foreign policy. Such a speech would have been out of context and the senator knew it. So he gave them the ballyhoo they wanted and they loved it. But you came along with a serious discourse on the problems of modern women. Wrong place, wrong time. It went over like a lead balloon because it was out of context."

She turned her head to stare at him. "You mean I should have truckled to the emotions of the audience?"

"Of course," he said. "Every two-bit salesman knows that. If you want to close a deal you have to brownnose the customer. Next time make sure you're in context, kiddo."

She gave no sign of how greatly she was angered by his indulgent smile and air of superiority. But she would not allow his disparagement to blunt her resolve.

That year people were saying, "Don't get mad—get even."

7

SUITE CHARITY...

The Folsbys registered at The Plaza in Manhattan and were escorted up to their reserved suite: sitting room, two bedrooms, two baths. Barbara appropriated the larger bedroom and disappeared to shower and change.

Emmet asked if his son intended to bathe. Brett replied all he planned was a washup. He had a fresh shirt in his attaché case that would do until he got back to Chicago.

"When does your plane leave?"

"I should be at the airport by ten. I'll have to eat and run."

"You'll make it. The limousine is standing by on Fifty-ninth Street."

Emmet started for the other bedroom, then paused. "You were a little hard on Barb about her speech, weren't you?"

"I don't think so," his son said.

Emmet made no response but went into the other bedroom and closed the door. Brett loosened his necktie, lighted a cigarette, slumped in an armchair. He smoked awhile and then turned on the TV set. It flickered and suddenly President Carter appeared trying to explain at a press conference why inflation was so high.

Brett leaned forward, turned off the set, and was startled when another image appeared: a man's head. It took him a second to realize the

40

dead screen was serving as a mirror; the face he saw was his reflected own.

He had the Folsbys' blond hair but his was paler than Barbara's gold. And he had his father's handsomeness, though his features were molded rather than chiseled. His lips were not quite lubricious but certainly sensuous. ("You're so bloody kissable!" an Englishwoman had told him.) In a previous time he might have been described as a matinee idol or likened to the man in the Arrow collar ads. Fortunately his face was saved from insipidity by bright, charged eyes and a quirky smile which sometimes became derisive.

That was the way he normally looked. But the television screen was convex and the image it gave back was distorted: a fun house mirror. Brett saw a bloated face, cheeks inflated, nose swollen, jowls of flab. It was, he fancied, the way he might look when his years had doubled to his father's present age. It was a macabre fancy and disturbing. He stared at his grotesque caricature a long time.

Emmet came from the bedroom freshly shaven and wearing a three-piece suit of gray sharkskin. His face, Brett noted, was hard, strong, purposeful.

"It's all yours," he said, gesturing toward the open door.

Brett carried his attaché case into the bedroom and left the door ajar. Emmet lighted a cigarette and moved to the windows overlooking Central Park. Street lamps were on, each haloed by the mist. The Park was deeply shadowed, budding trees waving limbs still skeletal. The sky pressed down.

Barbara came into the sitting room and he turned to look at her. She had pinned her hair but soft tendrils floated. She was wearing a one-shoulder gown of winy silk. Emmet's breath caught. There was a brief silence before he could say, "You look lovely."

"Thank you," she said, twirling. "Tonight I feel like I own the world." She joined him at the windows, looked down at 59th Street. "Em, after dinner can we take a ride through the Park in a hansom cab?"

"No."

"Why not?" she said indignantly.

He laughed. "Because there are no hansoms down there. I see barouches, victorias, and one cabriolet. But no hansom cabs."

"Gee, Pop," she squealed in a little girl's voice, "you know everything."

He smiled. "I do read books occasionally, you know."

Brett came from the bedroom. He had changed to a candy-striped shirt with a tie of raw coral silk. He stopped when he saw Barbara.

"Smashing," he said. "But you need a spark."

"Such as?"

"I have just the thing," he said and fumbled in his case. He brought out a small gift box with a red rosette fixed to the lid. He handed it to her. "Congratulations on your graduation," he said formally.

She held the present and stared at him. She was aware of his extravagance; he was perpetually in debt and it never seemed to bother him one whit. She wondered how a man so parsimonious with his emotions could be so profligate with his money. She opened the gift box. Within was a pavé diamond bangle bracelet. Barbara gasped. It was not one to be tossed in the sea.

"Oh my God," she said, "it's gorgeous!" She flew to him and kissed his lips. "Thank you, brother. It's just fantastic!" She slipped it on her wrist but it hung awkwardly, almost large enough to fall off.

Brett shook his head regretfully. "Too loose, Lautrec," he said. "I'll try to exchange it for a smaller size or something else."

"No, no!" his sister protested. She had placed the bracelet on the wrist of her bare arm. Now she pushed it up, worked it over her straightened elbow, and adjusted it on her upper arm. It fit comfortably, snug but not tight. "How does it look?" she asked.

Both men assured her it was stunning, and after consulting a full-length mirror Barbara agreed it was just the sparkle her gown needed.

"And different," she said. "I bet I'm the only woman in town with a jewel-encrusted bicep."

They went down to the lobby and checked raincoats and Brett's case. Then they entered the Oak Room, a family in a smiley mood.

After a round of Beefeater martinis they decided to simplify things and ensure speedier service by ordering identical meals: prosciutto

43

and melon, endive salad, beef Wellington. Brett selected the Burgundy, a 1971 Charmes-Chambertin Laboure-Roi.

During the salad course Emmet told his son that Barbara would be on a European tour for most of July—a graduation gift from her mother. But after Barb's return, the paterfamilias said, he hoped the three of them could coordinate their schedules so at least one would always be in Florida attending to the needs and wants of the ailing Constance.

"It shouldn't be a problem," Brett said. "Barb, if you choose to get a job—and whether you do or not is really immaterial—you do intend to live in Florida, don't you?"

There was a brief quiet. Then Emmet told his son, "Barbara has decided she wants to work for the Folsby Press."

Brett's lips twisted into a thin smile. He turned to his sister. He said, "Surely you can do better than that." He thought it would sound like a joke and they would laugh. But it didn't and they didn't. He strove to make amends, but matters worsened. "I mean, I would have thought you'd prefer a more glamorous career," he said to her.

"That's a sexist remark," she said tartly.

"Sexist? How so?"

"You're implying women should limit themselves to glitzy jobs."

"I'm implying nothing of the sort. My remark concerned you personally, not all women. I know of your interest in fashion, theater, the arts. Surely you'd be happier working

44

for, say, *Harper's Bazaar* than *Tunnel and Aqueduct Construction,* one of our quarterlies."

"What about *your* personal interests?" she demanded. "Don't tell me you're such a big fan of tunnels and aqueducts. But it's part of your job and you accept it. You went to work for the Folsby Press because it was a great business opportunity. That's exactly what I'm doing."

"You haven't the slightest idea—" he began angrily but Emmet held up a palm.

"Enough," he said sternly. "Stop your squabbling. This dinner is supposed to be a celebration. Please let me enjoy it in peace."

His children were silenced. Wine and beef were served. They ate and drank with no further conversation.

At a nearby table a dowager dining alone rose to depart. She wore a hat as large and varicolored as a Tiffany lampshade. Clutched under one arm was a geriatric Pekingnese observing the world through rheumy eyes. A waiter assisted her, but she insisted on stopping at the Folsbys' table. They looked up at her raddled face.

She addressed Barbara. "My dear," she said in a hoarse voice, "you're the loveliest thing I've seen in New York." She glanced at Emmet and Brett. "And the luckiest," she added, "with two such handsome escorts." And she continued her hobbling exit.

They waited until she was gone before they laughed.

"I don't much enjoy being called a thing," Barbara said.

"But you're a lovely thing," Brett reminded her.

"She meant well," Emmet said.

They skipped dessert but had coffee.

"Brandy?" Emmet asked.

Brett glanced at his Patek Philippe. "Like to," he said, "but I better run. I'll have my brandy at the airport if I have time. You two stay right here if you like."

"Not us," Barbara said. "We're going for a carriage ride in the Park, aren't we, Em?"

Brett smiled. "You horse-drawn and me jet-propelled."

Sometimes she found it difficult to know whether he was making a casual jest or if his comment had a deeper, perhaps sardonic, meaning she was missing.

A few moments later they were outside on 59th Street, the collars of their raincoats turned up against a damp, chilly wind blowing from the northwest.

"Call you Monday, home on Wednesday," Brett said to Emmet. "The trade show is going well. Heavy traffic at our booth. Thanks for the great feed. Sorry about the minor tempest."

He shook his father's hand and kissed his sister's cheek.

"Welcome to the Folsby Press," he said to her.

"Thank you, brother," she said. "It'll be fun working together, won't it?"

46

"Loads," he said, gave them an exaggerated salute, and walked down the line of waiting limousines looking for the Folsby Lincoln. He found it, talked a moment with the chauffeur standing alongside. They both got in, the limo pulled away. Barbara and Emmet, still standing on the sidewalk, waved, and saw Brett wave back. Then the Lincoln was lost in traffic.

"Well," Emmet said, "it turned out to be a pleasant evening after all."

"And the best is yet to come," his daughter said.

8

A MANY-SPLENDORED THING...

They chose a victoria with the hood raised. The driver was a scruffy oldster with a dented topper. He helped them step up into the carriage and told them there was a blanket back there if they became cold. Then he mounted to his perch, picked up the reins, and clucked. The fat, grayish horse turned its head to glance at him, then began a slow amble. More clucking produced a slightly faster gait but not a trot.

It was noticeably chillier in the Park. Emmet unfolded the blanket, spread it over their laps, tucked it around Barbara's legs. The blanket smelled musty and had a greasy nap, but the warmth it provided was welcome.

Car traffic was light. There were a few joggers, roller skaters, cyclists. But they clip-clopped along stretches of roadway completely deserted. The city had vanished as if a heavy felt curtain had descended around the Park and blanked out sounds, lights, even the acrid odor of teeming streets.

Barbara's hand snaked under the blanket, fumbled, found him, held him. Emmet turned to look at her. "Shameless hussy," he said with mock outrage and she laughed.

"Em, I don't think Brett was too happy to hear I'm joining the company."

"I believe he was surprised. But he certainly has no reason to be resentful."

"Brett is a Borgia," she said, and it was his turn to laugh.

"And who are you?" he asked. "Mother Teresa?"

She made no reply but pressed closer. He put an arm about her shoulders and they huddled. They were carried through the shadows, their silence more intimate than whispers.

The victoria completed a circuit and pulled up outside the hotel. They alighted and Emmet paid the driver. They walked toward the 59th Street entrance.

"You always overtip," Barbara told him.

"I know I do," Emmet said. "But it's a tribute; I've been so fortunate. Let's stop at the bar and warm up. They make great Irish coffee."

They were ushered to a secluded corner

48

banquette. Their coffees were brought, laced with Irish whiskey and topped with fresh whipped cream. They sipped contentedly.

"Em," she said, "if I'm going to work for the Folsby Press I'd like to know more about it. I know you publish trade magazines, but I'm awfully ignorant about how the company is structured. I'd like to ask questions, but if you feel I have no need to know, just tell me."

"Ask away," he said.

"Well, the Folsby Press is a corporation, isn't it?"

"Correct. A private corporation chartered by the State of Florida. It has ten thousand voting shares of which I am the sole owner."

She was startled. "Mother doesn't hold any?"

"Not at the present time. If I should predecease her—and I hope I do—she will inherit all my shares and control of Folsby Press. I hope that doesn't disappoint you. Not to worry. My shares in the company are just a portion of my net worth—the largest portion, I admit. But I have other assets—stocks, bonds, real estate, and so forth—which will provide more than adequate bequests to you, Brett, relatives, a few employees who have been with me a long time, my alma mater, and some selected charities. My will runs more than forty pages."

"But if you do predecease Mother," his daughter said, "will she be in any shape to run the Folsby Press?"

"A very cogent question," Emmet said, "and one I can't answer. Constance was with me every step of the way while I built the business. I never made an important decision without consulting her first. But now she is dreadfully ill. According to Dr. Steiner, improvement is out of the question unless a miracle cure is discovered. Her condition may stabilize or it may deteriorate. There is no way of predicting. But she may live many more years to come. We can only hope."

"What if she outlives you but is not mentally or physically capable of running the Folsby Press?"

"A problem I find increasingly worrisome. I have discussed it with my personal attorney and the company's lawyers. There are several options available, including having Constance sign a power of attorney authorizing a surrogate to assume all her duties and powers at the Folsby Press in the event she is incapacitated. But that brings up more problems. Who is to be designated as her surrogate and at what time and under what conditions does the power of attorney take effect? It's a can of worms, Barb, and I've made no final decision on how it should be handled. I want to talk it over with Judge Hampton. I need his counsel."

There were other questions she wanted to ask—including the size of her inheritance, and Brett's—but she felt she had pressed him far enough.

"Poor Mother," she said. "Life really is unfair, isn't it."

"No," he said. "It's just life, uncaring and nonjudgmental. Fairness and unfairness are

50

human concepts and relative. The millionaire thinks it's unfair because he's not a billionaire. Do you know the ancient saying—I think it's Persian—that goes: 'I had no shoes and wept until I met a man who had no feet'? Let's go up, Barb; it's been a long day."

"Not long enough," she said.

They entered, double-locked the hall door to the suite, and went to their separate bedrooms. Emmet undressed slowly and pulled on yellow cotton pajama pants with a drawstring top. He sat on the edge of the bed and waited. In a few moments Barbara entered. She was still clothed but her hair was down.

"May I borrow your pajama jacket, Em?" she asked. "I forgot to pack a nightgown."

"Deliberately," he said.

"Of course," she said saucily and caught the jacket he tossed to her.

He wondered why she, and Constance before her, enjoyed wearing his old shirts, sweaters, pajama coats. Sarah Demijohn, the Judge had told him, had a similar liking. It was one of the many, many things Emmet did not understand about women. He sat stolidly, awaiting Barbara's return, looking at nothing.

He recalled the beginning five years ago: place, time of day, weather. There had been a challenge and a response. But the recollection of who challenged and who responded had faded, become as vague as yesterday's dream. How strange, he thought, to remember the where and when but not the why.

He was not, he knew, her first man and

51

since the start of their affair had not been the only. But it was not important. The vital question was the nature and depth of her love.

His began as physical desire and had segued into something more, far more than paternal attachment and different from the love he felt for Constance and she for him. That was a potion to which another ingredient—Barbara's supernal beauty—had been added, changing its flavor and increasing its strength to an elixir which intoxicated him. It was a passion compounded of splendor and hopelessness.

She came into the room, bare legs gleaming. His eyes sought hard thigh and smooth curve of calf. She sat next to him on the bed, put a soft arm about his neck, blew gently into his ear. He turned so they were facing. They both leaned forward until they were almost nose to nose, staring intently into each other's eyes. It was a game they played. He was the first to blink.

He rose and began to pace slowly back and forth alongside the bed. She lay back, hair spread across two pillows. He could not avert his eyes from her cool, limpid body. He could not define the texture of her skin. Was it silk, satin, velvet? Her flesh and she herself were all mystery.

"Guilt?" she asked him softly.

"The only guilt I feel," he said, "is because I feel no guilt."

She sat up. "Oh, that's a brainteaser," she said. "We studied those in my philosophy course. If you say, 'There is no absolute truth,' it negates itself because you're claiming your statement is an absolute truth."

"What is your absolute truth, Barb?"

"You and me," she said immediately.

The quickness of her reply made him smile. She was shrewd, ambitious, resourceful. But those qualities didn't dismay him since they were his own.

"Here's another brainteaser for you," he said. "Is it better to love or to be loved?"

"That's old stuff," she scoffed. "Adam asked Eve the same question."

"What did Eve answer?"

"She said, 'Shut up and come to bed.' "

And so he did.

9

SHOULD AULD ACQUAINTANCE...

Brett Folsby left his sister and father standing on 59th Street. He walked down the line of parked limousines and found the Folsby Lincoln. A small, dapper black man was standing alongside. He wore a neat gray suit and a visored chauffeur's cap. The car's radio was on. Debby Boone was singing "You Light Up My Life."

"Good evening," Brett said. "I am Brett Folsby. You're replacing Ben?"

"That's right, sir. I'm on all night. Ben comes back at eight tomorrow morning."

"Uh-huh. Do you work full-time for the Folsby Press?"

"No, sir. I'm just a temp filling in. You going to the airport—right?"

Brett didn't answer. "What's your name?" he inquired.

"Lazarus."

"Beautiful. I wish I was Lazarus. Let's get rolling, shall we?"

They passed Barbara and Emmet, who waved farewell. "Which airport?" the chauffeur asked.

"Neither," Brett said. "The Seagram Building on Park Avenue. You know it?"

"I do, sir," Lazarus said.

Brett opened his attaché case, brought out a silver-plated hip flask, circa 1920. He had purchased it in a Boston antique shop attracted by the ornate monogram engraved on the side: J.B. He told all his friends the flask had originally been owned by John Barrymore. So many people believed him he began to believe it himself.

He lifted the hinged cap, tilted the flask to his lips. There was about an ounce of cognac remaining and he finished it in two gulps. He did not customarily carry a flask, but he feared flying and had sipped the brandy during his flight from Chicago.

"Here we are, sir," the chauffeur said, pulling to the curb on the east side of Park Avenue.

Before leaving the limousine Brett took a fifty-dollar bill from his wallet and handed it to the chauffeur. "I doubt if anyone will ask," he said, "but if anyone does, you drove me to LaGuardia."

"You got it," Lazarus said. "Have a nice evening."

"I intend to," Brett said.

He waited on the sidewalk until the Lincoln was out of sight. Then he walked around the corner to the 52nd Street entrance to the Four Seasons. He went directly to the men's room, took off coat and hat, relieved himself, washed his hands, combed his hair. He rummaged through his case until he found a small gold tie bar shaped like a phallus. He clipped his tie to his shirt front. He left the loo, checked hat, coat, and case, then walked upstairs to the Grill Room.

He paused briefly to observe the bar scene. There was a boisterous group of four middle-aged men drinking whiskey and comparing bill-fold photos with shouts of laughter. There was an elderly couple drinking white wine, both smoking from long cigarette holders. And there was a single young man, his head completely shaved, standing by himself with a small snifter of brandy before him.

Brett walked around the bar and took up a stance near the baldhead. He ordered a Rémy Martin with water on the side. He sipped, turned to examine the brandy drinker more closely. He was, Brett guessed, close to his own age, perhaps a year or two younger. He was decently dressed in navy blazer and gray flannel slacks.

He was not conventionally handsome but had pleasantly pert features set in a seemingly permanent half-smile as if he found the world both whimsical and entertaining. His shaved pate gleamed glassily and he wore something Brett had never seen before: a narrow fur necktie. It offered an amusing contrast to his hairless crown.

"Pardon me," Brett said to him, "but you're not *Kojak,* are you?"

The baldy turned. *"Kojak?* Why, no. But I'm sometimes mistaken for *Maude. "*

"Ah, yes," Brett said. "I can see the resemblance."

They traded smiles of discovery and agreement.

"I like your phallus," the other man said.

"I *beg* your pardon!"

"Your tie bar."

Brett glanced down. "A phallus? Are you certain? Heavens to Betsy, the clerk told me it was a carrot."

"Definitely a phallus. I know because I have one just like it."

"But larger I hope."

"Slightly. By the way, we've met before."

"In whose dreams?"

"Truly. Take a close look at my puss. Try to imagine me with a full head of mousy hair, a silly ponytail, and a sillier Fu Manchu mustache."

Brett stared at him a moment. "Well, damn me!" he exclaimed. "You're right! About three years ago in San Francisco. You were working in the art department of the Folsby Press. Your name is Simon. They called you Simple Simon."

"Very good. And my last name?"

"Ahh... Smith?"

"Close but no cigar. Smithson."

"Of course. Simon Smithson. Any relation to the Institution?"

"None whatsoever."

"May I buy us a round to celebrate an old acquaintance renewed?"

"Delighted."

Brandies were poured. They raised glasses to each other.

"You remember my name?" Brett asked.

"Folsby obviously. The boss's son."

"And my first name?"

Simon pondered. "Bert?"

"Do I look like a Bert?" Brett said indignantly. "It's Brett."

"Brett. Of course. Sorry about that."

"Are you still with the Folsby Press, Simon?"

"No, I resigned about two years ago."

"Oh? And what are you doing now?"

"Nothing."

"Nothing? How do you manage?"

"Very well. I had a wealthy aunt who was kind enough to die."

"Lucky you."

"I am lucky," Simon admitted. "It comes because I'm a Capricorn—the Goat. What are you?"

"A sybarite," Brett said.

"I guessed that, but under what sign were you born?"

"Coca-Cola. Actually I'm a Cancer—the Crab—but I wouldn't care to have it bruited about. Cancer the Crab—what a label! Why not Acne the Lobster?"

"Or Dandruff the Oyster."

They both smiled again, brought closer by their clownery.

"So you're a gentleman of leisure?" Brett inquired.

"At the moment. After I inherited and resigned I decided to become the new Picasso. My art teacher said I was an excellent draftsman, a fine colorist, and had an instinct for composition. I lacked only one thing: talent. The teacher was right. So I gave it up."

"And now?"

"Theater, ballet, opera, parties, travel. I've been thinking of making my entire life a work of art."

"Good idea, but I don't think Sotheby's would be interested."

"True."

"How old are you, Simon?"

"I'm twenty-six going on eighty-four. You?"

"The same. More eighty-four than twenty-six after today."

"A bad scene?"

Brett rolled his eyes. "Not the jolliest."

"Perhaps you need more of the old nasty,"

Simon said, staring at him directly. "Would you care to have your next wallop at my digs?"

"No, thanks. I'm really not interested in lava lamps."

"Pity. But I also have a fringed suede pillow printed 'Souvenir of Niagara Falls.' "

"In that case I'll be happy to join you."

"We can walk. It's quite close."

"Surely not the Waldorf?"

"More like the YMCA."

"Goody," Brett Folsby said.

They finished their drinks, paid their tabs, went downstairs to the checkroom. Brett retrieved his hat, raincoat, attaché case. Simon had checked only a maroon beret. He tugged it on over his naked skull and Brett laughed. "You look like a six-foot pin cushion."

Simon Smithson occupied the entire second floor of a handsome town house on East 53rd Street, scarcely a five-minute walk from the Four Seasons.

"I should warn you," Brett said, "whenever I visit a strange apartment that's been beautifully and expensively decorated I have the perfect put-down. I always say, 'Ah, yes, this place has great possibilities.' "

But when he entered the apartment and Simon switched on the chandelier in the living room, Brett could utter nothing but praise. The co-op was not done in any period style but was an eclectic selection of antiques, Victorian, Art Nouveau, Art Deco, Swedish modern, and Milanese avant-garde. Yet all these disparate elements were coordinated in an interior of grace, comfort, warmth. Wherever Brett's glance fell he was charmed and envious.

"Did you have it done?" he asked Simon. "Or did you do it?"

"I did."

"Fabulous! You're right: You know color and composition; your taste is faultless. It's a career you should pursue—interior decoration. You'd be a smash."

"It's a thought. Flop anywhere and I'll fetch us a brandy."

Brett sat in a brocaded wing chair, and two fat Persian cats, both snow-white, came from nowhere and began giving him ankle rubs. He leaned down to tweak their ears. They liked it.

Simon returned with crystal snifters of brandy. He handed one to Brett. "I see you've met the family."

"Beautiful animals. What are their names?"

"Hotsy and Totsy."

"Love it." He sampled the brandy. "Love this too. Sinfully good. What on earth is it?"

"Seven-star Metaxa."

"Bless the Greeks. There is so much we can learn from them."

"How true, how true." Simon sat on a leather hassock. "So you had a bad day?"

"Dreadful. My sister was graduated from college and I had to sit through a boring two-hour vaudeville. Then later I learned she's joining the company."

"What does that mean?"

"Trouble in paradise," Brett said.

"Sibling rivalry?"

"More like sibling hostility."

"What's she like?"

"Sugar and spice and everything nice. Outwardly."

"And inwardly?"

"A combination of Scarlett O'Hara and Agrippina."

"*Achtung!*" He was silent a moment, then said, "Brett, I'll give you an idea which might help you score some brownie points. Just before I came into all the loot and resigned, I was working on a memo detailing how the logos, typography, layouts, photos, and graphics in the Folsby magazines should be redesigned. Your magazines look like throwbacks to the nineteen fifties. There have been some really exciting developments in magazine design recently, but you'd never know it from looking at the Folsby mags. The logos are strictly buckeye, the typography stodgy, the layouts so cluttered they make your eyeballs glaze over. Even the feature headings are hokey."

"What do you suggest?"

"Bring in a top-notch design studio. Use the same hand-lettered logo type for all the Folsby publications. Ditto the inside fonts, layouts, photos, and graphics. Give the mags a fresh look, open and modern. Everything today is image. The Folsby Press should create and project a smart, bright image of an up-to-the-minute publisher. Right now it's dull, duller, dullest. You need a jazzier look, a bit of pizzazz."

"I think it's a wonderful idea, Simon, but I'm not sure the old man will go for it."

"Tell him a complete redesign will impress the media hotshots at advertising agencies, which means more paid ads. A thorough makeover will cost a mint, I admit, but it will be worth it in the bottom line. Convince your father he's got to position the Folsby Press for the future. And it's your future if you inherit the whole enchilada."

"By God, I'll do it!" Brett cried. "I can't just twiddle my thumbs now that my sister is coming aboard."

"Good lad," Simon said. "Save yourself."

"I intend to," Brett said determinedly.

Later, when they were undressing in the periwinkle blue bedroom, Brett said, "Gee, gosh, and golly, you have hair on your shoulders!"

"I know," Simon said mournfully. "After the hair on my head started falling out I tried all kinds of treatments: massage, hot oil, mange ointment, everything suggested. Nothing worked. And I refuse to wear a rug. So I opted for a total tonsure. It's really quite practical, especially in summer. And it does help me meet golden lads—like you! Anyway, at the same time I was losing hair on my head it was thickening on my shoulders. Now I notice I'm beginning to grow hair on my back. Do you suppose it's inching its way southward and will eventually cover my ass?"

Brett stared and admired. "That would be a tragedy," he said.

BOOK
2

1

FATHERS AND SONS...

The third-floor exercise room was a high cathedral chamber with exposed beams and joists. Tall arched windows faced north and the light was further muted by tinted glass. Walls were painted biscuit; the hardwood floor gleamed dully. It was an airy, spacious room but cluttered with several exercise machines, the newest of which had never been used. There was a long, heavy rope hanging from the ridgepole. It had never been climbed.

Judge Seth Hampton strode briskly on his motorized treadmill, gripping the handrails and glancing occasionally at the monitor to see how far he had walked. His doctor had recommended two miles four times a week with the belt set at three mph and adjusted to a three-degree incline. The Judge followed those instructions faithfully and never once had he considered the treadmill a metaphor for his entire life.

Across the room Noah Demijohn was strapped onto an old-fashioned rowing machine made of polished walnut. Noah, now seventeen, had set the resistance at the max. His skin glistened with sweat and his white spandex trunks had soaked through. It was the day after Thanksgiving 1981.

The Judge completed the two miles, switched off the treadmill, and retrieved his cane hooked over one of the handles. He walked slowly to a wooden bench and sat on one of the sailcloth cushions. He removed the top of his absorbent sweats. Sarah had provided fresh towels and he used one to wipe his face, neck, and arms. He watched Noah pulling the stubby oar handles, straightening his legs as he pushed back on the rolling seat.

The youth was nudging six feet but was still slender, muscles long rather than bunched. His upper body was well developed but not massive. Powerful legs had earned him the position of first-string quarterback on his high school football team. He was fast. Local sports pages had referred to him as "Nimble Noah."

"I'm not nimble," he had told the Judge. "I'm scared. You look up and see half a ton of beef barreling through the line just aching to sack you, why, you scramble as best you can so you don't end up in Intensive Care."

The Judge, remembering his own lost son, thought Noah a handsome young man. He had his mother's broad, sculpted features and when he grew older he'd resemble those Benin bronzes of kings with their air of regal gravitas. His skin was black with a ruddy undertone and he wore his hair cropped short. He had a wide, warm smile and a laugh so boomy Sarah said it rattled windows.

Noah finished his rowing, slid his feet from the stirrups, and went over to sit next to the Judge. He used Hampton's towel to mop head, neck, shoulders, and upper torso.

"No game this weekend?" the Judge asked.

"Nope. We got a bye and everyone's happy about it. Give us a chance to rest and mend. That last game was a killer. Sprains, strains, pulled this and pulled that, and one concussion. We can use the time off."

"Time to think about going to college."

"Sure, Judge. I still haven't made up my mind, but I figured it wouldn't hurt to apply, so I wrote some letters. No harm done if I finally decide to skip college and go to work—right?"

"It's your decision."

"Oh, sure. But if I don't go to college you'll figure me for a double-damned fool—am I correct?"

"You're quite correct," Hampton said. "Where did you apply?"

"Morehouse and Howard. And then, just for laughs, Harvard, Yale, and Princeton."

"Why for laughs?"

"Those big places? What would they want with a black boy from a little bitty town in South Florida, a kid whose father deserted him and ended up dead in an alley, probably in a drug deal that went bust. Can you see one of those Ivy League universities eager to take me on?"

"You can't tell," the Judge said. "Send in your applications and see what they say."

"I know what they'll say: No, no, and no. And besides, I could never afford it."

"There are scholarships available. And grants. And naturally I'll be willing to help out."

Noah turned to look at him. "That's another reason I want to go to work and earn a salary as soon as I can—to pay you back. You've done a lot for me and Mom. We can't sponge on you forever."

"Well, of course I'm keeping track of every penny you owe me," Hampton said. "I mark it down in a big ledger."

Noah's laugh boomed. "You'll get it all back," he said. "Someday. With interest."

The Judge made no response.

The boy stood up. "Got to shower and change. Mr. Folsby wants me to sparkle up his boat this afternoon. Now there's a man I'd like to work for. He pays good money. I wonder if he'd give me a regular job in his company after I get out of high school."

"I doubt it," the Judge said. "Emmet's company employs only people with a college degree."

Noah shook his head. "You never give up, do you?"

"Never. Go to college, Noah, if you expect to have a future."

"I'll think on it," the boy promised and started to leave.

"Ask your mother to come up, please," Hampton called after him. "If she's not busy."

Noah gave him a wave and final smile, then he was gone. He knows, the Judge thought, of course he knows about his mother and me. But he's a smart, sunny boy and accepts it. Hampton hoped he had Noah's respect. Not adulation—he neither expected nor wanted that—but a decent respect would be welcome. For esteem is a kind of affection, is it not? the Judge asked himself. Perhaps even a kind of love.

2

REBIRTH OF A BRAHMIN...

Seth Parnell Hampton had been a judge, his father had been a judge, and his grandfather had been a judge until he was killed while taking part in Chamberlain's bayonet charge at Little Round Top.

The Hampton wealth did not come from the practice of law, of course. Prior to the judge-ships, the Hamptons had been New England merchants who sent sailing vessels laden with beads, tin pans, and calico to West Africa. There the cargo was sold or bartered for slaves. They were conveyed to the West Indies and sold or bartered for rum which was returned to New England.

The profits from this triangular trade were used to buy farmlands, mills, factories, and shipyards. During the course of these acquisitions, the Hamptons became closely involved in Massachusetts public affairs, and though no Hampton ever ran for elective office the family grew a behind-the-scenes political power. Vestiges of their influence survived, tended and nurtured by Seth Parnell, now the oldest of a clan scattered over the world with a variety of surnames.

The Judge was a graduate of Harvard Law and had a distinguished career as a corporate attorney before being appointed to the bench. Everyone agreed he was a personable man, an articulate and talented jurist, and might have been considered for a seat on the Supreme Court except for a flaw which became more apparent as his career progressed: He was a heavy drinker, sometimes classified as a functioning alcoholic.

The problem worsened with his marriage to Matilda Lenore Lowell, a large, florid woman almost as wealthy as he. Mrs. Hampton was also a habitual drinker, matching her husband martini for martini. Members of their private club referred to her as Waltzing Matilda, not for her dancing skill but for her gait when inebriated.

Seth and Matilda had one child, a son named Jonathon Osgood Hampton, called Joe: a slight corruption of his initials. His father planned on a Harvard degree and the legal profession for Joe, culminating in appointment to the bench. But the boy insisted on a military career. He was graduated from West Point third in his class and was assigned to an infantry regiment (at his request) shortly after he was married to a young woman of whom neither of his parents approved. Sally Mae Kincaid was from Georgia and had, as Mattie said, "large breasts and a tiny mind."

Jonathon Osgood Hampton went to Vietnam a captain and returned a corpse. His widow remarried within a year ("Unseemly haste" was the Judge's verdict), and his parents' drinking increased as their marriage crumbled. It became obvious to Seth's friends and compeers he was no longer capable of performing the duties of his office. It was gently suggested he resign before his behavior in the courtroom became a public scandal. Seth agreed; he was a realistic man—when sober.

Still devastated by the death of their son, the Hamptons moved to South Florida. They purchased a mansion on the Hillsboro Mile—the section of Hillsboro Beach inhabited by the wealthy who sought security behind locked gates. The house was much too large for the now childless couple, but they were convinced the indoor swimming pool, exercise room, and sauna would enable them to establish a disciplined and abstemious lifestyle.

It didn't, of course. They soon joined a raffish crowd of retirees who drank as much as they. Life became a dissolute routine of three-martini lunches, three-martini "happy hours," and bibulous dinners at Boca Raton restaurants followed by confused nights of partying. Lost in an alcoholic haze, Seth and Matilda became strangers to each other. Despair at their son's death, which should have brought them closer in shared grief, only served to drive them farther apart.

The Judge returned to his home one morning after an early round of golf to find his wife seated on a stack of luggage in the foyer. She was smoking a cigarillo.

"I'm waiting for a cab," she announced. "I'm leaving."

He stared at her. "Is it Florida?" he asked.

"No," she said, "it's you. Why did you let him go?"

It was an argument repeated a dozen times in almost identical words.

"Mattie, I couldn't stop Joe from going to West Point and I couldn't stop him from going to Vietnam. He *wanted* to go."

"You could have put your foot down."

"He was a man, not a boy. You know how independent he was. And intelligent enough to accept the consequences of his own decisions."

"You could have pulled strings, had Joe assigned to someplace safe."

"And incur his anger and scorn? No thank you."

"You could have done *something!*" she cried. "But you did *nothing!*"

He was weary of these endless quarrels, which left both more embittered.

"Go then," he told her. "Leave. I'm past caring."

"You've never cared in your life. Never."

They traded short, sharp curses until he stomped away. And that was how their marriage ended, assailing each other with gutter language. Within a year they were legally divorced, and Judge Seth Parnell Hampton rattled around the big house by himself, served by a ruffianly crew who stole from him and laughed when they found him lying on the lawn, sprawled in a drunken stupor.

On a steamy day in 1975 he was playing golf in a foursome of drinking companions. He holed out on the seventh green, leaned down to take his ball from the cup, and suddenly was on the grass, prone, his heart pounding at such a rate he was certain it was about to explode.

His last conscious thought was that he had wanted to die as gallantly as his grandfather at Gettysburg. But he was dying on a golf course, not a battlefield. And the men standing around him were not wearing uniforms and carrying muskets; they were wearing lime-green slacks and carrying putters.

He awoke in a hospital bed. His arrhythmic heart required cardioversion to shock it back to a normal beat. A strep infection of the urinary tract was treated with antibiotics. And he was told his liver was turning to a rock and if he wished to continue drinking he'd be wise to bring his last will and testament up to date.

Two weeks later he returned home in an ambulance. For the following month he was visited thrice weekly by a nurse who took his blood pressure, temperature, pulse. And a physical therapist came twice weekly to help him walk again by assisting him in a series of mild exercises.

By the time the month ended he was walking slowly with the aid of a cane, feeling so fragile he feared his body might simply shatter and fall in a scatter of small pieces. With no overseer he neglected his daily regimen and stretching and bending exercises. He became stiff and creaky, and one day he phoned his physician and asked if massage would help unkink the knotting in his neck, shoulders, and back.

"Couldn't hurt," the doctor said. "I can recommend a good masseuse. But she's black. Do you have any objection to that?"

"None whatsoever," the Judge replied, amused by the question.

An appointment was made and Sarah Demijohn showed up on time in a battered pickup. He instantly thought he had never before seen such a primitively beautiful woman. But there was an edge of severity in her carved features.

He guessed. "Are you part Indian?" he asked.

She nodded. "Chickasaw. On my mother's side."

"Chickasaw? They're from Alabama and Mississippi, aren't they?"

She was pleased and he saw her ecstatic smile for the first time. "Now how'd you know that?" she marveled.

She lifted a folded massage table from the pickup. It was about the size of a card table, had a carrying handle, and was obviously heavy. But Sarah Demijohn had no trouble lugging it up three flights of stairs. She walked ahead, wearing white shorts, and he saw the muscles flexing in her solid legs. They paused a moment to allow the Judge to rest.

"Were you ever a dancer?" he asked her.

She was amazed. "You do see things, don't you?" she said. "Yes, I did some dancing. It was years ago."

"Ballet?"

"Not likely. Not with my legs, behind, and

bosom. I was with Katherine Dunham. You know her?"

"I certainly know her work. I went down to New York from Boston to see her dance. She was a revelation. I was used to classical ballet, the cool serenity and bloodless elegance. The *Swan Lake* kind of thing. Dunham showed me how stirring dance can be, its physicality and vitality. Why did you give it up?"

"Got married," she said shortly.

In the exercise room she took off her jacket, unfolded and set up the massage table, assuring him it wouldn't collapse. She told him to undress, leaving on his underwear if he liked or using a towel or sheet to conceal what she called his "private parts."

He undressed in the bathroom adjoining the sauna. He was ashamed of his body. Since his illness and the end of his drinking he had lost almost twenty-five pounds. His crepey skin hung in blotched folds, his legs had become hairless and shiny, his shoulders were bowed. There had been a time when he was proud of his physique. Now a glance at his nakedness in a mirror frightened him.

He came out with a large towel knotted about his waist. Sarah looked at him and shook her head. "You too skinny, Judge," she said.

"And flabby," he added.

"You eating?" she demanded.

"Not much," he admitted. "I don't have any appetite."

"Gotta eat," she said. "Maybe it's the food you're getting turns you off."

He couldn't mount the high massage table. They solved the problem by having him first step up on the wooden bench, steadied by Sarah's strong arms, then sliding onto the table. He lay facedown. She rolled up the sleeves of her shirt and started on him.

"You ever have a massage before?" she asked him.

"A long time ago."

"Well, I'll take it easy and not go too deep. You just skin and bones anyway. Can't go deep in that. Now you try to relax and let me pry you loose."

He felt her hard fingers probing his neck and shoulders. Then his arms. Then his back. It was a joy to feel her touch, a rhythmic caress.

He asked about her life and she spoke freely. She had given up dancing when she married. Her husband got in trouble with the law. Then he abandoned her and their son, who was eight years old. She went to school to learn massage and eventually got her license. Now she was getting by. Not becoming rich, mind you, but putting food on the table.

Speaking of her husband she said, "He was a bad man, but I loved him," and the Judge admired the easy way she could live with contradictions. He wished he had the gift.

He told her he was divorced and his son had died in Vietnam. She was the first person he had spoken to about the illness which had shaken him.

"I was at death's door and knocking," he said.

He told her of his current problems with the

thieving, inefficient domestic staff. The indoor pool had a leak, the house needed hurricane shutters, the landscaping was in execrable condition. There was a long list of things needing to be done, but he had neither the desire nor the energy.

"No friends to help you out?"

"I have no friends," he said, "since I stopped drinking."

She helped him turn onto his back, the towel tied loosely across his loins. As she worked on his shoulders, chest, waist, being very slow and tender, they chatted of many things: Florida weather, favorite foods, dancers they had seen perform. He told her more about his dead son and she told him more about her living child. They were both survivors, exchanging tales of wonder and travail.

"I'd like to take your towel away," she said, "so's I can get at your thighs."

"Go ahead," he said.

She unknotted the towel and spread it open. "Well, well," she said, "what have we here?"

"Two prunes and a noodle," he said faintly, mortified because he was quoting his ex-wife.

"Nah," Sarah said. "Where there's life, there's hope." And she leaned over him.

He closed his eyes. Memories stirred, first in his mind and then in his body. Warm pleasure replaced cold pain and he loved the woman ministering to him.

Judge Hampton had always believed in free will and its unfettered expression. He thought only chance and accident might interfere with one's planned destiny, but through deliberate actions we make our way. Now, swimming in bliss, he wondered for the first time if divine intervention might play a role he had ignored all his life.

He laughed silently at such an absurd notion and moments later reached up to pull Sarah close so he might embrace the woman who had given him life.

He paid her double the fee she asked.

"You don't have to do that," Sarah said.

"I know I don't *have* to do it, but I *want* to. Will you return next week?"

"Only if you promise to exercise," she said. "Every day. A little bit. Keep your juices flowing."

"I'll do it," he vowed.

When she came back the following week, the Judge took her to his library, sat her down, offered her a drink, which she declined.

He recited the speech he had prepared. He wanted her to move into his home, become his majordomo. She would fire the present domestic staff and hire new people, especially a good cook. Have hurricane shutters installed, the indoor swimming pool patched, cleaned and filled, all necessary repairs made, and the landscaping restored to its original verdancy. She would be the honcho of his estate, make all household decisions, keep a record of all expenses. He would pay for everything, including a handsome salary for her plus health insurance.

She asked only one question: "Will my son live here?"

"Of course," Judge Hampton said. "And have his own room."

She began to weep.

Within six months all had been accomplished. The house shone. The grounds looked beautiful. The new chef provided a varied and appetizing menu. The indoor pool became a neighborhood attraction, used by his few new friends and, once a week, by the new staff.

The Judge gained weight, his grayish skin attained a healthy flush. He exercised regularly, used the pool (never alone), and occasionally went for walks along the beach, wading in the frothy ocean up to his knees and laughing with delight.

The years passed—so quickly!—and soon Noah was thinking of college and the Judge was planning. There had been a time when his interests were solely devoted to the practice of law, Boston politics, his church. Now he had become fascinated and engrossed by the gritty interactions between people, their motives, and why they acted in the queer ways they sometimes did. That, he decided, was where the drama of life lay. He ceased to brood on his own mortality.

On Thanksgiving Day of 1981, having finished their turkey dinner, the Judge, Sarah, and Noah moved outside to an umbrella table on the terrace. They drank iced black coffee, nibbled on petit fours. They watched fishing boats and pleasure craft moving slowly in the sunlight spangling a calm sea.

Suddenly, almost with a shock, Judge Seth

Parnell Hampton realized he was content. And sharing his happiness were the people responsible for it: a beautiful woman, a handsome son. The Judge looked at them and the word "family" came into his thoughts. It was such a sweet word he wanted to utter it aloud. Family.

3

BEST LAID SCHEMES...

A few moments after Noah departed on Friday morning Sarah arrived at the exercise room. She was carrying a gallon jug of chilled water and a stack of plastic cups. The Judge was continually awed by her ability to anticipate his needs.

"Yes, the sauna," he said, smiling. "Would you care to join me?"

"For a while," she answered. "To sweat out my wickedness."

"That won't take long," he said.

They didn't bother locking the hallway door. The staff, like Noah, was undoubtedly aware of their intimacy and respected their privacy.

They sat naked on towels spread over the rough wood platform in the dry sauna. The heat rose rapidly and both hunched over, forearms on knees.

"I spoke to Noah this morning," Hampton said. "About going to college. He's betwixt and between. Sarah, he *must* go."

80

"I know. But he cannot be forced. He wants to be independent."

"Like my son," the Judge said. "Noah thinks he should go to work when he finishes high school. He wants to pay me back for what I've provided. It's admirable but ridiculous. I neither expect nor would I accept any money from him."

"Sweet Daddy," she said, moving so their slick shoulders pressed.

"I want him to go to Harvard, my alma mater."

"Harvard? You think he has a chance?"

"A very good chance. He is earning an A average. He is computer-literate. He is president of his class and captain of the football team. Most important, he is black. Universities and corporations are currently under pressure to diversify. At the moment, qualified minority applicants are hard to find. I think Harvard will welcome Noah's application."

"Judge. I am not as certain as you. And if he is rejected he will be hurt."

"And blame me for raising his hopes. I'm willing to risk it. Sarah, I must tell you I am not without resources. Perhaps I cannot pull strings the way I once did, but I can still give them a gentle tug. The first step is to convince Noah to attend college and include Harvard in his applications. Then I intend to write letters and make personal telephone appeals on his behalf. I am acquainted with several highly placed individuals in the University hierarchy. In addition, there are many alumni who will help Noah since I have gladly assisted them in the past in similar situations. Finally, I have made many donations to Harvard and have served as trustee on several of their funds. All these things count, Sarah. There is no substitute for personal relationships, for chits earned and eventually paid. It's the way the world works."

"What can I do?" she asked.

"Convince Noah he must attend college. Don't base it on his need for more learning per se. Express sympathy with his desire to repay me. But emphasize he can never hope to do it without a college education to prepare him for a good job and an income impossible to earn with merely a high school diploma."

She thought of what he had said for a silent moment. Then: "Yes," she said, "it might work. I will do it."

"Good," Hampton said. "Noah's agreement is only the first step, but everything else depends on it. He is a smart, intellectually curious boy, Sarah, and I know he will succeed at Harvard. I remember the first day he arrived to live here. He wandered into my library and his eyes widened. 'So many books,' he said. 'Have you read all of them?' I told him I had, some two and three times. He asked if he might borrow some to read. I told him of course he could, and he wanted me to pick out books he might like. I started him on such things as *Treasure Island, King Solomon's Mine,* Conan Doyle. Then he began making his own selections."

"He reads a lot," Sarah said proudly. "And studies hard."

"I know he does. It's been a pleasure to see how his tastes have changed and matured as he's grown older. He's gotten away from light fiction. Now he prefers history, biography, philosophy—and poetry! Harvard will broaden his horizons even further."

"I will do as you say," she repeated. "Now I must leave you because the man is coming to replace the cartridges in our water filters. I must be there to make certain there are no leaks."

The Judge didn't smile. He knew she treated her housekeeping duties seriously, and he was grateful she kept his home functioning with a minimum of mishaps. They enjoyed a sweaty embrace, a kiss, and she called him "Sweet Daddy" before departing for a shower in the adjoining bathroom.

The Judge remained in the sauna awhile longer. He drank two cups of water (now tepid) and poured two over his head and shoulders.

He was satisfied with the way things had gone. He had told Sarah nothing but the truth. Noah's agreement to attend college was necessary before the Judge could begin to engineer his enrollment at Harvard. But Hampton had not told Sarah—or anyone else—the full extent of his intentions.

He had witnessed the growth of Noah from boy to youth to young man. The physical changes had been apparent and a delight.

Less apparent but more delightful—even exciting!—had been the development of Noah's intellect, evidenced by his choice of books, his scholastic record, and by many, many long conversations during which the Judge and Noah discussed and sometimes argued about a variety of topics: politics, the Civil War, the effectiveness of President Reagan, the future of the Cold War, the enigma of female behavior.

Gradually, as Hampton came to recognize the potential of this stripling, he envisioned a fitting future for him. At first he called it a dream but *dream* implied a fantasy and the Judge's thoughts were not fanciful but rooted in reality. Similarly the word *scheme* was not correct since it connoted craftiness and connivance. The Judge tentatively settled on *plan* as the word to describe how he intended to shape the destiny of Noah Demijohn.

For the time being he would keep it secret, knowing if it was to succeed he would eventually have to solicit the assistance and cooperation of others. But the beginning he could manage by himself, hoping when the time came to enlist aides his design would be so advanced and successful it would not be rejected out of hand as impractical, impossible, foolhardy, or even insane.

But then, alone in a timbered room, naked and sweating, Seth Parnell Hampton suddenly thought of a word more accurate than *plan* to represent his project. The word he chose with much satisfaction was *campaign*. He would engage in a campaign which might take years to complete, might end in failure, but which would give his life purpose and meaning.

Yes, he decided, it would be a campaign. And he would be the Commanding General. With an army of one good soldier.

4

ANCHORS AWEIGH...

Barbara Ann Folsby had had her hair bobbed! After internships at the Folsby Press offices she realized long tresses were simply unsuitable for the corporate world. Either she spent too much time putting her hair up each morning or she left it down and had to endure occasional strokings by coworkers and, in New York, from wild-eyed strangers on the street.

So she told an exclusive Manhattan hairdresser she wanted a "Jackie Kennedy cut." He sniffed but did as requested and the result altered her appearance remarkably. Her features emerged from the mass of tousles, becoming sharper, clearer. There was less prettiness in her face, more knowing elegance.

Brett defined the change. "Now you look like Nefertiti," he said.

Her father was saddened by the loss of her long hair as she knew he would be. "I've saved you a curl," she told him. "You can wear it in a locket about your neck." He accepted her mockery without comment.

She was working in New York when she flew home for the Thanksgiving weekend. Brett had come in from an assignment in Dallas, so the family was assembled for the holiday. On Friday morning, seeking privacy, Barbara carried a briefcase of confidential documents down to the Folsby yacht moored at their dock on the Intracoastal Waterway.

The boat was a 1972 fifty-eight-foot Hatteras motor yacht with three staterooms, two shower stalls and heads, and a galley. Emmet was not a man who, like many owners of boats—and motorcycles!—was compelled to trade in every year for a larger, more powerful, and more expensive toy. But the '72 yacht had been completely refitted in 1977 and updated every year with the latest electric and electronic gear. The name of the craft, painted on the stern, was *Folsby's Folly*.

Barbara had hoped to be alone on the boat, but when she darted across highway A1A to the dock she saw Noah Demijohn swabbing the afterdeck of the *Folly*. He was stripped to the waist and wearing white duck cutoffs. His wide feet were bare. As she drew closer she heard him trying to sing "Bette Davis Eyes" and she laughed.

He turned, flashed her a broad smile. "Hi, Miss Barbara," he said. "Happy holiday!"

"Same to you, Noah," she said. "Have a good turkey?"

"The best. Ate myself silly. You?"

"Scrumptious. You working off the calories?"

"Just sprucin' things up. Your father knows what this sun and salt can do to a boat."

"I have some work to do myself. Hope I won't be in the way."

"Nah. I'm done below deck... it's all yours. I want to finish swabbing and shine the brass. Then I'll be on my way, Miss Barbara."

"Noah," she said, "how old are you now?"

"Seventeen."

"And how long have we known each other?"

"Oh lordy, seven years at least."

"Don't you think it's time you dropped the 'Miss Barbara' jive? Just plain Barbara will suit me fine."

He leaned gracefully on the mop handle and they looked at each other gravely, both sensing a sea change in their relationship. She saw a big, strong boy with noble features which made him seem older than his age. He might have been muscular, but he moved with a lilt. She liked his Afro; it fitted his head tightly: a helmet of black curls.

"Tell you what," he said. "Suppose I call you Barbara when there's just the two of us and Miss Barbara when other people are around."

She smiled. "Noah, you're a born diplomat. All right, let's play it your way."

She boarded the *Folly* and went down to the master stateroom, the only one of the three with desk and chair. She sat a few moments, not moving herself but feeling the hull shift in the wakes of passing boats. In the same way she felt a shifting of her thoughts after the brief

87

encounter with Noah. She reckoned a youth as handsome as he must have a dozen girls clawing after him. Girls his own age. Or younger.

She realized with a small pang she was now twenty-five. It seemed a milestone but on what road she could not have said. Three years and four months ago—just yesterday!—she had been wearing cap and gown. Now she was competing in the gritty workaday world with its endless revelations, dangers, and opportunities. For instance...

She had been surprised to learn of her father's ruthlessness in his business dealings. During their lovemaking he was tender, complaisant, sometimes even suppliant. But Emmet was a different man in the office. Despite his camaraderie with his employees he ran a tight ship and did not suffer fools gladly. He had summarily fired a magazine editor who had twice addressed him as Emmy.

Brett, to her astonishment, had proved to be both talented and efficient. And creative. Two years previously he had suggested a thorough redesign of all Folsby magazines. In a brilliant presentation to the Executive Committee, which Barbara had attended, he had displayed samples of recommended changes in logos, type faces, layouts, and graphics. He was prepared with cost estimates, and his proposal had earned enthusiastic approval. When the makeover was completed, the Folsby Press won a design award and advertising revenue increased 19 percent for the year.

But her brother, Barbara was convinced, had made a fatal error.

The Folsby Press was structured with an administrative department at the top, headed by her father of course. Farther down the pyramid were the two main operating divisions: editorial and advertising.

Barbara learned magazine publishers, trade and consumer, did not make money selling magazines to readers. Profits came from selling readers to advertisers. In fact, some of Folsby's periodicals had "controlled circulations," meaning the magazines were given away to a selected list of influential readers.

The sale of advertisements was the engine driving the Folsby Press. And, Barbara noted, most of the executives in the ruling management echelon had started their careers and gained experience in the advertising department.

Brett had opted for the editorial side of the business. His sister thought him a fool. Her instinct was: Follow the Money! She had told her father she'd like to be assigned to the advertising division. "It's fascinating," she said. "And I think I have a real talent for selling." Emmet agreed to give her the opportunity to prove it.

Selling advertisements would be the main path to success at the Folsby Press, but there were other actions to be taken to aid the growth of her career. One was to cultivate a coterie sympathetic to her feminist views and loyal to her because of their shared faith.

And there were those who flocked to her banner because, after all, she *was* the boss's daughter. Emmet had said firmly no nepotism and no special favors. His employees knew better. They wanted only to be counted as dependable friends to a potential heiress.

Barbara opened her briefcase and drew out the documents for review. There was a one-page letter addressed to her and signed by Judith Kopp, executive assistant to Tom Jessup, manager of the New York office. The letter detailed a sad story of sexual harassment by Jessup over a period of several years.

Also included were raunchy notes and letters written to Judy by Tom, and two recent tape cassettes containing short conversations between the two, which had taken place in Judith's office. The tapes had been made on a miniaturized, voice-activated recorder concealed in the EA's desk. The verbal suggestions made by Jessup were obscene.

Barbara had dictated the letter Kopp had signed and had purchased the hidden tape recorder. The total result was a damning indictment of an executive using his power to coerce an employee and threaten her if she resisted. The phrase "If you know what's good for you..." occurred on the tapes and in the notes. The evidence was conclusive. Jessup's career at the Folsby Press was finished.

Barbara had first intended to present this material to her father with an impassioned plea he *do* something to end the poor woman's anguish. But now, after careful consideration, she decided it would be wiser to mute her role lest she be suspected of being an agent provocateur. She would merely hand him the package and say something like, "Emmet, I think you better review this. It could be trouble."

She repacked the briefcase but didn't immediately leave. She sat in the swivel chair, swinging idly side to side, and wondered why a man as intelligent as Tom Jessup would risk career, income, marriage, future, everything—for an affair with a subordinate. Judith Kopp, Barbara acknowledged, was pleasant, personable, but hardly a raving beauty. She was, in fact, rather plain. But Jessup had lost all sense in a berserk pursuit of a plain woman. The man was besotted.

And as she swung idly, side to side, Barbara's glance fell on the bed in the master stateroom. She stopped swinging. "The scene of the crime," she said aloud but softly, softly.

The night of July 4, 1973. Her mother ill. Brett out of town. She and Emmet had taken *Folsby's Folly* down the Waterway and out to the ocean through the Hillsboro Inlet. To watch the fireworks from the Pompano Fishing Pier.

She had been seventeen. Noah's present age.

A hot, close night. Many boats anchored offshore. A crowd on the beach waiting for the show. Then it began. Rockets. Stars. Flowers blooming. The black sky sequined. Reds, yellows, blues, greens. Silver and gold. Explosions and the cheers of spectators.

Then they saw only each other and after a while heard nothing but their own cries. How had it happened? Who had made the first move, the first suggestion? Mutual. It had been mutual, a rare and wonderful celebration of the nation's birthday. He was not the first man she had bedded but the oldest and most practiced.

There had been no guilt then and none since then. They made love in a moral void. She with her dewy body. He with his hard strength. Joy for both but no blame for either. Natural, she decided. It was all so natural there was no need to ponder its significance. It had none but rapture.

She smiled at the memory. Sex with fireworks. A B movie. She took up her briefcase and went topside. Noah was still working, polishing the yacht's brass bell.

"All finished, Miss Barbara?" he said, then grinned. "I mean, all finished, Barbara?"

"I've had my fun and now I'm done," she recited.

"Barbara, you think there's any chance of our going fishing again? Sometime soon? I hear grouper and snapper are just jumping into the boats out there."

"No barracuda?" she teased. "Like last time."

He laughed. "I had to cut my line or that sucker would have taken my arm. No more barracuda for this boy, I swear."

She looked at him thoughtfully. "Don't be so sure," she said. "Will you be free tomorrow?"

"For fishing?" Noah said. "Anytime of the day or night. You'll ask your daddy?"

"I sure will."

"You think he'll say yes?"

"No problem," Barbara said.

5

FUTURE SHOCK...

The day was a glorious meld of hot sun and cool breeze. There was a scattering of tiny clouds—confetti tossed high in the delft-blue sky. The sea lapped gently. Pelicans sailed, dived suddenly, soared aloft again with the catch flopping in their long beaks. The outside world was vibrant, charged with movement and hope.

The sickroom of Constance Folsby was still, dim, almost painfully chill. She sat motionless in her wheelchair, a pallid wraith, head tilted to one side as if it were too heavy a burden to be borne.

"It *is* a good day," she insisted to her husband. "I feel a bit stronger and I haven't had a single muscle spasm since yesterday. And I'm speaking clearly, am I not?"

"Clear as can be," Emmet assured her and reached for one of her limp hands. He sat in a straight chair close to her. On the floor was a current bestseller she had been reading when he entered: *Noble House*.

"Constance," he said, "I was so happy you

could join us at the table yesterday. I know it was a chore for you, but we did have fun, didn't we? Brett's jokes! And you ate very well I noticed."

"Just some white meat."

"And some yams and some stringbeans," he said, laughing.

"Well, I was hungry," she admitted. "And it all looked so good. But to tell you the truth, I hardly knew what I was eating. Something has happened to my tastebuds."

"I had a talk with Dr. Steiner," he told her. "He says a lot of research is being done and several drugs are being developed to treat the symptoms."

"But no cure," she said.

"Not yet. But one may be discovered. And if your spasms and weakness and depression can be lessened—well, that's something to be thankful for, isn't it?"

"Of course it is," she said, looking away, and he realized she was humoring him.

They were silent awhile in that desolate room. He sought the courage to broach the subject which had brought him to her side, but it did not come easily.

"Emmet," she said suddenly, "what are the children doing?"

"Dressing for the party. Didn't they tell you?"

Her face froze for an instant, then relaxed as she remembered, and it made her happy.

"Of course," she said. "Gracie McCall is engaged, and they're going to her party in Palm

Beach. I'm glad for Gracie. She's a sweet girl even if she is scatterbrained. You know, I always thought she had eyes for Brett."

"Wouldn't doubt it."

"But she's going to marry a stockbroker. Emmet, I wish Barbara and Brett would find someone."

"They have plenty of time. They're both young."

"You and I were married at their age."

"But we were in love."

"You were," his wife said, "but I wasn't— until later. I just thought you were a good catch."

He was delighted with her feisty mood. "And was I a good catch?" he asked.

She flipped a palm back and forth. *"Comme ci, comme ça,"* she said, and they both smiled.

He thought he could bring it up now. "Constance," he began, "do you remember our talking about signing powers of attorney in case either of us becomes incapacitated?"

She nodded.

"Well, I've had umpteen conferences with our lawyers and even asked Judge Hampton for his advice. That is what I'd like to do... "

He spoke slowly, trying to keep his voice expressionless, trying not to reveal these matters were as disheartening to him as they must be to her.

If he should predecease her, she would inherit all the shares of the Folsby Press and control the company. If that happened and she became physically or mentally incapacitated,

95

her powers would be delegated to a board of five persons: Brett, Barbara, and Folsby's Chief Executive Officer, Chief Financial Officer, and Chief Legal Officer.

Similarly, if Constance should predecease him, he would retain control of the company until such time as he resigned or died. If, during his reign, he became physically or mentally incapable of performing the duties of his office, his authority would be delegated to the same five-person group named in her power of attorney.

He started explaining the conditions which must exist before the powers of attorney were put into effect but stopped when he saw he was losing her.

She had slumped in the wheelchair. Her eyes had almost closed and her head drooped farther to one side. Beneath the white peignoir and gown her body seemed flaccid, a husk. She who had been so vital was now shrunken and empty. One of her knees trembled uncontrollably.

"Constance," he called sharply, fearing his talk of their mortality had darkened her bright mood.

Her eyes opened halfway; she looked at him dimly.

"Will you sign the power of attorney, darling?" he asked her. "I'll have the attorney come here and we'll both sign our documents at the same time."

"Whatever you think best," she said weakly.

He could not recall her ever having said that

before. She had been as much partner as wife, had helped him grow the business—a smart, energetic executive. She had been decisive and her judgments invariably proved correct. Now her will had shriveled, she had surrendered to his.

"Would you like to be in bed, dear?" he said. "Naomi must have finished her tea by now. Shall I call her to help you?"

"Please." But when he kissed her cheek and started away she said, "Emmet, I'm sick and tired of being sick and tired."

"I know," he said.

"No," she said. "You don't."

6

ARRIVALS AND DEPARTURES...

Brett Folsby was in his bedroom, fully dressed for the party, chatting on the phone with Simon Smithson in New York. Simon had spent the past two years attending classes in interior decorating and interning (at no salary) with several Manhattan professionals. He was telling Brett about his most recent course of instruction.

"Wallpaper!" he cried. "Can you imagine spending a month studying wallpaper? Believe me, laddie, there's less there than meets the eye. Anyhoo, part of our final exam was to create a new, novel, and original use for wallpaper.

Most of my fellow wannabes suggested book jackets or framed squares of abstract patterns displayed as artwork. I became the teacher's pet by recommending wallpaper be used as a floor covering."

"Surely you were jesting."

"*Au contraire,* sweetie. Use it like carpeting, tile, or linoleum. Lay it wall-to-wall and put coordinated area rugs in the trafficked places. Most of a floor never gets walked on anyway. What do you think?"

"Loony. But I've learned to trust your crazy ideas. Listen, Simon, Colorado had a heavy snowfall and the runs at Aspen are open. How about meeting me there next weekend and we can share a schuss or two."

"Sounds good to me. I could use a little fresh air. To say nothing of your estimable company. How long has it been?"

"Too long," Brett said. "A month at least. I'll make the reservations at Aspen and give you a buzz next week."

"Super. Before you hang up I've got an incredible story to tell you. About a week ago I got a frantic phone call from an old pal in San Francisco. Haven't seen him in years. He told me he's got cancer. Of course I was all tea and sympathy. Then yesterday I got an equally frantic call from *another* old friend in Frisco and guess what—he's got cancer, too! Two golden lads stricken at the same time. How's that for a weird coincidence?"

"It *is* weird," Brett said. "What is it—lung cancer?"

"That's the kicker," Simon said. "Both of them have a rare form of the disease. I forget the name, but you get purplish blotches all over your body."

"Gruesome," Brett said. "Ah well, the docs will probably clear it up with chemotherapy or radiation or something. Hey, sport, I've got to run."

"What are you doing tonight?"

"A bash up in Palm Beach. My sister's best friend has become engaged and her family is tossing a shindig to celebrate getting rid of her."

"What are you wearing?"

"A putty-colored linen suit with an embroidered waistcoat you've never seen. And my Sulka ascot."

"Sounds fabulous. Well, have fun. Behave yourself. The choice is yours."

They both hung up laughing.

Brett bounced downstairs, carefully opened the door of his mother's sickroom, peeked in. She was in bed, awake, staring at the ceiling. She turned her head slowly when he entered, gave him a soft smile. He swooped to kiss her cheek.

"How are you feeling, sweetheart?" he asked.

"In the pink," she said ruefully. "Can't you tell? Oh my, don't you look nice."

"Too flashy?"

"Not at all. Just right. What did you do today?"

"Saw a movie. *On Golden Pond.*"

"Good?"

"Not my cup of oolong, but I think you'll like it. I'll get you the video, darling, just as soon as it comes out. Henry Fonda and Katharine Hepburn."

"Then I *will* like it. Hepburn is my favorite."

"How so?"

"She's so independent."

"Just like you," he said. "I better be on my way, love. Get a good night's sleep. I'll stop in tomorrow and read to you awhile if you like."

"Oh, yes. That would be nice."

He leaned to kiss her again and she clutched his arm.

"Brett," she said, almost whispering, "be kind to your sister."

"I'm always kind to her," he said with a stretched smile.

His mother released him and he paused at the doorway to give her a farewell waggle of fingers. Then he went out to the garage.

He was driving a red 1980 BMW M-1. He was a poor driver with a penchant for jackrabbit starts and squealing brakes. He traded in every two or three years and invariably his used car was in wretched condition. He had once totaled a Jaguar XKE, being half-squiffed at the time, and had staggered away from the crackup with nary a scratch.

As Brett was driving toward Palm Beach, certain the party was going to be a bloody bore, Barbara Folsby was talking with her father in his second-floor office. She was wearing a white tuxedo pantsuit, and pinned to her lapel was the jeweled bird Judge Hampton had given her as a graduation gift.

"You look lovely, Barb," Emmet said, but she was aware of his distraction. "About this Judith Kopp matter..."

"Sorry I dumped it in your lap, Em," she said. "You have weightier problems than this."

"No, no. I'm glad you did. We can't let it become public. Tom Jessup will be allowed to resign for personal reasons or whatever he wants to put in his letter. He'll get severance pay and his pension—the idiot! Does Kopp want to keep her job?"

"I'm sure she does."

"Well, she'll get a raise, a special bonus, and a transfer to another city if she likes. That leaves only the selection of Jessup's replacement. I'll make some calls tomorrow asking for recommendations. I'd rather promote from within than go to a headhunter."

"Em, may I suggest someone?"

"Of course."

"Phil Horwitz, the advertising director of the northeast division. You know I've been working with him for the past six months and he really impresses me. He's knowledgeable, energetic, and a dynamite salesman."

Her father nodded. "I know his record. Yes, I'd say he's a candidate."

She didn't want to push it harder. "By the way, Em, I met Noah Demijohn today and he asked when we might go fishing again. Any chance of your taking time off tomorrow?"

"I doubt it," he said. "I'll be tied up on the phone cleaning up the Jessup mess. Look, you and Noah are good sailors. The two of you can easily handle the *Folly* in a calm sea. Why disappoint the boy just because I can't make it."

"I hate to go without you, Em."

"Nonsense. Take the *Folly* out and bring back some nice pompano. It'll be a treat for young Noah."

She smiled and patted his cheek.

Before leaving for the party she returned to her bedroom and phoned Phil Horwitz at his home in Connecticut.

"Barbara!" he said, surprised by her call. "Don't tell me you're working on a holiday weekend."

"Not exactly," she said. "Phil, I have something to tell you, but it's got to be strictly confidential. Okay?"

"Of course. I don't blab."

"Tom Jessup is leaving for reasons I can't tell you on the phone. The old man is going to consult with top execs about Jessup's replacement. I gave you a heavy plug and you're one of the candidates being considered. If you're interested in the job, now is the time to use whatever influence you might have."

There was a long moment of silence. Then he said, "Yes, I'm interested and there are some chits I can call in."

"Well, you better get busy. But for God's sake, keep my name out of it. You heard about it through the grapevine—understand?”

“Of course. And Barbara, thank you for giving me the plug. I won't forget it.”

“I know you won't,” she said. “I won't let you.”

Then she went downstairs and slid into her '78 Corvette. It was still in mint condition. She was a skillful driver and cosseted the Corvette as her father did the *Folly*.

She wished she could age as admirably as her car. That evening, preparing for the party, she had found two silver hairs among the gold and plucked them out. And was it her imagination or were there tiny lines appearing at the corners of her eyes and lips?

She reckoned she could always challenge age with cosmetic plastic surgery. She knew the importance of maintenance.

7

PARTY FAVORS...

The President was shot. The Pope was shot. Prince Charles married Lady Diana Spencer. Sandra Day O'Connor became the first woman appointed to the Supreme Court. American hostages held by Iran were released. Space shuttle *Columbia* returned successfully to earth. William Saroyan and Ann Harding died. Israel destroyed an Iraqi atomic reactor. And on the evening of November 27, 1981, Mr. and Mrs. Dennis McCall of Palm Beach,

Florida, hosted a party to announce the engagement of their daughter Gracie to Mr. Eric Warden of Boca Raton, Florida.

Brett fulfilled his social obligations as quickly as possible after entering the McCall mansion on Ocean Boulevard. He figured if he completed his duties immediately he would be able to slip away early if the party proved as dull as he anticipated.

He shook the plump hands of Mary and Dennis McCall, proud parents of the fiancée, and thanked them for inviting him to such a festive celebration. They accepted his good wishes with beaming gratitude since he was one of the few guests who did not remark, "Remember, you're not losing a daughter, you're gaining a bathroom."

He left them hastily, found the open bar, and had a small chilled vodka to give him courage to continue.

He sought out Gracie and her fiancé. He delivered a cheek kiss and felicitations to the former and a handclasp and congratulations to the latter. Eric Warden, affianced stockbroker, was a chesty young man wearing a necktie Brett considered venomous. His manner was brusque, his voice loud.

"How about those Dolphins?" was his greeting.

"Ah, yes," Brett said.

Apparently piqued by the lackluster response, Warden demanded, "You follow football?"

"Not closely."

"Baseball? Basketball?"

"Afraid not."

"Hockey?"

Tiring of this, Brett said, "Actually my favorite sports are curling and tossing the caber."

Gracie and her fiancé were bewildered. Brett smiled at both, murmured, "Bless you, my children," and started away. But Warden stopped him long enough to hand him a card. "In case you're thinking of investing," he said.

Brett made his escape pitying Gracie for pledging her troth to a churl who distributed business cards at his engagement party. Wandering through the throng, pausing occasionally to chat with acquaintances, he moved slowly back to the bar. He saw Barbara talking—or rather listening—to Oliver Pendragon. Brett thought his sister was looking about desperately for someone to rescue her. He derived great pleasure from her plight and wondered, not for the first time, how she could possibly endure such a lumpish man.

There was a crush at the bar and he continued exploring rather than join the mob. He found a room where a trio was playing tunes from Broadway musicals and couples were dancing. He sauntered on to a cavernous dining room. The caterers had laid out a banquet on the McCalls' table and supplied a number of small bistro tables, each with two wire chairs.

Brett examined the bravura display of viands but ignored sliced beef, ham, turkey, salads, and crudités to concentrate on the iced seafood: a tempting selection of stone crabs, shrimp, lobster claws, and king crab legs. He decided to delay his departure long enough to enjoy a light dinner.

He returned to the bar and waited patiently until he was able to obtain two glasses of chilled Sancerre. He carried his wine back to the dining room and snagged one of the few bistro tables still available. He heaped a plate with seafood and sat down to enjoy a crustacean feast.

From where he sat he could view the doorway to the dining room. He was halfway through his meal when his attention was caught by a very young woman standing just outside the entrance and peering in. It was her height which intrigued him. Brett guessed she had to be at least six feet tall, perhaps taller than he, and she was wearing sandals on bare feet.

Her dress was a simple shift of what appeared to be a coarse sand-colored fabric; Brett wondered if it might be burlap. It was hemmed a few inches above the knees of her slender legs and the shift was so loose, almost a teepee, it gave no hint of her figure; she could have been obese or anorexic.

What amused Brett was her gleaming black hair scissored in a gamine cut. It was remarkable to see a six-foot-tall waif. He rose and approached her.

"I beg your pardon," he said, "but if you are looking for a place to dine you're welcome to share my table."

A pixieish smile came and went so rapidly he wasn't certain it had existed.

"Thank you," she said in a breathy voice. "I don't want to eat, but I would like to sit down for a moment."

He escorted her to his table and she saw the two wine glasses.

"Oh," she said, "are you with someone? Am I interrupting?"

"Not at all," he said cheerfully. "I ordered a double so I wouldn't have to wait in line for a refill."

She would not let him fetch her a drink or food. But she consented to sample one shrimp and one king crab leg from his plate.

"I don't drink alcohol," she explained in her wispy voice, and he couldn't decide if she were shy or timid. "And this really isn't my kind of food. I do eat fish and chicken occasionally, but mostly I'm a vegetarian. I work in a health food store, you see."

"And practice what you preach," he said, smiling. "Allow me to introduce myself. My name is Brett Folsby and my sister Barbara is a close friend of Gracie McCall, which accounts for my presence. You?"

"My name is Zenobia Plummer and my sister Zoe is the assistant to Oliver Pendragon, who works for Mr. McCall's pharmaceutical company. Zoe invited me to come with her tonight."

Brett laughed. "So we both have sisters to thank for our meeting. Zenobia and Zoe. Greek?"

"Our mother is, not father."

"Ah. You live with your family?"

"No. Father died about five years ago and Mother moved back to Athens."

"Ever go over to see her?"

"Once. About three years ago. She's got a boyfriend. He's a pig."

"And you're a vegetarian."

Zenobia nodded and took the last shrimp from his plate. He started on his second glass of wine.

"Do you know Oliver Pendragon?" she asked.

"I do but not well."

"What do you think of him?"

Brett shrugged.

"Zoe is in love with him," she said casually. "I think he's a pig."

Brett took a deep gulp of wine. "Do you think all men are pigs?"

"Oh, no. Some are horses, very strong. And some are beautiful birds."

"And what am I?"

Her quick smile flickered. "Perhaps a fox. Or maybe a gazelle. I don't know you well enough to decide."

"Easily remedied," he said and stared at her over the rim of his wine glass.

She had a smooth face, nary a sign of line or wrinkle. Her lower lip was full, a short upper lip revealed a glisten of white teeth. Brett thought it was a new face which had never been used. Her eyes were her best feature: large, dark, liquid.

She became aware of his scrutiny. "How old do you think I am?" she challenged.

Twelve, he thought. "Sixteen?" he said.

"Nineteen."

"You do look younger."

"I intend never to grow old," she said determinedly.

"Easy to avoid," Brett said. "Die young."

He could not cease staring. An innocent, he thought. Something of a nut but artless and trusting. A dear. Truly a dear.

He was curious about the fine gold chain around her slender neck. Whatever was suspended from it had been tucked into the bodice of her tent, which had turned out to be corduroy, not burlap.

"What's at the end of your chain, Zenobia?" he asked.

She hauled it up and held it out to him. It appeared to be a chunk of clear glass, perhaps two inches long, with faceted sides.

"What an enormous diamond," he said. "And so oddly cut."

"Crystal," she said. "The rays bring peace and enable you to find your inner self. I always wear it and put it under my pillow when I sleep. It's a link to the universal oneness, the divine harmony."

She slipped the crystal back into her neckline and closed her eyes.

"Sleepy?" Brett asked.

"I'm trying to sense your aura," she said. Her eyes opened and she shook her head. "Too many people here. Too noisy. Auras can only be glimpsed in private and quiet. Otherwise you just see a clash of auras, all colors."

"What exactly is an aura?"

"Emanations of the inner spirit. All things have auras, even stones. They may be strong or weak, in all different colors. I have been told I have a very strong aura. Pink."

"Mine is probably weak," Brett said. "And muddy."

"Oh, no," she protested. "I'll bet you have a lovely aura."

She said she really wished she could go home and meditate. But she depended on her sister for transportation and Zoe wouldn't want to leave the party so soon. Brett asked where she lived and it turned out to be a condo in Pompano Beach, not far from his Hillsboro home. He said he was also ready to depart and would be glad to drive her home. She accepted eagerly and went off to tell her sister she was leaving. Brett took advantage of her brief absence to down a small brandy at the bar. He hoped it would improve his aura.

Twenty minutes later they were tooling southward in Brett's BMW. Zenobia had brought no coat or jacket but didn't seem bothered by the cool night breeze. He turned on the radio and she told him of an experiment she was conducting: playing music for her house plants—a ficus and a philodendron.

"I think they respond to classical music," she said. "Perk right up and get new shoots. But hard rock makes them droop."

"Me too," Brett said. "I prefer Cole Porter."

"Who's he?" she asked and he felt dreadfully old.

She lived in a three-story beach condo a mile south of Atlantic Boulevard. It was a nondescript building with a parking area larger than the scabrous lawn. Its single palm tree had died. Denuded of fronds the spongy trunk leaned drunkenly.

"Would you like to come up?" Zenobia asked.

"Do you wish me to," Brett said, "or are you just being polite?"

"Of course I wish you to," she said, astonished he could think she'd say something even remotely insincere.

"All right," he said. "And when you want me to be gone just say so; I won't be offended."

Her small one-bedroom apartment was on the third floor at the rear, windows facing the highway rather than beach and sea. The rooms were sparsely furnished with inexpensive maple pieces. The sisal rug on the living room floor had seen better days. There were several pyramids scattered about: large and small; wood, plastic, and tin. Taped on the wall was a poster of John Lennon.

"He was very spiritual," Zenobia said. "I cried when he was killed. Would you like a glass of carrot juice?"

It would be easy, Brett reflected, to top almost everything she said with a one-liner: a joke, a put-down, a biting gibe. But he found her simplicity and openness bewitching and resolved to curb his corrosive wit. One simply did not use irony with a child.

"No carrot juice, thanks," he said. "But you go ahead."

"Perhaps later. I'd like to do my meditation now. Do you mind, Brett?"

"Of course not," he said, realizing it was the first time she had used his name, and it pleased him. "How often do you meditate?"

"Twice a day, morning and evening."

"What exactly is the purpose?"

"When you meditate you contemplate the infinite, seek enlightenment, attempt to achieve tranquility and become one with the eternal universe."

She rattled this off so rapidly he was certain she had read it and memorized it—or maybe learned it from a master of Soto.

"Zenobia," he said, "may I call you Zen?"

"Oh, yes," she said. "I'd like that. Brett, I usually meditate naked. Will it embarrass you?"

"I'll try not to blush," he said, thinking— What a naif!

She came close to him and turned her back. "Please unzip me," she said.

Obediently he drew it down and it hissed at him. She shrugged the tent from her shoulders, stepped out, and left the corduroy crumpled on the floor. She was not totally naked; she was wearing white cotton briefs. She had no brassiere and there was nothing to warrant one.

He had seen many unclothed women, but

Zen was surely the most enchanting. She was supple as a young boy, her figure as new and unused as her face. Hip bones and rib cage didn't jut but were cushioned with soft flesh and satiny skin. He envisioned a peeled twig or sapling, just as smooth and pliant, and imagined if he could lift her and wave her body it would crack like a whip.

She sank to the floor, crossed her long legs, and easily assumed the lotus position, back straight, head upright. She closed her eyes. "Oom," she intoned.

Brett slumped in a white canvas butterfly chair. He wished he had a brandy in one hand, a cigarette in the other. But he had neither and could only sit still, smile at the bare infant folded on the floor, and muse on the strangeness of life.

"Oom," said Zenobia.

It *was* strange, Brett affirmed, and ruled solely by chance and accident. That year people were saying, "Go with the flow," but was there any other choice? Ambition, plans, hope—all were dependent on happenstance and only dreams provided an escape from the cruelty of the unpredictable—unless one opted for "the mouth of a revolver or the foot of the Cross."

"Oom," said Zenobia.

Contrarily, Brett acknowledged, chance could also provide totally unexpected opportunities and joys. Life was, after all, a matter of dumb luck, a crapshoot. And if Zenobia sought cosmic enlightenment, he wanted only his good fortune to continue. Why, he might have been born poor or, even worse, destined to become an Oliver Pendragon or an Eric Warden.

"Oom," said Zenobia.

Trying to find meaning, he finally decided, was a fool's game. Go with the flow. Try to avoid pain. Try to court pleasure. Play the hand dealt you and never complain. Accept All. If there was any answer that was it: Accept All.

Zenobia opened her eyes, uncrossed her legs, and rose from the floor, just floated up without using hands and arms to support herself. Brett struggled from the butterfly chair.

"Did you have a good meditation, Zen?" he inquired politely.

"Marvelous," she said in her whispery voice. She came close, took his face between her palms, looked deep into his eyes. "You know what I'd like to do now?"

"What?"

"Make love."

"OOM!" said Brett Folsby.

8

CAUSA BELLI...

He arrived home shortly before midnight. On the drive northward to the Hillsboro Mile he had recalled Simon Smithson's wonderful collection of Noel Coward's recordings. They agreed Coward's rendition of "Someday I'll Find You" was his best, and Brett was still humming the tune when he went directly to the deserted kitchen and mixed a strong brandy and soda.

He took a deep swallow before carrying the glass out to the terrace. There he found Barbara sprawled in one of the cushioned wicker chairs, bare feet up on a tiled table. She was staring moodily at the churning sea. She glanced briefly at her brother, then returned her gaze to the choppy surf.

He moved a chair so he could also face the ocean. The moon had moved westward out of sight, but there was still a dim glow overhead and, far out, the bobbing lights of fishing boats. The wind had strengthened; they heard the pound and gush of waves hitting the strand.

"You're home early," he said. "Have a good time?"

"No," she said. "You?"

"So-so."

"I saw you leave with Zenobia Plummer."

"Did you?"

115

She turned her head to stare at him. "Brett, for God's sake, she's a *child!*"

"Ah yes," he said. "I made the same mistake—at first. Admittedly she appears to be quite young and her manner may seem ingenuous. But that is her public persona. Actually she is nineteen, an emotive and sensitive adult."

"As I'm sure you discovered later," his sister said, "since your ascot is missing."

Silently cursing his carelessness he took the folded silk from his jacket pocket and dangled it before her. "I removed it when I entered our house," he said. "Satisfied?"

"No," she said, "but I'll bet you are."

"Try not to be gross," he admonished. "Why are you interested in my driving Zenobia home?"

"You have a depraved taste in women, Brett," she said.

Accept All, he exhorted himself. Go with the flow. Never complain. But prideful anger won.

"You mean," he said stonily, "you resent my resisting the vulgar come-ons of your brainless friend Gracie McCall. Having met her fiancé I can understand how you feel. The man is a clod."

"She's messing up her life," Barbara said darkly.

"Why are you so pissed?" he demanded. "Because she's marrying an oaf? Because she prefers being a homemaker to the nine-to-five routine? Or is it because she isn't as rabid a feminist as you profess to be?"

"*Profess* to be?" she repeated wrathfully. "What a rotten thing to say."

He drank off half his highball. Then, still furious, he said, "I can't believe you're not intelligent enough to recognize it, but I suppose you do admit it to yourself and are too shrewd to let others glimpse the truth. You're like Zenobia Plummer in that respect: projecting a social image totally at odds with the private reality."

"What the hell are you talking about?"

"Feminism is a legitimate ideology in which I happen to believe. But to you it is merely a vehicle for your own ambition, your need to control, your lust for power. Your essential ideology, superseding feminism, is you, you, you. But to reveal it in public would be counterproductive; you'd be damned as a hard, grasping, covetous bitch. So you don the cloak of a feminist to conceal your true nature from the world."

She jerked to her feet. "You bastard!" she spat at him and rushed back into the house.

"Good night, *Barbie,*" he called after her and essayed a laugh.

He sat awhile longer, finishing his drink. He was vaguely ashamed of his condemnation of his sister. Not because it was a falsehood; he was convinced it was accurate. But what troubled him was his motive for accusing her of a masquerade.

He had always sought to have no illusions about his own character. Now he was forced to admit his attack had been partially due to fear. He was daunted by her resolve, her energy, her ability to skillfully plan and forcefully do. No metaphysical vaporings for her. She was completely self-centered with a demonic drive he knew he could never match. His present was secure—but what of his future?

He might have had additional cause to worry if he had witnessed what occurred in Barbara's bedroom shortly after she left him. She went directly to her dresser. From the third drawer, from under a stack of lingerie, she extracted the juju doll given her by Sarah Demijohn.

She examined the nude male statuette a few minutes, turning it in her sweated palms. She put it aside a moment while she removed the jeweled bird from her lapel. Then, using the pin of the brooch as a dagger, she repeatedly stabbed the wooden manikin in the chest.

And all the while, as she stabbed and stabbed, she concentrated on her brother—his venom, lies, treachery, and the slashes he had inflicted on her portrait of herself.

BOOK

3

1

MEMORY LANE...

Mrs. Constance Louise Folsby continued to suffer short-term memory loss. But the instances of forgetfulness usually concerned recent or current happenings. She found, to her wonderment, that as her physical condition deteriorated her memory of long-ago events became sharper, more vivid. She could recall details of the past she thought forever lost. She remembered...

...when Emmet came into her father's drugstore for the first time he was wearing a scruffy leather jacket and his blond hair was cut so short she could see his pink scalp. Constance was helping out behind the soda fountain after school and Emmet ordered a cherry Coke from her.

...when her father died she worried no one would come to the funeral but the church was filled and the overflow had to stand in the back. The largest floral tribute, a beautiful arrangement of white roses, bore no card. Constance and her mother never found out who sent it.

...when the entire town took to the streets on V-J Day there was dancing, hugging, kissing, and lots of drinking. Constance tasted alcohol for the first time—two glasses of sloe gin and Dr. Pepper. She then threw up over her new organdy dress. Her mother had to undress her and put her to bed.

...when Emmet proposed he did not say, "Will you marry me?" as hopeful swains did in movies and novels. He said, "I want to marry you."

Constance had many other strong, clear memories, some happy, some sad. There were deaths and births, good luck and bad, growth and decay, and change, always change. Her life was a tapestry sturdy enough to last, a fabric of value: husband, children, home, a growing business, security, and hope.

Then it began to unravel. In February of 1963 she had her first attack. In November of 1963 President Kennedy was assassinated. Constance always linked the two as the tapestry of her life began to shred away and so did the life of the nation.

She awoke one morning with frightening sensations: Her face was tingling, arms and legs were numb. Her vision had dimmed and when she tried to get out of bed she almost fell. She had difficulty urinating and her thighs knotted with muscle spasms.

She told her husband and the children she was feeling poorly, probably the flu, and better stay in bed with aspirin and hot tea for breakfast. After Emmet left for the office and the kids for school, she called Dr. Rivkin, hoping for an immediate appointment. But he was making hospital rounds. Constance described her symptoms and Dolly, the nurse, told her to come in at two P.M.

Constance wasn't certain she'd be able to

drive her Chevy, but by two o'clock she was back to normal, vision clear, no more spasms, everything in her body as it usually was. She kept the appointment and told Dr. Rivkin how she had felt when she awoke. He nodded, made notes, did the usual tests, and said he could find nothing amiss. But if she had another attack she was to call him immediately and he would come to the house.

Gradually the recollection of how she had felt faded and she believed it had been a one-time thing: a virus or food poisoning or even an insect bite. But about eighteen months later she had an almost identical attack. She phoned Dr. Rivkin and he arrived within half an hour while she was still suffering. He took pulse and temperature, listened to breathing and heartbeat, tested her vision and muscle response. Then he phoned for an ambulance. Emmet accompanied her to the hospital.

She was there for five days of tests, including a tap of her spinal fluid. Specialists were called in. Finally Dr. Rivkin said he and the consultants concurred: she had multiple sclerosis.

"It is a chronic disease," he told the Folsbys. "The insulating covering of the nerve fibers—called the myelin sheath—is deteriorating. But it is not a fatal disorder."

"Is there a cure?" Emmet asked.

"No," Rivkin said. "We can treat only the symptoms."

No one knew the cause. No one could predict the number or severity of attacks. Continued deterioration was possible. Complete remission was possible. Active mobility was possible. Total disability was possible.

The list of possible symptoms was frightening: memory loss, tremors, muscle spasms, double vision, emotional instability, wild mood swings, numbness of the extremities, and weakness, always increasing weakness, deteriorating sexual function, difficult urination.

"And depression," he added.

"I should think so," Constance said. "With symptoms like those."

"Medication will help," the doctor said. "At first you must be prepared for alternating periods of remission and relapse, with corresponding feelings of elation and hopelessness. Some MS patients seem to arrive at a plateau after which no further deterioration occurs."

"But some continue to deteriorate?" Constance asked.

"Yes," Rivkin said, then repeated, "but it is not usually a terminal illness."

"Unlike life," Emmet said. "You say it is not *usually* a terminal illness. Does that mean it is sometimes fatal?"

"When there are complications," the doctor explained. "Heart problems for instance. Diabetes. But Constance is not diabetic. And her heart is strong."

"Thank you," she said with a twisted smile.

Now, twenty-two years after her first attack, Constance's condition continued to deteriorate but at a slower rate than earlier.

"Probably because there's not much left to deteriorate," she said to Emmet. Gallows humor had become a necessary habit—a defense against utter despair.

She was still able to get out of bed—assisted by a nurse's aide—and move about in her motorized wheelchair. But reading had become difficult and when she tried to watch *Dallas* the TV screen blurred. Her bodily functions had ceased to be an embarrassment; they were just one more indignity to be endured.

She swallowed a variety of medications: antidepressants, muscle relaxants, pills for tremors, fading vision, weakness, painful urination, loss of appetite, occasional slurred speech. She asked Dr. Jacob Steiner if some of her symptoms might be due to side effects of the drugs or perhaps the interaction of two or more.

"We can only keep trying," he said—which was no answer at all.

She had long ago given up trying to describe to family members and friends her physical weakness, mental confusion, and emotional inconstancy. They were all sympathetic, sincere in their concern for her condition, eager to assist any way they could. But healthy others—even the doctor—simply did not *know*. They lived in a charged world of action and desire. She existed in a universe of fatigue and apathy where no one else dwelt.

But early in 1985 a small degree of succor came from an unexpected source.

2

TEA FOR TWO...

Brett had been dating Zenobia Plummer with increasing frequency. She was now twenty-three and no one could accuse him of robbing the cradle. But there was no evidence of passing years in her unlined face and trim body; she still looked like a teenager. Brett accused her of selling her soul to the devil in return for eternal youth.

"I don't believe in the devil," she said quite seriously.

They dined at restaurants in Fort Lauderdale, Boca Raton, Palm Beach, and even drove down to Miami to spend a day exploring South Beach, which was just beginning to be transformed to an *in* place of trendy boutiques and ethnic cafes. They went to movies, concerts, art galleries, and flea markets. They were happy together: laughing, casual, affectionate.

Brett gave her gifts: a Hermès scarf, tarot cards, Shalimar perfume, a chain of gold links for her crystal. In return, she allowed him to keep a bottle of cognac in her apartment. She never sampled it but once consented to sniff it.

"It smells like medicine," she pronounced.

"That's exactly what it is," Brett assured her. "A cure-all."

There was a week of unseasonably warm

weather in January. The sky was spotless, the sun a glowing delight. A mild northerly breeze kept the humidity low and gently rippled the sea. Zenobia expressed a desire to spend a few hours on the beach and Brett invited her to visit the Folsby home. They could loll at an umbrella table on the terrace, he told her, and take a dip or walk along the shore whenever they pleased.

That year he was driving a new Porsche 911 Carrera convertible in Signal Red and had already collected a few dings in the fenders and side panels. He called for Zenobia about eleven o'clock on Saturday morning and drove back to the Hillsboro Mile. Traffic was heavy; *everyone* was going to the beach on such a splendid day.

They had the wide terrace to themselves and removed their outer garments and shoes. Brett's brief swimming trunks were printed in a combat camouflage pattern. Zenobia was wearing a whiter-than-white Lycra maillot, the sides cut high on her hips. She had no suntan at all and it was difficult to tell where fabric ended and skin began.

"Let's go swim to Morocco," Brett said.

They ran down to the water, hand in hand, and took a brief dip in the chilly ocean. Neither was an accomplished swimmer but both wallowed blissfully. They emerged to jog along the beach for about five minutes and then loped back to the terrace.

"That concludes our physical exercise for the day," Brett announced. "Now it's time to eat. Sit in the shade, Zen; you'll get enough burn from the reflected glare. I'll fetch our refreshments."

He went inside to the kitchen where the cook had, as requested, prepared a big pitcher of iced tea with slices of orange and a sprig of fresh mint floating. And there was a platter of cucumber sandwiches and chocolate lace cookies. Brett carried the lunch outside and found his father standing at the umbrella table, listening to Zenobia's chatter and smiling.

"Ah," Brett said, "here you are. I'm sure you have plenty to talk about."

"We do," Emmet said. "This lovely young lady was just telling me about the wonderful properties of her crystal."

"Didn't mention your aura, did she?"

"Not yet," Zenobia said. "But I sense a very bright, vigorous aura."

Brett put down his burden. "Will you join us for a snack?" he asked his father.

"Can't, sorry to say. The Judge has invited me for a swim in his pool and lunch afterward. Brett, I hope you'll introduce this charming young lady to your mother. I think Constance will be as happy to meet her as I am. Have fun, you two, and please visit us again, Zenobia."

"Thank you, Mr. Folsby," she said in her faint voice. "You have a lovely home."

She and Brett drank iced tea, ate all the sandwiches, nibbled on cookies. The wind freshened in early afternoon and both dressed. Zenobia was wearing one of her tent dresses which she told Brett she made from a pattern she had found in a magazine called *Basic Living*.

Half the tea was still remaining when Brett suggested they take it with them to his mother's room; perhaps she'd enjoy a glass. He was standing with pitcher in one hand, plastic cups in the other, when Zenobia came close to kiss his cheek.

"I like you," she said.

He laughed. "What's not to like? Do you know any other man who supplies you with cucumber sandwiches?"

"And other things," she said, looking into his eyes.

They found Constance sitting up in bed, her back against two heavy pillows. Naomi was dozing in a corner armchair. The sickroom was cold, as usual, but Brett knew Zenobia would not object. She was truer to his dictum "Never complain" than he.

His mother visibly brightened when he introduced Zenobia, and he realized how she welcomed the opportunity of meeting someone new, having a new experience, forming new reactions, perhaps feeling new emotions. The new signified growth, did it not?

Brett moved a chair for Zenobia close to the bed. He poured tea into the glass on the night stand and adjusted the jointed plastic straw. Then he excused himself—for a few minutes, he said, to change from his damp swimming trunks. In truth, he hoped the two women might become closer if he was absent. Also, he needed a gin and tonic to kill the aftertaste of the iced tea.

"Did you have a good swim?" Constance asked.

"Beautiful," Zenobia said and described their jog on the beach and the nice lunch they had on the terrace. "And I met your husband," she told Mrs. Folsby.

"I know. He stopped in to tell me. He said you were lovely—and he was right. What did you think of Emmet?"

"Oh, he's so handsome!"

Constance smiled. "I think so," she said. "He's aged very well. How old are you, dear?"

"Twenty-three."

"Are you! I would have guessed much younger. Do you work?"

"In a health food store. It's in a strip mall on Atlantic Boulevard. I'm the day manager now. I was promoted about six months ago."

"Good for you. I suppose you sell herbs and vitamins and food supplements—things like that."

"Yes, and we have a juice bar and we're starting to sell organically grown fruits and vegetables and grains. Our little place is becoming very popular. People want food without all those awful chemicals and additives. After all, the body is a holy temple and should not be desecrated."

Constance sipped her tea. "Some bodies may be holy temples," she said with a wan smile. "Mine is more like a run-down tenement."

"Oh, no, Mrs. Folsby, you—"

"Please, Zenobia, call me Constance."

"All right. I don't mean the body is all that

important, Constance. It's the spirit within which counts. The spirit can be in a ramshackle country church or a stone cathedral in a big city. The body is like an envelope and the spirit within is the letter. The letter has meaning. An empty envelope is nothing."

Constance looked at her curiously. "Do you belong to a church, dear?"

The younger woman finished her tea, set the cup on the floor. She hitched her chair closer to the bed and took up one of Mrs. Folsby's limp hands. "Not an organized church, no. But I do have faith."

"Do you? In God?"

"Not in an old man with a white beard. But in life everlasting."

"Heaven or hell?"

"Oh, no. But I believe the soul is immortal; we cannot know why. And we are born to be reincarnated in a different form—human or something else—depending on our spiritual enlightenment and moral purification. Do you have faith, Constance?"

"I did. I was a regular churchgoer. And so were my husband and our children. Every Sunday. But when I became ill I stopped going. And so did my family. I felt my faith had let me down; I think they felt the same way. The minister visited me and tried to explain why the innocent—even babies!—must endure pain and suffering. And I read many books on the subject. It was all sludge. I no longer have faith, but I remember when I did and how serene it made me. So I know how you feel,

Zenobia, and I am happy you have found a faith that gives you hope."

"Are you always in pain?"

"Not so much as weakness, perpetual weariness, a truly terrible lassitude."

"Am I tiring you, Constance? I'm sorry."

"No, no," the older woman said, finished her tea, grasped Zenobia's hand as tightly as she could. "It does me good to talk of these things. I'd like to learn more about your faith. Will you visit me again?"

"Of course. As often as you like."

Mrs. Folsby smiled. "Tell me, Zenobia, do you like Brett?"

"Oh, yes."

"Do you love him?"

A long silence as they locked stares. Then, in her whispery voice, Zenobia said, "Yes."

"Have you told him?"

"No. I'm afraid he might be—well, you know."

"He might be frightened off? I don't think so. He'll accept it as his due." Constance laughed briefly and quietly. "My son doesn't lack ego. But I believe Brett feels something very special for you. Did you know you're the first woman he's brought to our home?"

There was no mistaking the younger woman's delight. "I am? Really?"

"You are," Constance said. "Really. Another reason I hope to see more of you."

Zenobia blushed. She leaned forward to kiss Brett's mother.

3

CHIAROSCURO...

Barbara had been promoted to the position of advertising director of the northeast division—partly due to the enthusiastic endorsement of Phil Horwitz, manager of Folsby's New York office. She now supervised a staff of seven men and four women selling advertising space in the trade magazines of the Folsby Press.

Her rise had been rapid but not without difficulties. She had solved the problems herself, having too much pride to ask her father and others for information and advice.

She began her selling career by accompanying experienced reps during their calls on advertisers, potential advertisers, and media directors of advertising agencies. Barbara listened, observed, and thought she had learned how to become a successful salesperson.

But when she began making solo calls she discovered the selling techniques she had studied proved worthless for her. She thought the reason was obvious; she was a woman. Her tutors had been men, and those in a position of power reacted differently to the presentations of salesmen and those of saleswomen—even if their pitches were identical! E.g.: An executive might endure a "hard sell" from a man—and even be persuaded by it—but resented or was amused by a hard sell from a woman.

Barbara had always believed women, if they so desired, could be as assertive, aggressive, and even as macho as men and needed to exhibit those characteristics if they hoped to succeed in the male-dominated business world. It seemed a logical supposition. There was only one thing wrong with it; it didn't work. Trying to ape the exaggerated confidence and virile forcefulness of her male counterparts proved a disaster. Prospective advertisers had little interest in listening to those they considered impersonators. It was as if she appeared in their office in drag.

An epiphany came quite by accident. She was calling on the advertising manager of a corporation which produced machine tools. She had scarcely started her spiel when she saw the balding executive's eyes glimmer with tears and he slumped over his desk. He asked chokingly that she excuse him and postpone their meeting for another day. She asked the cause of his distress and offered any assistance she could provide.

He told her the sad story of his eighteen-year-old daughter who had been twice arrested for possession of hard drugs. She had spent a year in rehab and had recently been released, allegedly cured of her addiction. But she had stolen money from her parents and was now apparently back on the streets again, her present whereabouts unknown. The girl's mother had suffered a nervous breakdown and was currently hospitalized.

Barbara conversed with the distraught executive for more than an hour, not offering advice but commiserating, exploring options with him, suggesting sources of professional help. They went to lunch together and continued their discussion of his predicament. By the time they parted his gratitude for her interest was profuse. She was, he told her, the first person he had found to whom he could unburden himself and he would never forget her kindness.

A week later his gratefulness took a tangible form in the purchase of twelve ad pages in Folsby magazines devoted to the machine tool industry.

Bemused by this unexpected bounty, Barbara began cultivating a quieter, more personal approach to prospects. She inquired solicitously about their health and that of their families. She found many business executives ready— even eager—to discuss their private lives and especially their problems with wives, children, mistresses, girlfriends, relatives.

How those lords of American industry loved to talk! And how pleased they were to have a good listener and sympathetic confidante. A warm rapport usually led to the purchase of advertising space in Folsby magazines.

Barbara was well aware of the traditional view of women as soft, tender, responsive, emotional, empathetic. She was convinced men had promulgated those attributes to conceal the quality they most desired in women: docility.

But mistaken or not, if traditional female characteristics succeeded in the hard masculine business world, Barbara was willing to adopt them. Brett had accused her of masquerading as a feminist to clothe her naked ambition. She thought him totally mistaken, but she was willing to disguise herself as a member of the "gentle sex" to further her career.

Even more surprising to her was that her ersatz femininity did not attract unwanted physical propositions. She endured only one incident of crude bargaining: An advertising VP told her plainly he could "throw some business your way" if she would join him for a weekend in Montreal. He accepted her cold rejection calmly. "Nothing ventured, nothing gained" was the bearded VP's comment. Of course his company's ads never appeared in Folsby magazines.

With her playacting came a change in the way she costumed herself for work. She had always thought the "power dressing" of the early 1980s with its man-tailored skirt-suits, ruffled blouses, and outsize ribbon bow ties was a frumpy look. She wore severely elegant pantsuits in navy or gray flannel (occasionally pin- or chalk-striped) with cashmere turtleneck sweaters in subdued hues of terra cotta and deep plum.

Befitting her new role she selected a softer silhouette for her jackets and wore skirts long enough to cover her knees. And although still rejecting flounces, frippery, and pastels, she lightened her wardrobe with brighter, more vibrant colors and used a bit more makeup than heretofore. Her new appearance seemed to delight her father.

Her assignment to the northeast division enabled him to continue their clandestine affair since Emmet routinely flew the *Constance* to New York once or twice a month as he did to other Folsby regional offices. Occasionally he would entertain longtime advertisers at lunch or dinner in Manhattan, Boston, Hartford, and Philadelphia. No one thought it odd his daughter accompanied him on these business trips.

In March of 1985 Barbara flew to Boston to chair a sales meeting of staffers covering the New England area. The Folsby office was high in a building on State Street with sealed windows overlooking the harbor.

She ended the four-hour conference at precisely five P.M. Sales personnel and office employees departed by five-thirty. Barbara lingered after telling the others she had phone calls to make and would catch a late shuttle back to New York. Alone, she made certain the hallway door was securely locked and then settled down in the largest of several individual offices.

The one she chose had a black leather couch. She unbuckled and slipped off her suede chukkas and lay down to unwind after a hectic day. She flipped on a table radio. Madonna was singing "Material Girl." She listened to the end, switched it off, and wondered if it could be her theme song.

She reviewed the day's activities to make certain nothing had been neglected. The meeting had gone well and she was gratified her salespeople were pleased with a new program she had initiated. The Folsby Press customarily sent Christmas cards and corporate gifts to their advertisers. Barbara was compiling a computer file of the birthdays of advertisers in the northeast division and each received a con-gratulatory card (personally signed by her) and a small remembrance. The program was proving so popular she planned to recom-mend it be expanded nationwide.

At six P.M. she heard a tapping at the cor-ridor door. She went padding in stockinged feet, peered through the peephole, and unlocked. He entered and she closed and relocked the door behind him. Then they embraced and shared a warm kiss before pulling apart to grin at each other.

"Hi, honey," Noah Demijohn said.

"Hello, Black Beauty," she said.

He held up a palm. "Whoa! Haven't you been reading the gospel according to St. Jesse? I am no longer a black. I am an African-American, a foursquare, hyphenated Yankee-Doodle dandy."

"I don't know," she said doubtfully. "African-American Beauty just doesn't have the zing of Black Beauty."

"Call me anything you like, honey," he said. "Just keep calling."

He took off his olive drab parka. He was wearing a brass-buttoned navy blazer, khaki slacks, scuffed buckskin shoes.

"Hey," Barbara said. "Joe College."

"You betcha," he said. "Rah-rah-rah. Got

anything to drink in this citadel of capitalism?"

"No hard stuff. I don't let my people keep booze in this office."

" 'My people,' " he mocked. "Love it. The plantation mentality at work."

She laughed. "I can always depend on you for a reality check."

"Just trying to keep your feet on terra firma, hon. Look what I brought us."

He fished in the side pocket of his parka, brought out two miniatures of Grand Marnier, each little bottle containing about an ounce and a half of the orange-flavored cognac.

"Beautiful," she said. "Just what I need. It's been a long day."

"How much time do we have?"

"Maybe two hours. Then I have to get to Logan and back to Manhattan."

"Time enough," he said. "I've got a meeting later tonight at Harvard Yard."

"Your Black Caucus?"

"That name's just a joke. It's an ad hoc committee of soul brothers and sisters who meet once a month to whine in unison. But I enjoy the politicking."

"Judge Hampton sure knew what he was doing when he talked you into pre-law."

"Bless the man. He knows me better than I know myself."

She sat in a swivel chair behind the desk. Noah sat atop the desk facing her and close enough to put a hand lightly on her knee. They both took small sips from their tiny bottles.

"Yummy," Barbara said.

"Are you addressing me, madam?" Noah said. "Hey, what do you hear from Florida? I write to the Judge regularly and phone my mother once a month—but what's the gossip?"

"Gossip? Well, my friend Gracie McCall— you met her at the Pompano Boat Parade a few years ago—well, she's getting a divorce. I can't understand how it lasted this long, her husband's such a schmo. And Brett is now assigned to our Boca headquarters. His title is Deputy Editor-in-Chief."

"What does that mean?"

"The national editorial exec has two assistants: Brett and a brainy woman named Sally Lucas. Of course Brett figures he's next in line for the top slot—but we shall see what we shall see."

"Uh-huh. And how is your mother feeling?"

"About the same, I guess. No better, no worse. Recently she started taking acupuncture treatments."

"Acupuncture? Did her doctor suggest it?"

"No. Brett's been dating a bubblehead who works in a health food store and she persuaded mother to try it. Her neurologist said it can't hurt and if it makes her feel better it's probably the placebo effect: If you're convinced a certain treatment will help, then it probably will."

"That's the way I feel about you," Noah said. "The placebo effect."

"You dog!" Barbara said, laughing. She rose and switched off the overhead light. Dim illumination came from the interior hallway. They moved to the windows and looked down at the lighted boats moving across the harbor. They stood close, Noah's arm about her shoulders.

"Reminds me of our first time on the *Folly*," he said. "Remember that?"

"Why, no," Barbara said. "I've forgotten all about it."

"Liar, liar, pants on fire," he said. "Except the pants on fire were mine."

"You were a nice, sweet, respectful boy. I ruined you."

"As Hamlet said, 'For this relief much thanks.' "

"Oh, my, the college kid is quoting Shakespeare. I think I liked you better when you were a barefoot fisherman."

"Nothing's changed. Except our age."

"Please! Don't mention it!"

They remained in silence a few moments, mesmerized by the glittering darkness of the harbor, slowly moving shadows, occasional flashes of white foam.

"You still seeing the guy in Florida?" Noah asked. "The one with the hots for you?"

"Oliver Pendragon? I date him now and then when I'm home. He's becoming famous. Wrote an article on how genes affect physical and mental illness and may possibly control behavior. It was published in a technical journal and caused quite a stir. Want to hear something weird? Pendragon works for the pharmaceutical company owned by Gracie

McCall's father. And she heard through the grapevine that Oliver collects porn videos. The great scientist watching porn—isn't that a hoot?"

"We shouldn't blame him," Noah said. "His genes make him do it."

"Or maybe it's just his glands," Barbara said. "Talking about that, you still seeing Patricia what's-her-name?"

"Not Patricia—Priscilla. And her last name is Johnson. Yes, I'm still seeing her."

"I hope you're careful."

He stared at her, not smiling. "As careful as you are," he said.

"That's okay then," she said hastily. "As long as neither of us does anything stupid. You told me Priscilla wants to be an archaeologist?"

"Anthropologist."

"And she's starting by studying you?"

"You've got it," he said, smiling again. "She calls me the Missing Link."

"She's a—an African-American—right?"

"Yep. Lighter than I am."

"Love her?"

"Nope. I admire her. I respect her. Enjoy being with her. But I don't love her. I love you, honey; you know that. I've told you often enough."

"Not recently."

"We haven't been together recently. You want me to put it in writing? Notarized?"

"God, no! Noah, why are we talking?"

"Beats the hell out of me."

"The couch," Barbara said. "Not the desk. I'm not in a kinky mood."

"The desk can't be any harder than the bunk on the *Folly*," he said and they both laughed.

Then they were naked, embraced, kissed.

"I do love you, honey," he said. "No shuck. Deeply and truly, I do love you."

"My Black Beauty," she said breathlessly.

He leaned to feel the resilience of the couch cushions.

"Black leather," he said, lying down. "Are you sure you'll be able to find me?"

"I always have," Barbara said.

4

OPENING GAME...

In the 1940s, 1950s and 1960s, during his career as an attorney and later as a jurist, Seth Parnell Hampton was deeply engaged in public affairs and the politics of metropolitan Boston, the State of Massachusetts and, to a lesser extent, in national policies and federal programs.

He had come to the conclusion the term "political science" was an oxymoron; there was no science involved in the practice of politics. Nor could it be called an art since imaginative creation rarely played a part. Hampton finally decided politics was a craft, similar to constructing an attractive and comfortable chair—although there had been politicians so proficient history now referred to them as "statesmen." Bismarck was one, Lincoln another.

The Judge's definition of politics as a craft may have been valid during the decades of his activity. But in the few years he had conducted a campaign to fashion a splendid political destiny for Noah Demijohn he had come to realize it was a different era; there was an ongoing revolution in the process by which officeholders were selected, nominated, and elected, and if he failed to recognize and use the new techniques his efforts were doomed.

His first moves were modest: He sought to reacquaint himself with the politics of the Bay State. He subscribed to Boston newspapers and periodicals. He employed a clipping service to supply him with information on the activities of the Massachusetts legislature and the state's congressional representatives. And he resumed correspondence with old friends: attorneys, politicians, jurists, government employees, financiers, church dignitaries.

Noah was now at Harvard and earning a noteworthy if not brilliant record. To make certain, the Judge wrote to several faculty members and college officials of his acquaintance, identifying Noah as his "protégé" and asking their confidential assessment of the young man's intelligence, personality, and prospects.

The replies he received convinced the Judge his selection of Noah as his Army of One was justified. There were two mild caveats suggesting Demijohn was, at times, too much given to levity and, also occasionally, seemed inordinately intent on seeking the favors of young women. But all the correspondents commented favorably on his charm (one student adviser used the word "charisma") and predicted a successful future.

The Judge immediately moved to ensure Noah's admittance to Harvard Law and then turned his attention to what was to follow.

Cordial letters and phone calls to attorneys at the white-shoe law firm at which Hampton had formerly been a partner alerted them to his personal interest in a young man soon to enter Harvard Law and asked for their aid. He requested no promise or guarantee—only an assurance they would be willing to interview Noah and invite him, if he proved a likely prospect, to clerk during the summer months.

"You should know," Hampton told one of the senior partners, "the boy is black."

"No problem, Judge," the man replied. "We are making an intense effort to increase our diversity. We now have a staff of more than a hundred in our Boston office and already it includes four women, two blacks, and an Asian."

"Excellent!" the Judge said heartily.

Having completed what a military tactician might term reconnaissance and advance, the Judge thought it proper to inform Sarah Demijohn of his plans for the young man.

Not *all* his visions, of course, or she might well think him demented. But he felt Noah's mother should be aware of the preliminary actions he had taken and how they might affect her son.

On a rainy afternoon in April, the sky pressing down, an easterly wind clattering the shutters, he suggested they enjoy a dip in the heated indoor pool before dinner, and she readily agreed.

The Judge changed in his bedroom, pulling on pleated khaki swimming trunks, a loose T-shirt, and an old-fashioned rubber bathing cap to protect his billowy white hair from chlorine in the pool. Then he donned a terry robe and before flip-flopping downstairs remembered to swallow his daily medication. The pill was said to help prevent atrial fibrillation and possibly a stroke. Hampton had been amused to learn the same drug was also used as a rat poison.

When Sarah sunned on the public beach or used the pool with domestic staffers she usually wore a modest one-piece bathing costume with a high neckline and attached skirt. When only she and Hampton swam she wore a sleek silver spandex bikini, the bottom French-cut, the bra so scanty the Judge advised her not to sneeze.

The pool was enclosed by walls and an arched ceiling of glass panels set in a steel framework. The greenhouse effect was accented by potted palms and a lattice of ivy. Overhead illumination was available but rarely used. The pool itself was equipped with bottom and side lights casting a wavering aqueous glow and giving the entire vaulted chamber the appearance of an underwater grotto.

Neither Sarah nor the Judge was an accomplished swimmer; both were content to remain at the pool's shallow end. Occasionally they essayed a splashing swim across the width but generally they just floated, gripping the tiled gutter, kicking their legs gently, stretching arms and shoulders.

They engaged in this mild but enjoyable exercise as Hampton told Sarah of the things he had done to further Noah's career. He was surprised when she expressed doubts. Their voices echoed faintly in that greenish cavern.

"Judge, are you sure my boy can be a lawyer?"

"A very capable lawyer," he assured her. "He has the brains and the temperament. You and I know—and his professors agree—he can charm the birds from the trees. He has a lot going for him, Sarah." Then he added as if the thought had just occurred to him, "He'd be a whiz in politics."

"Politics? Noah? Where would he politick—in Florida?"

"Wherever he pleases, dear. It's up to him."

"He could be a lawyer down here," she said hopefully.

"Of course he could. If that's what he wants. Sarah, I don't wish to dictate how Noah

147

should live his life. I just want to open doors for him. It's his decision whether or not to step through."

She stared at him directly. "It's for you too, Judge, isn't it?"

She was street-smart; he could not attempt deceit. "Surely it's a pleasure for me," he agreed. "To help a young lad make his way— it's a joy. And it helps give my own life a purpose. Is that so awful?"

"No," she said. "It's kind and decent of you. As long as you don't push him where he really doesn't want to go but does it because he thinks he's beholden to you."

She was getting close to the quick. "I'm no puppeteer," he protested. "I don't mean to manipulate Noah. I don't believe anyone can. He has a mind of his own; you know it."

"It's true," she affirmed. "But he's an honorable boy. He wants to pay you back for all you've done for him. And me."

"And you fear he may act in a way contrary to his nature from a feeling of obligation?"

"Yes," she said determinedly. "It's possible." He looked at her and saw her ordinarily impassive expression had taken on an implacable set.

"Becoming an attorney and seeking a political career is a serious matter," he argued. "And I don't think Noah would attempt it on my say-so if he didn't feel it a future he desires and one in which he had a good chance of succeeding. Your son is confident, Sarah. He knows his own worth just as you and I know it."

She wasn't convinced. "I just want him to be happy," she said. "If he wants to be a short-order cook, that's all right too."

"It might be all right," the Judge said, controlling his anger, "but it would be a tragic waste. Like a great artist settling for drawing cartoons. I want Noah to be as much as his talents and labors permit. And I think he is capable of making a name for himself."

Perhaps she sensed his stubborn resolve, for she didn't reply but turned and dog-paddled to the other side of the pool, then waded back, glaucous pearls of water dripping from her strong shoulders.

"But he's black," she said with finality as if it were a solution, not a problem.

"If you think that's going to limit his hopes," the Judge said, "you don't know your son."

She was suddenly saddened. "Maybe I don't," she mourned. "I did when he was a boy. But now he's beyond me."

"Be proud of him," Hampton urged. "He's come a long way and has a long way to go."

"I guess," she said, sighing. "But when I talk to him on the phone, sometimes it's like talking to a stranger, not my own flesh and blood."

"He *is*," Hampton insisted, "and he'll never forget it. When did you speak to him last?"

"About a week ago."

"Any news?"

"Just things he's been doing: classes, exams, meetings with other black students. He's been dating a young woman he likes. He wants us to meet her."

"Is he serious about her?"

"I don't think so. Just a friend. And Barbara Folsby was in Boston for a day and Noah had a drink with her."

Judge Hampton blinked. "Barbara Folsby?" he repeated slowly. "That's nice."

5

COME TO DUST...

Saturday had begun with an enameled sky. Now the blue was smudged with a jaundiced haze. The July sun was a blur. They were trapped in a bell jar of still heat, the air smelling of sulfur. Sweat leapt to the skin; their silk bikini briefs were soaked through. Movements were languid; lassitude conquered muscle and mind.

"Enough funerals," Simon Smithson said. "No more for me. Except my own of course." His elfin grin had become an old man's grimace.

"How many?" Brett Folsby asked.

"Funerals? Seven this year."

"Gawd!"

"I thought I could cope, but I can't," Simon said. "I've used up all my compassion. I just sit there, a blank, and can't wait to leave the church and see if the world still exists."

They sipped iced negronis and looked about vaguely. Smithson had rerecorded his blues collection, all old 78s, onto tape cassettes. The volume was turned low but they heard Hot Lips Page wailing "Blood on the Moon."

"What are you going to do?" Brett asked.

"Celibacy is not an option," Simon said. "You want to say ta-ta?"

"No—but be careful, chum."

"You mean safe sex? What a stupid label that is! As if sex has ever been or ever can be safe. Not just disease but unrequited love, emotional hurt, guilt, shame, and a dozen other dangers. That's the lure—the gamble, the risk, the hope."

It was a vacation week for Folsby. He had flown to New York on Monday and he and Smithson had driven out to the Island in Simon's '82 Aston Martin Volante, the top down. The summer home was on a dirt road near Amagansett, closer to the bay than the ocean but with a view of neither.

The weathered two-story house was owned by a movie producer who was spending the summer with his mistress in Provence. He had given Smithson the keys and engaged him to redecorate throughout, including a new kitchen and master bedroom. So far Simon had done nothing but junk most of the old wicker furniture, now yellowed and splintering.

They had loaded up with provisions and, both being good cooks, prepared most of their meals. They had visited a few local disco bars and met several golden lads who had escaped the plague. On Wednesday night they had a party, which culminated at three A.M. with a naked conga line dancing desperately across the parched front lawn.

Brett took their empty glasses inside to mix fresh negronis. When he returned, Muddy Waters was singing "I'm Your Hoochie-Coochie Man." The porch was shaded but the sultriness was debilitating. They flopped themselves bonelessly in canvas directors' chairs.

"Did you see *Kiss of the Spider Woman*?" Simon asked.

"Not yet."

"Good stuff, but you may not dig it." He stared broodingly down at his drink. "Sometimes I wish I could swing both ways. Like you. It would solve a lot of my problems."

"It's an acquired taste, old buddy. Like black olives."

"Or chocolate-covered cat litter."

"That too."

"You still seeing your chickadee in Florida?"

"Zenobia? I am. My *belle di notte.*"

"What's she like?"

"A space cadet. She believes in a weird mixture of Asian religions and the occult. Plus bean sprouts and tofu. Her latest is something called New Age music. From California. A sure cure for insomnia."

"Good body?"

"A boy."

"The best of all possible worlds," Simon commented.

"If you say so."

"Good sex, sport?"

"Super," Brett said. "For me at least. And I believe she enjoys it. Although sometimes I have the feeling she thinks of it as horizontal t'ai chi."

Smithson laughed and rose to change cassettes. Slim Harpo began singing "Baby Scratch My Back."

"Well, she sounds like a winner to me," he said. "You call her 'Zen' of course."

"Of course."

He gave Brett a mocking glance. "And what do you call your sister?"

"Dunt esk."

"Why this nasty hostility betwixt you and Barbara?"

Brett rose and switched off the cassette player in the midst of "Billie's Blues."

"Not Lady Day," Smithson protested. "She's my favorite."

"What's with you and the blues?"

"They're my songs—all about love and longing. The story of my life. But don't try to change the subject, you sly devil. What about you and the kid sister?"

Brett shrugged. "Just mutual dislike. It may be irrational, but there it is. You've met people you have an immediate aversion to, haven't you? It doesn't require logical reasons— just bad personal chemistry. Result: instant antipathy."

Simon stared at him. "I think there's more to it than that."

Brett held up a palm. "Stop!" he said with

153

a twisty smile. "I know exactly what you're going to say: That I have a subconscious letch for Barbara, I dream of her when asleep and fantasize about bedding her when awake. And I'm so horrified and ashamed by my incestuous yearnings I overcompensate by pretending an intense distaste and making her out to be a ravenous monster. All horsefeathers, Dr. Freud. You're totally wrong."

"I wasn't going to suggest any such thing, sonny boy. My analysis of your enmity is more complex than mere lust. No, I don't think you want to play doctor-nurse with sis; I think you want to *be* her. It's not sexual desire fueling your antagonism, it's envy. Knowing your private proclivities I'm guessing you'd love to have her beauty and her body. But more than possessing her physical attractions you ache to have her strength of character, her resolve, ambition, her forcefulness. Compared to her you see yourself as a wishy-washy creature, a drifter and, as you have confessed, a shallow hedonist. You believe you have no serious purpose, no drive, no real passion. You admit, secretly, she is stronger than you. And so you envy her and transform your covert admiration to overt dislike."

Brett had listened intently to these accusations. When they were done he took a deep breath, drained his drink, and held out the empty glass to Simon.

"It's bloody hot," he said. "Get us a refill, will you, please."

When Smithson returned with fresh drinks

154

he found Brett perched on the porch railing, his head lowered, shoulders slumped.

"Careful," Simon warned. "The whole thing is liable to collapse. It's worm-eaten."

"So am I," Folsby said and took a sip from his tumbler.

Smithson slid into his chair and regarded his disconsolate companion with concern. "Well?" he said.

Brett raised his head, looked at him. "You're too clever by half," he said. "The business of my wanting to have Barb's beauty and body is garbage. I'm quite content with my own phiz and physique, thank you. But the rest of what you said is close to the nub. It's true; I'm envious of her vigor. The woman is a damned dynamo!"

"What's she been up to lately?"

"Well, she's got the company sending birthday cards and gifts to all our advertisers. It's a smart merchandising ploy and I'm surprised no one thought of it before. But she did. All right, it's an advertising gimmick and part of her job. I can't fault her for that. But recently she circulated a long memo suggesting our magazines publish personality profiles of industry bigwigs. You know most of our editorial content is technical stuff: new machinery, effective manufacturing techniques, managerial organization, and so forth. Dull stuff unless you're employed in the industry being written about. But Barbara wants to personalize the magazines with bios of the big shots. All puff pieces of course.

She claims it will increase reader interest and result in heavier advertising."

"What do you think of it?"

"Good idea—but that's not what rattles my cage. She's moving in on editorial content, y'see, and that's my bailiwick. If the executive committee okays her idea—and I think they will—she'll have her foot in the door, the first step to eventually dictating or at least influencing everything we print. And if it happens I'll end up a peon working for the advertising department. They'll have the yea or nay on every word in the Folsby magazines. I think it's exactly what she's plotting."

"You're not being paranoid?"

"I swear I'm not!" Brett said furiously. "I'm guessing within a year she'll be promoted to deputy national advertising manager and transferred to our Boca Raton headquarters."

Simon struggled from his chair and gently tugged Brett off the porch railing. The two men began pacing, their leather sandals slapping on the warped flood boards. They moved slowly, carrying their drinks, pausing occasionally to sip.

"Can't you come up with an idea that might clip her wings?" Smithson asked. "Or at least slow her down. Perhaps a strong memo pointing out the benefits of an independent editorial department might help."

Brett said, "I detest these power games, *detest* them! But I'm forced to play. I have expensive tastes, as you well know, and what can I do other than work for my father? Who else would have me? At the salary and perks I get from the Folsby Press? No way! So I'm locked in. Money! It's so vulgar and so important, isn't it? Enough to make one despair."

Smithson shuffled along in silence a moment, then said, "But even if your sister achieves her goals it doesn't mean the end of your salary and perks, does it? I mean, you won't be tossed out in the street. The Folsby Press will continue to be your cash cow regardless of your title and status. Correct?"

"I suppose so. But..." His voice trailed away.

Simon stopped and faced him. "Aha!" he said. "Your 'but' speaks volumes. Your dislike of your sister doesn't spring only from envy. Fear is also involved. You're thinking of the future, your parents deceased—what happens to the Folsby Press then? What happens to your merry life, the expense account, use of the corporate jet? In short, who inherits? Who controls? Who wins the power game? You fear if it's Barbara you're in deep do-do. Poverty looms—or at least a radical downsizing of your lifestyle. Is that what's driving you to drink, old buddy?"

"You're too effing smart," Folsby grumbled. "And right, as usual. My parents are antiques, but Mother is incurably ill and the old man is facing the big six-oh next year. Things can happen. Awful, unexpected things, and who knows where they'll leave yours truly."

"Who inherits the company—do you know?"

"No. Father has said Barbara and I will receive cash bequests. The amounts not stated. But he has said nothing about how he intends to bequeath his shares of the Folsby Press and I haven't the nerve to ask."

"Don't," Smithson advised. "He might consider the question impertinent, if not objectionable. Hey, let's go take a shower. We're both beginning to smell like goats."

They bathed singly since the shower stall in the master bedroom was too small to accommodate two. They donned fresh white cotton briefs and padded barefoot down to the kitchen. They mixed tall gin and tonics and sat at the bleached pine table directly beneath a whirring ceiling fan. It stirred the humid air and gave the illusion of a cooling breeze.

"Brett," Smithson said, regaining his quirky grin, "do you trust my judgment?"

"Completely," Folsby said promptly. "You've given me some grand ideas and not one has flopped."

"Good, because I have another suggestion for you. You may find it outlandish at first but hear me out."

"Sure. Let's have it."

"This tootsie of yours in Florida..."

"Zenobia, known as Zen."

"Yes. You've already told me a little about her. But you didn't mention her disposition. What's it like?"

"Her disposition? Everything nice. Obliging. Generous. Sympathetic. Nothing strident or pushy about her. A wispy voice. Modest. She has, as I told you, these crazy enthusiasms for health foods, crystals, Oriental religions, the occult, pyramids, and so forth. Unsophisticated. I think she understands about one percent of my jokes, but she's fun to be with. Relaxing. She makes no demands whatsoever and is grateful for kindness. There is no malice in her."

"Is she in love with you? This is no time for false modesty, lad."

"Yes, I do believe she's in love with me."

"Has she met your parents?"

"Of course."

"What is their reaction?"

"Father is much amused by her prattle. He treats her like the charming naïf she is. Mother is totally smitten. Zen visits her two or three times a week and they have long, soulful, and utterly incomprehensible conversations on spiritual enrichment, self-awareness, and the bliss of universal love."

"Has your sister met her?"

"Yes."

"What is Barbara's reaction?"

"Usually she ignores Zen. She thinks her a featherbrain, my floozy du jour."

"Uh-huh. You know what I think, Brett? I think you should marry Zenobia as soon as possible."

"What? You goof!"

"Let me finish. Marry Zenobia as soon as possible and beget a child as quickly as you can."

"But I—"

"Will you *please* let me finish? Your parents

are in their late fifties—right? Take my word for it—they're aching for grandchildren. Of course they hope you and your sister will be happily married, but they really want you to *breed*. They'll simply dote on the sight, sound, and smell of grandchildren. And why not? A grandchild is a promise of family immortality."

Brett hunched forward, listening intently. His hands were clasped loosely on the tabletop. He stared at the other man. "You're serious about this, aren't you, Simon?"

"Of course I'm serious. And you should be too; it's your future. Use your brain, kiddo! Your marriage will please your parents. The arrival of a bundle of joy will send them into ecstasies. And as a proud daddy you'll immediately take the lead in the inheritance sweepstakes. Your sister will be checkmated."

"A remarkable idea," Folsby said slowly. "Two objections spring immediately to mind. *Primero,* I've told you I believe Zenobia is in love with me. Perhaps madly. But I'm far from being madly in love with her. Affection, yes. Love, no."

"Come off it, buster. You'll never be madly in love with anyone—except possibly yourself."

"Touché. In other words you're suggesting a marriage of convenience."

"Oh, laddie, all marriages are convenient—for the woman or for the man, or ideally, for both. I'm merely recommending a way to cement your parents' favor and ensure you—and your heir, of course—will be first in line when it comes time to distribute the goodies."

"All right, assuming I sacrifice myself by marrying Zen—and believe me it would be a sacrifice to listen to her endless gobbledygook about karma and transmigration—we arrive at my *segundo* hesitation: What happens to you and me, our relationship, if I become a paterfamilias?"

Smithson stared at him. Not a hard stare but something lorn and vulnerable in his eyes. His hand inched across the table, palm upward. Brett took up the hand in his. Their fingers intertwined.

"The decision is yours," Simon said, his voice sounding old and quavery.

"I thought you and I had come to an unspoken agreement," Brett said softly. "Promiscuity is out, commitment is in. But my marriage adds another factor to the equation. I must know how you feel."

"You know how I feel, darling," Simon said in a low voice, looking down at their linked hands. "I've told you often enough and have proved it. From a purely practical point of view I think you should marry and father a child. If that means the end of us, then my sacrifice would be greater than yours."

Brett withdrew his hand and stood up suddenly. He moved to the other side of the table, leaned down. He put a bare arm about Simon's bare shoulders. He turned the other man's face and kissed his lips firmly.

"We'll manage," he said. "That's my decision."

Simon lurched up to embrace him, nuzzled

into his neck. Brett stroked his bald pate, seeing his lover's tears.

Smithson pulled away. He held Brett's face between his palms. "We'll manage," he repeated happily. They kissed again, and both drew a deep breath and sighed as if they had escaped a mortal danger.

"Now then," Simon said, "what shall we make for dinner tonight?"

Brett gave him a dazzling smile. "Reservations!" he said.

6

BELLES LETTRES...

10/4/85

Dear Judge Hampton,

Greetings & salutations, & hoping this finds you & Mother in good health & good spirits. Please excuse errors in punctuation, grammar, & spelling in this letter. I am still trying to figure out all the bells & whistles on my new word processor. Even if I succeed, I know the result won't equal your fine copperplate handwriting.

Can't believe I am starting my senior year! The time sure went swiftly. I look back at my freshman year, recall my first reactions to being in college, & can't believe I was so innocent. I remember my depression because for the first time in my life I met men my own age who, I had to admit, were smarter than I was. I had the same feeling of inferiority when

I saw the guys who turned out for football. They were all bigger, faster, & knew more moves than I did. The end of my football career!

But as for the more intelligent guys, it turned out most of them weren't smarter—just more knowledgeable in certain subjects—like English lit, Renaissance art, French poetry, et cetera. In other words, they had specialized expertise in limited areas, but that didn't make them great brains or heavy thinkers. In fact, some of those specialists turned out to be dweebs compared to generalists.

Got some good news for you, Judge—actually for both of us. You told me last summer how you mistrust the label "political science." But it is the designation of one of my courses. I think you'll be amused & perhaps gratified to learn the deeper I get into pol-sci the more I agree with you: Politics is more craft than science or art.

Studying The Prince *(assigned reading) confirmed what you said about modern politics being more method than theory. Machiavelli's treatise really has little relevance in our current zeitgeist.*

But when, on your urging, I read All the King's Men, *I was totally convinced you are correct. What a great narrative it is & much more revealing than any dry-as-dust political history. Judge, can you suggest any other novel you feel will help me understand the inner dynamics of local, state, & national politicking?*

To get back to my good news, my pol-sci prof has okayed my request to write my term paper on new methods of electioneering. Again, this was your proposal & I thank you for it. Tentative title is "Emerging Trends in the American Election

Process." Sir, any recommendations on how it might be organized will be most welcome &, I'm certain, will be put to effective use.

With love & respect,
/s/ Noah Demijohn

My dear Noah,

As usual it was a delight to receive your letter, the most recent being of the 4th inst. Your mother and I enjoy good health and I have been enjoined to remind you to dress warmly during the coming winter. Remembering New England's fierce snowstorms I add my admonition to hers.

A few replies to your comments...

While it is true few of Machiavelli's practical instructions have application in modern politics, his amoralism remains a basic tenet of all professional pols I've ever met. Believe me, dear boy, the ruling passion of most politicians is to be reelected, and its accompanying maxim is "the end justifies the means."

I was happy to learn your term paper will be devoted to new trends in electioneering—a fascinating subject. I hope you intend to make it more than a journalistic account of methodology. It would please me, and your professor as well, I'm sure, if you draw conclusions—no matter how opinionated—on how modern political techniques are being created to meet the needs and wants of the general population and in turn are influencing the shape of our government and changes in social morals and behavior.

American politics have evolved greatly since I played an active role. I refer particularly to the grow-

ing activism and power of minorities: blacks, women, Hispanics, and so forth. In this regard, you and I have never had a frank discussion of racism—how it affects the social structure and, more important to me, how it affects you personally. I can only guess at the extent of your victimization and would be most interested to learn how you deal with the prejudice to which I am certain you have been subjected. What solutions can you offer to this dreadful problem which continues to befoul our society?

Noah, you ask me to suggest another political novel which might give pol-sci (as you call it) a human resonance. I recommend most heartily The Last Hurrah *by Edwin O'Connor. It is one of my favorites since the main character is said to be based on James Michael Curley, who was elected mayor of Boston five times! I was involved in Massachusetts politics during Curley's final two terms and can testify this novel accurately mirrors the excitement, hilarity, and outright villainy of that rambunctious era.*

Finally, you ask for a recommendation on how your thesis may best be organized. I suggest your subject matter requires a temporal progression: past, present, future. Or specifically, how elections were managed yesterday, how they are conducted today, and how you predict they will be orchestrated tomorrow.

If you wish to do personal research on election methods of the past I urge you strongly to interview Terence and Timothy Dooley, twin brothers, now nonagenerians and, I understand, still working proprietors of a "social club" in South Boston. The Dooley brothers were extremely influential in local and state politics for more than fifty years and contributed mightily to the successful elections of Mayor Curley.

I'm sure the Dooley boys will be happy to keep you fascinated with tales of the old days in Boston electioneering. Of course you may refer to me as an old friend to help them start spinning their yarns—many of which may be true! And don't neglect to mention my middle name, dear boy. It should help you win their eager cooperation.

> *With love and best wishes for*
> *your continuing success,*
> */s/ Judge Seth Parnell Hampton (Ret'd)*

10/18/85

Dear Judge Hampton,

Please excuse my not having written last week— but it's partly your fault! Your questions on racism caused much soul-searching on my part & I found it difficult to organize my thoughts in any kind of logical order. This is the third—& final!—version of this letter & I can only hope you find it well reasoned even if you don't agree with my conclusion.

There is one thing I'm certain we agree on: Most American whites harbor a deep-seated prejudice against blacks &, in some cases, a virulent hatred. Whether this hostility springs from racial enmity (an atavistic antagonism) or sexual fears can be debated endlessly. But causes should not be part of our discussion; we are concerned with effects. I must add the obvious: Blacks can be just as guilty of racism as whites, & the prejudice of many African-Americans is not due solely to resentment of white oppression.

166

I'm sure it will surprise & perhaps shock you when I say I believe a great deal of white prejudice results from a serious error made by black leaders, past & present, & by the black intelligentsia. Almost without exception they have written & preached equality can be achieved only by fostering the ethnic self-esteem of blacks.

I reject the weaseling term "self-esteem." To me it smacks of self-satisfaction, conceit, & even hubris. Worse, by concentrating on racial self-esteem, our leaders have neglected the individual in favor of the tribe. If "self-esteem" is ever to mean confidence in one's self, as it should, it cannot be taught by continually heralding the race, its history, values, & attributes.

Blacks should be & eventually must be treated & judged as individuals, not a race, tribe, or clan. I am, first of all, Noah Demijohn. My color is important to me & to others but not as important as my mental, moral, & emotional nature. Whites will never come to accept each black's unique individuality until our leaders cease emphasizing black racial identity.

I think the label "African-American" is a disaster. It merely reinforces ethnic identity of the many to the detriment of the distinctive one. I do not consider myself an African-American. Unhyphenate me! I am simply an American who happens to be black. Africa is as foreign to me as Lapland; I have nothing in common with either.

Needless to say, these views on recognizing the disparateness of blacks do not set well with my soul brothers & sisters at Harvard. We meet about once a month to listen to visiting speakers or engage in ferocious debate. I have become something of a pari-

ah by denigrating the importance of our ethnic identity.

Curiously, the only person supporting my ideas is my good friend Priscilla Johnson, the young woman I have mentioned in previous letters. Her major is anthropology & you'd think she'd be a fervent believer in the need to stimulate racial pride in blacks. But she is as convinced as I am that equality will become a reality only when blacks think of themselves as individual Americans & not a foreign people who were victims of forced immigration.

Of course I have been the target of many attacks of mean & spiteful prejudice. What black hasn't? But personal confidence (not racial self-esteem) enables me to endure these mindless insults. Believe me, Judge, I work hard to keep my ego intact. So far I have succeeded.

I have already given a partial answer to your question on how racism may be overcome: By de-emphasizing black racial solidarity & preaching the doctrine of individual sovereignty and responsibility. There is another factor at work to lessen racism in our nation & I expect you may think me a fool to mention it since there is little statistical evidence to support it.

But I believe possibly within fifty years interracial marriage will be so prevalent as to have a profound effect on American society. As I said, there is only the scantiest anecdotal evidence to confirm such a view. But I now see interracial couples almost daily & it amuses me that all our deep, complex solutions to racism may become moot by the triumph of romance! Amor vincit omnia—& I'm heartily in favor of it!

168

By the way, Judge, I know you & Mr. Emmet Folsby are close friends & meet frequently. Has he mentioned his daughter has been promoted to Deputy National Advertising Manager of the Folsby Press & will be assigned to their headquarters in Boca Raton?

Barbara was in Boston recently for a farewell dinner with her northeast area sales staff. But she assures me her job will require occasional visits to New England advertisers, so I expect I will see her again up here—as well as in Hillsboro during my visits home.

I trust you & Mother enjoy good health & happiness,

/s/ NOAH DEMIJOHN

OCTOBER 23, 1985

My dear Noah,

Your letter of the 18th inst. is at hand and I find your well-expressed ideas intriguing and provocative. Let me start by saying I agree wholeheartedly with your belief that racial equality can only be achieved by the empowerment of the black individual and not by appeals to ethnic or genetic solidarity which are sure to lead to increased separateness and alienation from the mainstream of American society.

However, I do have a caveat best expressed by telling you of my personal experience.

I was born into a class now somewhat derisively labeled as WASP. There is no need to characterize this breed and detail its virtues and vices. Suffice to say that prior to and during my undergraduate years at Harvard I was as scornful of the strict formalism of my class as you are now of black leaders' empha-

169

sis on racial identity.

But while at Harvard Law I gradually came to realize my iconoclasm would prove self-defeating and a hindrance to my career. The solution, I found, was not by renouncing my views and accepting without question the traditions, habits, and unwritten rules of my class. The answer lay in retaining my doubts in private while publicly giving allegiance to the WASP philosophy and expressing respect for the attainments and views of WASP panjandrums.

Some may term this conduct opportunistic or hypocritical. I prefer to consider it simple prudence. It would serve no useful purpose to defy openly the conventions of my class, to challenge the leaders and mock the powerful—including my father. And so, wanting to succeed, I "went along" without ever losing my inner contempt for the code by which I ostensibly lived. That this personal dichotomy may have been a contributing cause of my alcoholism I shall leave to others to decide.

It is true, dear boy, my experience concerned class while yours involves race. But I feel the problems are similar if not identical. While your espousal of "individual sovereignty and responsibility" is, I concur, the best and swiftest path to complete integration, I must warn you against proclaiming your views publicly with too much certitude, no matter how sincere you may be. You have already found yourself a pariah with your peers because of your belittling their eager search for ethnic identity.

I assure you, Noah, that should you continue to espouse your views publicly you will earn the enmity of many liberals, the pied pipers of black power, who have devoted their careers and mortgaged their futures to the concept of African-Americanism and the negroid diaspora.

I strongly urge you to be realistic. The time may come when you have the position and power to challenge the current black leadership. You do not have either position or power at present. I suggest you act with circumspection and mollify your public image without altering the views you hold—which I find admirable.

I also admire your cool, intelligent reaction to the ill-treatment you suffer from bigots. It is a relief to know you have not become embittered. To be continually galled by senseless prejudice can adversely affect your physical as well as your psychic health. Are you aware of the high incidence of hypertension amongst black males? I am certain constant exposure to intolerance is a factor.

I was somewhat taken aback by your suggestion that interracial marriage will eventually result in equality. I trust you were joking. Perhaps interracial dating and marriage are increasingly popular in the metropolitan areas of the Northeast. I assure you in Florida and other southern states the marriage of whites to blacks is still an anomaly. I think most Americans (white and black) harbor a prejudice against it that will not be overcome in your lifetime.

Noah, the young lady you mention, Priscilla Johnson, sounds interesting. I have spoken to your mother and we agree it would be nice if you invited her to accompany you down here for the long Thanksgiving weekend. There is plenty of room and we would welcome her visit. I am eager to meet a modern young lady who plans to become an anthropologist. And the fact she agrees with your views is another mark in her favor! Please do invite her.

Yes, Emmet Folsby told me of the promotion of his daughter and her transfer to the Folsby Press headquarters in Boca Raton. Barbara is obviously a capable, determined, and forceful young woman— someone to be reckoned with.

With love and best wishes for
your continuing success,
/s/ Judge Seth Parnell Hampton (Rt'd)

7

CONJUGAL RITES...

The long hall of the Folsby manse, bare and gleaming as a bowling alley, stretched from the front door through the entire ground floor to the terrace overlooking beach and ocean. Doors along both sides of this polished corridor—smelling faintly of lemon—opened to Constance's sickroom, living and dining rooms, kitchen, lavatory, linen closet, and a "Florida room" furnished with large-screen TV, hi-fi equipment, a walnut game table, and wet bar. Couch and chairs were burnished rattan with cushions of white duck.

Walls of the long hall were papered in a light green oriental toile design. There were two groupings of identically framed watercolors depicting American sailing vessels at sea. Illumination in the corridor was provided by bronze sconces cast to resemble ships' lanterns.

At the east end were sliding glass doors leading to the tiled terrace. A flight of concrete steps led down to the beach. Alongside the stairway was a gently sloping ramp Emmet Folsby had designed and constructed to accommodate his wife's wheelchair. The ramp ended on a small platform where Constance could sit in her chair and view the sea and activity on the beach. Shade was provided by a large sky-blue market umbrella held erect by a steel socket attached to the platform.

On a keen, nippy day in December 1985 the Folsbys sat on this little platform—she in her motorized wheelchair, he on a folding canvas stool—and admired the spangled heave and draw of the surf. The temperature was less than sixty degrees, the sun a banked blaze, the air astringent as gin. Both wore sweaters, and Constance had an Afghan across her lap and tucked around her legs.

They watched a vee of pelicans go swooping by. There was a line of fishing boats anchored offshore and in the distance a tug was plodding southward, hauling a barge carrying an oil drilling rig.

No swimmers were in the water, but there was a single sailboard with a crimson sheet fighting the rough chop. The sailor, a young man in a yellow wet suit, was obviously a beginner. His slender craft tipped continually, dumping him into the water. He would clamber back aboard, haul the sodden sail upright, and try to get his board moving only to capsize again almost immediately. The Folsbys watched his efforts with some amusement but admired his tenacity.

"He won't give up until he turns blue," Constance commented.

"I hope it won't be this chilly for the wedding," Emmet said. "We might have to move it indoors."

"Zenobia would be disappointed," his wife said. "She has her heart set on a beach ceremony. She believes the ocean signifies everlasting life."

He had learned not to laugh at Zenobia's pronouncements or his wife's ready acceptance of their meaningfulness. The two spoke a language he thought highfalutin gibberish. They used metaphysical words and phrases to impart cosmic significance to something as mundane as a sneeze. But he forbore to criticize or deride their enigmatic jargon: If it gave them comfort, as it apparently did, who was he to sneer?

"Constance, has Zenobia said anything about having children? Brett hasn't mentioned it and I haven't asked."

"Oh, yes. I didn't ask either, but she volunteered the information. She said they both want a large family."

"Good," he said contentedly. "The larger the better." He took up one of her withered hands and pressed it between his palms. "How will it feel to be a grandmother?"

She turned to smile at him. "Wonderful. And

174

you'll be called Granddad or Grandpop. How does that sound?"

"Can't wait," he said. "Do you want a boy or a girl?"

"A boy," she said promptly. "First. And then a girl."

"But we'll take whichever we get."

"Of course we will. With joy and love. Brett's marriage makes me so happy; Zenobia is such a dear, sweet girl." She paused, then added fretfully, "I wish Barbara would find someone."

He released her hand slowly. "She's still young. People are getting married at an older age these days."

"Well, she'll be thirty next year; that's old enough if she wants to start a family. I know Oliver Pendragon has asked her several times, but she won't have him. Emmet, aren't there any nice eligible young men at headquarters?"

"If there are she'll find them. I wouldn't attempt to influence her. You know Barbara—Miss Independence."

"Sometimes I think her career has become too important to her. It's all she talks about. She never seems to be having any fun."

He was silent.

"I wonder if she's happy," Constance mused. "Do you think so?"

"I wouldn't know, dear. She's living the life she wants to live. I presume she finds satisfaction in that."

His wife turned her head to look at him directly. "What about you, Em—are you happy?"

"I'd be happier if you were well—you know that."

She was silent a moment. Then: "I hope you've found a woman. Or preferably, several women. I told you after I became ill I'd accept it and understand."

"Let's not talk about it."

"I *want* to talk about it. I want us to be completely open and honest with each other. Don't you?"

"Of course," he said, watching the hapless sailboarder fall off his tipped craft, climb back, pull the mast upright, and try again.

"Em, there is something I want you to promise."

"What is it?"

"When I die before you do—as I know I shall, and sooner rather than later—I want you to promise to remarry."

"Constance... please. This is painful."

"No, it isn't; it's practical. I know you're a passionate man, darling, and if you meet someone you can love after I'm gone I want you to marry her with no silly notions you're being unfaithful to your memory of me. I don't want any nonsense like that. Do you agree?"

He made a small sound, less compliance than dismay.

"There!" she said brightly. "I've been thinking about it a long time and I'm glad I finally told you. Whatever you do now with other women or whatever you do when I'm gone—why, that has nothing at all to do with what we had together. That can't be spoiled or even touched because it belongs to us alone. It's ours, isn't it, dear?"

"Yes," he said, nodding vigorously, "it's ours."

"Now I think I'd like to go inside," Constance said. "A chill is beginning to seep into these old bones. Don't help me, Em; I want to do it myself."

He folded his little canvas stool and stood aside as she started the wheelchair. She turned it skillfully and moved slowly up the ramp. He followed close behind the chair, ready to aid with a push if needed. But she maneuvered easily off the ramp and across the terrace. Then he went ahead to slide open the glass doors.

They moved down the long hall toward her sickroom. A radio was playing in the kitchen; they heard Lionel Richie's "Say You, Say Me."

"You know," Constance said, "I think I'll have a nice hot cup of beef bouillon."

BOOK
4

1

TAINTS AND TRAITS...

The juju statuette given to her by Sarah Demijohn was now set atop the dresser in Barbara's bedroom, more curious bibelot than magical talisman. She still stuck pins into the carved wood manikin while concentrating on a particular male: her brother, Noah Demijohn, her father, other men of her acquaintance. But never having achieved any results of which she was aware, her attempts at hexing had become infrequent, serving only to soothe a temporary snit.

On Friday evening, August 4, 1989, Barbara dressed carefully, donning a black silk teddy and then a long slinky tube of mauve jersey, a Donna Karan, with deep décolletage and a totally open back. Her hair, trimmed quite short, was now artfully tinted to preserve its golden sheen. She stroked her neck with a drop of Joy. She adjusted a silver cuff by Elsa Peretti. And before adding the jeweled bird brooch— Judge Hampton's long-ago gift—she used the pin to stab the naked figurine while she thought fiercely of Oliver Pendragon.

Then, tugging on a black velvet cloche and taking up her newest Judith Leiber minaudière, she went downstairs wishing Emmet was there to see her zingy gown. She paused briefly to peek into her mother's sickroom. Constance was in bed, watching a summer rerun of *In the*

Heat of the Night. Barbara closed the door softly and went out to the garage.

The Corvette had been redesigned the previous year and Barbara had traded in her '78 for the new model: black with a beigy leather interior. She started the engine, flipped on the AC, and waited a few minutes until the car cooled. It was a witheringly hot summer; humidity a gummy fog that never lifted.

She drove northward to a black-tie affair at The Breakers in Palm Beach. She had been invited by Oliver, and since the dinner was in his honor she thought it too cruel to refuse. She envisioned a noisy dinner spent with older men, suety faces bourbon flushed, and older women frumpy in expensive sequined cocktail dresses. The evening turned out to be a totally unexpected and revelatory occasion.

Gracie McCall's father, owner of a successful pharmaceutical company, had endowed a new department at a local university. It was to be called the McCall Center for Genetic Research. Ostensibly it would be devoted to basic rather than applied research, but Dennis McCall had made certain a licensing agreement was part of his gift; his firm and the university would share equally in profits from any discoveries, drugs, or medical techniques developed at the facility.

Oliver Pendragon had been named director of the research center, and the dinner that evening was to serve as a farewell to his employment at McCall's company and to celebrate his appointment as chief of the new laboratory.

Barbara was impressed by the number of sober and well-dressed guests attending this event and was even more startled to find herself seated next to Oliver on the dais along with Dennis and Mary McCall, the university president, a lieutenant governor, a U.S. Senator, and several other male luminaries and their wives. The ornate, high-ceilinged chamber was a brilliant scene: fresh flowers on tables with gold-edged place settings, crystal glassware, and an abundance of opened wine bottles. A harpist played softly during the meal.

The dinner served was, Barbara thought, appetizing but heavy for that time of year: sliced tenderloin with bordélaise sauce, roasted potatoes, and broccoli parmesan. Dessert was individual sundaes: three flavors of ice cream with a chocolate-mint sauce and whipped cream. Brandy and liqueurs were available.

There was a brief intermission before the speeches, and Barbara found her way to the ladies' room where she encountered Gracie McCall. The two women embraced and kissed the air. Barbara noted her friend had put on weight and lightened her fiery red hair.

"I like the new shade," she said, although she didn't. "What's it called?"

"Peach sorbet," Gracie said. "Alan *loves* it."

"Who's Alan?"

"My third husband," Gracie giggled. "Or will be as soon as his father dies. Right now the boy hasn't a *sou*. Hey, I hear Brett's a proud papa."

"I don't know how proud he is, but he's a papa all right. A son. Two and a half years old now. Anthony Scott Folsby. Cute kid. He's got the family's blond hair."

"Somehow I never figured Brett as a daddy."

"No," Barbara said shortly. "Nor did I. Especially with that ding-a-ling he married. Gracie, what's all this fuss about Oliver? They're treating him like he invented frozen ravioli."

"Sweetie, haven't you *heard?* The man is *famous.* Books and magazine articles and TV talk shows. Barb, he's an effing celebrity! They're calling him a *genius.*"

"Oliver? My God, Gracie, he's a booby!"

"To you and me maybe, but right now he's the Boy Wonder of science. He's good for a quarter-million a year, and my pop says if some of his research proves out he'll be Daddy Warbucks and maybe win a Nobel. Who'd have *thunk* it? Not me!"

"And not me," Barbara said thoughtfully. "Let's do lunch one of these days, hon, and compare war stories."

"You betcha," Gracie McCall said, and they traded winks.

She returned to her place on the dais and for half an hour listened to mercifully short speeches by several men of power extolling the intelligence, theories, and vision of the personage they had come to honor. Then he rose to speak and was greeted with prolonged applause.

Oliver Pendragon had, she noted, slimmed

down—perhaps for his appearance on television. His dinner jacket was obviously bespoke and helped eliminate his former porcine appearance. And he had shaved off his ridiculous toothbrush mustache. But the transformation was not complete; his face was still round and meaty, his manner mirthless and stodgy. And his voice remained solemn and sonorous as if he had just descended from a mountaintop with a stone tablet of new commandments.

"We thank you for your presence here tonight," he started, "and for your continuing interest in and encouragement of our work."

Barbara thought at first he was referring to himself and his research staff. But as he proceeded she was appalled to realize he was using the royal first-person plural. He was speaking of only one person—Oliver Pendragon.

"Our search has been long and arduous and we expect it to continue so. We are merely on the threshold of truly amazing discoveries revealing the influence of genes on human development and physical and mental well-being.

"We now have incontrovertible evidence tainted genes are the source of many if not all human physical and mental disorders. Please note we use the word 'tainted' rather than 'faulty.' The latter implies a malfunction beyond repair—which is rarely the case. 'Tainted' indicates a failure to function normally, a condition which can frequently be corrected by medication or genetic engineering.

"In addition to determining physical and

mental health, genes play a vital role in ordaining human behavior, including personality, emotive traits, aptitudes, and talent. This is, we acknowledge, a revolutionary concept. Yet all our preliminary research indicates its validity. If proved, the results have the potential to remake our society and our culture.

"So you see we are venturing into an unknown world where problems and dangers undoubtedly lurk. But we are confident our discoveries will eventually lead to a brighter future for all humankind.

"We thank you for your goodwill and humbly ask for your cooperation and aid in making our vision a reality. We cannot fail if we have the courage to dare."

Pendragon concluded his speech and was given a prolonged ovation. Moments later he was surrounded by guests shaking his hand, patting his shoulder, assuring him of their fealty and best wishes for his success. It was almost twenty minutes before he could grasp Barbara's arm and draw her aside.

"Do you have your car?" he asked.

She nodded.

"Let's go to my place for a nightcap. Just the two of us. I need to unwind."

She didn't hesitate. "All right," she said.

The parking valet brought her Corvette and Oliver stroked the roof. "Beautiful car," he said. "For a beautiful lady."

"Thank you," Barbara said. "You still have the antique VW?"

"Good Lord, no! I have a 1983 Rolls-Royce

Silver Spur. But I didn't drive it to the hotel tonight. Bad for my image."

"Your image," Barbara repeated, much amused. "Of course."

He lived in a high-rise condo in West Palm. As they drove across the bridge Barbara said, "Oliver, I'd like to talk to you about your speech."

"Ah, yes. It went well, don't you think?" He sounded exultant. "Excellent response."

"It went very well," she agreed. "But I'd like to discuss some of your ideas."

"Did you see the table of reporters? Not just locals. The *New York Times* science man was there and two stringers from news syndicates. I should get good coverage. The TV people wanted to tape, but McCall thought the cameras would be intrusive. So we settled for studio interviews tomorrow morning."

"About your ideas—" she started again.

"I have a bottle of champagne in the fridge. We'll kick off our shoes, have a glass or two, and then you can ask whatever you want. All right?"

"Sure," Barbara said. "Right now you're wired; I can tell."

"Wouldn't you be? Did you hear the tremendous applause?"

His two-bedroom apartment looked like an upscale Danish dwelling: all blond wood, glass, leather cushions, and what seemed to Barbara an excess of mirrors. The floors were cluttered with stacks of books, science journals, newspapers, consumer magazines. A computer installation filled one wall of the second bedroom, along with desk, swivel chair, file cabinets, large-screen television, fax, answering machine, color copier, and three telephones.

"My home office," he explained. "I get more work done here than I do at the lab. There it's mostly administration. Here I can think and create."

She glanced at him to see if he might be joking. He wasn't.

They went into the kitchen, which appeared to be the only tidy room in the apartment. He unwrapped the wire from the neck of the champagne bottle and, rather than prying the cork loose with his thumbs, used a small towel to grip it tightly and twist it free, a swift and expert performance. Barbara wondered where and when he had learned to do it.

They sat on a wood and calfskin couch in the living room. They sipped champagne and Oliver stared at her bosom swelling the jersey sheath.

"I've been traveling a great deal lately," he announced. "New York, Paris, London, Rome. Even Copenhagen. I've met a lot of people everywhere, a lot of women. Barbara, you're still the most beautiful and I still love you as much as I did fifteen years ago."

"Thank you," she said faintly.

"I've changed," he said. "Don't you think I've changed?"

She was tempted to comment, "Not enough,"

but she said, "You certainly have. You're more confident now. More assertive."

"And polished," he added. "I think I've gained a great deal of polish."

"It comes from being famous," she told him, deciding his priggery was unlimited. "Can we talk about your speech now?"

"It surprised you? Shocked you perhaps?"

"I hadn't realized you were such a strong believer in biological determinism."

"I'm not."

"You certainly gave that impression. In the nature versus nurture debate you seem totally committed to the faith that anatomy is destiny. You said genes not only cause physical and mental disease but dictate behavior, personality, and aptitudes. Do you really believe that?"

He laughed, took her free hand, turned it up. He began to stroke the lines of her palm with a forefinger.

"Darling, the first duty of a politician is to be reelected and the first duty of a research scientist is to obtain grants. They may come from the government, foundations, universities, charities—wherever. But research such as mine requires a great deal of money. A constant supply. Now Mr. McCall has been very generous. But his endowment covers only the establishment and equipment of the new research center. But the continual operation will require fresh funding from other sources. How will I obtain that? By publicity. By creating and maintaining the image of an inspired and inventive scientist. By proposing revolutionary theories which excite the grantors and make them want to be partners in fashioning a bright new world."

She was beginning to understand. "So your speech was essentially a fund-raising ploy? Public relations?"

"Not completely. But to attract funding I must appear to be more enthusiastic and certain than I actually am. This is strictly confidential, you know. Just between you and me. Understood?"

"Of course."

"So I find it necessary not to lie about my theories and my discoveries but to exaggerate. Do I believe genes are the sole determinant of human disease and dictate behavior and personality? No, I do not. But I do believe they provide an inclination, a propensity, a learning, a proclivity—whatever you wish to call it. I prefer terming it a disposition."

He repeated the word with evident relish, articulating it slowly: "dis-po-zish-on."

"Are factors other than tainted genes involved in disease and violent or immoral behavior? Of course there are. Environment, education—both secular and religious—the society and culture in which the individual exists, the familial relationship, all these things may exacerbate or mollify tainted genes. And similarly they may deaden or enliven those genetic traits which produce great artists, writers, musicians, political leaders. And lovers."

"But you didn't mention those other influences in your speech."

"Of course not! Why should I? I don't seek grants to improve the environment, education, or family relationships. My only interest—my *obsession!*—is investigating the role and power of genes. And to do that I must overstate their importance and ignore the influence of other factors. I've given the reporters a strong, exciting story with no caveats and no complexities to dilute my message. Ready-made headlines and leads."

"Shrewd," Barbara said. "You've become a very shrewd man, Oliver."

"A politician," he said. "I've learned the politics of science. But enough about me. Let's talk about you—and us."

Still stroking her palm with his index finger he began to mutter in broken sentences glorifying her beauty: sleekness of legs, nakedness of back, succulent lips, mysterious eyes, an inventory of torrid attractions.

She sat with bowed head, watching his fingers scribble on her palm. But she wasn't listening to his compliments. She was thinking—as she had so often in the past three years—how clever Brett had been to marry and produce a son who delighted and infatuated his grandparents. It had been a cunning move on her brother's part.

But the game was not ended, and it occurred to her the man now droning his passion might somehow enable her to score—if not immediately then in the future. Oliver had not suddenly become a paragon; he was still physically undesirable. But he was now knowing and astute, capable of functioning in the real world. At least he was endurable.

His mumbled praise faded away and she raised her eyes to give him a complaisant smile.

"Barbara," he said throatily, "I have some naughty videos. Would you care to watch them?"

"Love to," she said.

2

CAROMS, CUES, AND KISSES...

Emmet Folsby dubbed his final shot—but he left Sarah Demijohn a tough split: the cue ball almost equidistant between the two object balls in the center of the green baize. She studied the lay a long time, then leaned far over the table and the two men noted her strong bronzy legs.

She executed the draw perfectly: left hand spread firmly, right hand holding the stick almost vertically. She struck the cue ball sharply below center. It spurted forward to hit one object ball. The spin took control and the cue ball rolled slowly back to kiss the other object gently.

Folsby hung up his cue stick. "Sarah," he said, "you're too good for me."

192

"Nah," she said with her ecstatic smile, "I'm too *baad* for you. Don't you know how kids talk these days? Bad is good and ug is beautiful."

"The world turned upside down," Hampton said. "Em, I gave up trying to beat Sarah at billiards years ago. She can put English on a cantaloupe."

"Sarah skunks me at billiards and my daughter outshoots me at skeet. Never underestimate the power of a woman." He said it with a wry laugh, but Hampton knew his defeats rankled.

The Judge was seated on a rustic settee made of deer antlers, with suede cushions. The massive billiard table was an ornate antique with carved griffin heads, lion legs, claw-and-ball feet. Everything in the room was old and mellow. The high arched windows were now splattered with a Saturday morning shower, streaming with fat, dusty drops. The paneled chamber was illuminated by a multi-branched brass chandelier suspended over the billiard table.

Folsby joined the Judge on the settee. They watched Sarah set up and practice three-cushion caroms. Her strokes were light and deft. She moved around the table nimbly, pausing occasionally to chalk her cue. She never used the wooden bridge but stretched her limber body effortlessly. Most of her shots ended with gentle kisses.

"Sarah," Emmet called, "Barbara and I are taking the *Folly* out this afternoon. If we have any luck you can plan on a fish dinner tonight."

"Great," she said. "Fresh is always better than store-bought."

"How *is* Barbara?" Hampton asked. "Not getting bored with Florida, is she?"

"I don't think so. She travels a good deal, you know. For instance, on Monday morning I'm flying up to New York with the national advertising staff. We have a new rate card with special discounts that have to be explained to advertisers. Then after New York the director and I will fly on to San Francisco while Barbara goes to Boston. So she's not stuck in Florida all the time."

"Boston?" the Judge repeated. "Lucky Barbara. Noah reports they're having a cool summer."

"How's he doing?" Folsby asked.

"Excellently," Hampton said. "He's living in Cambridge, studying for the bar exam at night, and clerking during the day. His law firm wants him to join them after he passes."

"Tell Emmet about the new department," Sarah said.

"Oh, yes. The firm plans to start a pro bono division and wants Noah to organize it and head it."

"That *is* good news," Folsby said. "I'll tell Barbara and perhaps she'll have a chance to phone Noah and congratulate him while she's in Boston."

"That would be nice," the Judge said. "Is she still seeing Oliver Pendragon?"

"Apparently. Went to a dinner in his honor last night."

"The reason I ask is because he was interviewed on a television talk show this morning. He has some remarkable ideas. And some I find disturbing. He believes human behavior is determined by our genetic makeup. I wonder if he realizes what that would do to jurisprudence. Laws are based on the concept of free will. If it is proved our actions are dictated by our genes I predict a catastrophic revolution in our courts, especially in criminal cases. Every defense attorney will argue his client is not responsible; his genes made him do it—an enormous expansion of the M'Naughten Rule."

"I hope it never comes to that," Emmet Folsby said. "And I doubt it will. I don't believe in any form of determinism—and that includes God's intervention. Our lives are the result of choices we make—or fail to make. If Pendragon is the genius he's alleged to be, I wish he'd spend his time finding the cause and cure of human diseases, starting with multiple sclerosis."

Sarah Demijohn racked her cue stick. She stood with her crupper pressed against the ledge of the billiard table. She leaned back and put out her arms, palms down, to support herself. She faced the two men on the settee. Her posture was not deliberately seductive, but they found it so.

"How is Constance feeling, Emmet?" she asked.

He frowned. "I really can't tell you," he said fretfully. "I just don't know. The doctor says her physical condition continues to deterio-rate. Slowly, thank God. But she's never been in a better frame of mind since she became ill. She appears bright-eyed. Talks more and faster than she has in years. She has a kind of fervor. That's the only way I can describe it—a fervor. Sometimes it's almost hyster-ical and then it scares me. It's like she's drunk. Happy-drunk. Her medication hasn't been changed so it can't be the cause."

"Perhaps," Hampton suggested, "it's a wild happiness due to the birth of her grandchild."

"No," Folsby said, "it started before that. Even before Brett was married. I think it began when she met Zenobia and they became close. You know Zen is always talking about the universal oneness, the divine harmony and other things I don't understand. But apparently Constance finds great comfort in such ideas and so I can hardly object. But I must admit her excitement—it's the way I see it: an excitement—makes me a little fearful."

"What do you fear?" the Judge asked qui-etly. "Mental derangement?"

Folsby made no answer.

"Don't be scared, Emmet," Sarah said softly, and he looked up at her. "You've never been to a black church or you'd recognize what's happened to Constance. She has the spirit. I've seen it so many times. Men and women and little children. They get the spirit and, as you said, it's like they're happy-drunk. They sing, shout, clap their hands. Maybe they even dance in place or speak in tongues. They have the spirit in them and it gives them strength. Their bodies may be wasting away, but they get the spirit and know they shall live forever in love and glory."

"I'm not a religious man," he said in a low voice. "I don't understand all that. What exactly is this spirit you're talking about?"

"Faith," she said. "In whatever god you want. It's complete faith in that god, and you know the god is in you, and you are part of the god, and so you shall have life everlasting."

He sighed. "I've never had the spirit, as you call it, but if Constance has it and it makes her happy, then I don't question it. Apparently it's real for her; that's all that matters."

"A wise attitude," the Judge commented. "Would you care for a drink now, Emmet?"

Folsby rose. "No, thank you, and thank you, Sarah, for your words of wisdom. I better go back now, visit with Constance awhile, and then get the boat ready for this afternoon."

"I'll walk you down," Sarah said and accompanied him when he departed. She returned a few moments later. Hampton was still on the antlered settee and she sat close beside him. He put an arm around her shoulders and she nestled into him.

She was wearing trig-white Bermudas and a Harvard T-shirt Noah had sent her. She wore it proudly, her bosom bulging the university seal bearing the imprint "Veritas." Hampton thought her a bonny woman and knew how fortunate he was to have her close.

"I think you made Emmet feel better," he said. "He's a troubled man."

"No cause," she said. "Constance has found the spirit is all."

"Do you have the spirit, Sarah?"

"I do. I don't go stomping my feet and shouting 'Amen!' but I got it. Deep down and quiet."

"There's something we must talk about, dear," he said, voice faltering. "We've been avoiding it, but we can't any longer."

"I know," she said, reaching up to smooth his fluffy white hair. "Noah and Barbara Folsby."

"What is your guess?"

"My guess is yes," she said, her face impassive again. "For years now. I thought he'd outgrow her or she'd tire of him. But it hasn't happened; they're still meeting."

"Do you believe it's serious?"

"It may be with Noah, not with her."

Hampton made a grimace. "She's eight years older."

"And smarter," Sarah said. "I don't mean book learning. I mean more experienced. In a lot of ways my son is still a boy."

"A foolish boy," the Judge said angrily. "My Lord, Sarah, he has Priscilla Johnson. I think she's a splendid young woman."

"She is."

"Tell me honestly, is it the color thing? He

has a beautiful white woman. A blonde. Does he see her as a trophy? Is it his ego?"

"No. He doesn't think that way."

"Then what *is* it?"

She straightened, pulled away, turned to look at him directly. "I do believe he's in love with her."

Hampton groaned. "And is she in love with him?"

"I don't think so," Sarah said. "To her he's just a pet. I like Barbara. I consider her a friend. But I know way down she's cold."

"She hasn't got the spirit?"

"No. Like her father. But at least he knows it, accepts it in others, maybe even wishes he had it. Barbara couldn't care less."

"What *does* she care about?"

"Herself."

"Would you object if Noah married a white woman?"

"No. But I'd object if he married Barbara. She'd break his heart."

The Judge nodded. "This is a problem I hadn't anticipated. Sarah, please believe me when I say I would not have objections and would not be offended if Noah married Barbara or any other white woman—provided he wanted to be a garage mechanic, restaurant owner, or even a business executive or corporate attorney. A white wife would have little effect on those careers. Might even be an advantage. But as you know I envision a brilliant political future for Noah and I've worked long and hard to make the dream a reality. Yes, I have benefited from my campaign. It has given purpose to my remaining years. But in today's society I think a white wife or white mistress would doom Noah's political destiny and my hopes. I just do not believe American voters are willing to elect an interracial couple to the mayor's office, governor's mansion, or White House."

"I think you are right," she said. "Marriage to Barbara would destroy him personally and professionally."

"Well put," Hampton said. "And exactly correct."

She was silent a moment, then said, "What can be done? I thought time would be on our side; they would drift apart. Now I am not sure."

"The first thing to be done," the Judge said briskly, "is to determine the facts. At the moment all we have are suspicions. They must be confirmed or proved incorrect."

"How can it be done?"

"There is a Boston company calling itself an Inquiry Agency. I have used them very successfully in the past."

"Detectives?"

"Investigators. Very low-key, very discreet. Emmet said Barbara will be in Boston next week. I can employ this agency to report on her activities and those of Noah while she is there. But I won't do it without your permission."

Sarah pondered a long time, features set in a polished mask. Finally she drew a deep breath and said, "Yes. Do it."

He drew her closer, kissed warm lips, smooth cheeks, tip of nose. The years had faded her jetty hair; he caressed her cap of tight gray curls. He put tongue to neck, bare arms, palms. He leaned to kiss her dimpled knees.

"You keep me alive and frisky," he told her. "At my age I should be eager only for warmth, comfort, and coddling. But I still have desire, flickers of passion. They prove to me I live. I owe my life to you."

She said, "You give me more than I give you, Sweet Daddy."

He saddened suddenly and blinked several times as if to stanch tears.

"I wish I was younger," he said huskily, "and could give you the kind of loving you deserve."

3

HOME, SWEET HOME...

Shortly before his marriage Brett Folsby purchased a three-bedroom apartment on the tenth floor of a beachfront condo in Boca Raton. His father provided an interest-free loan for the down payment although he secretly felt the apartment too large, the building too grand with its marble lobby, Olympic-size swimming pool, and private tennis courts.

Simon Smithson came down from New York and stayed two weeks to help furnish and decorate the newlyweds' home. He was introduced to all the Folsbys and their friends, and everyone agreed he was an exceedingly pleasant young man but eccentric with his shaved head and small gold earring. However, he fitted the general preconception of a Manhattan interior designer and no one showed any particular interest in his sexual orientation.

Zenobia was particularly charmed by Simon's wit, his elfish grin, and the warm, sympathetic manner with which he listened to her decorating ideas—before regretfully rejecting them. He did agree to one of her suggestions: an inlaid vaguely Oriental pentagram in the center of the tiled living room floor. Zenobia said it would ward off evil demons and Smithson said that was exactly what the marriage needed.

He did the apartment in a fey mix of Victorian and Industrial Modern. The concept sounded bizarre to everyone, but so sure was Simon's taste the final result was pronounced a triumph of design by guests at the housewarming. In fact, it was featured in local newspapers and magazines, which hailed it as a welcome relief from the banal semitropical decor and sorbet colors of most South Florida homes.

After the Boca apartment was completed, Smithson returned several times for short social visits. He was always welcomed and made a number of new friends, including some who engaged him to redecorate their homes, offices, and in one case a duplex cabana.

On Sunday, August 6th, Smithson flew to Lauderdale, arriving early in the afternoon and planning a stay of only two days until continuing his vacation trip to Curaçao. Brett picked him up at the airport and Simon observed his dusty black Allante with some amusement. "It needs a good wash and a wax job," he commented.

"So do I," Brett said.

"Somehow I never saw you as the Cadillac type, luv."

"It's the family," Brett explained. "I needed something heavier and safer. My sports car days are over."

"Ah," Smithson said. "Middle age lurks."

"Sometimes I feel it's already here," Brett said, and on the drive up to Boca he said, "I've missed you, dear."

"And I you, sweetie," Simon said. "We're being defeated by damnable logistics."

"How true, how true. Any ideas how to remedy the situation?"

"I do," Smithson said. "We'll discuss it later. Anything special planned for today?"

"Nope. A quiet evening at home."

"Domestic bliss. Exactly what I crave."

"Zenobia's sister Zoe has joined us for the day. They're taking Tony over to my parents for a visit. We'll have the afternoon alone until they return in time for dinner."

"I've never met Zoe. What kind of woman is she?"

"She adores paisley," Brett said.

"Oh-oh," Smithson said.

He had brought a New York present for Zenobia and Brett (two dozen bagels) and a little wooden train for Anthony Scott Folsby. When he was introduced to Zoe Plummer he apologized for having no gift for her.

"Your presence is gift enough," she said, and Simon thought it a gracious thing to say even if her smile was flinty.

Zoe was an extremely tall woman, an inch or two taller than her younger sister. Everything about her was long: nose, chin, fingers, feet. She wore a Laura Ashley–type outfit: a loose floral dress down to her ankles. It had a square neckline revealing a bony chest. Perched on her head was a wide-brimmed straw hat, beribboned, with the brim turned up in front. She looked as if she might be going to a garden party where watercress sandwiches would be served.

She towered over Simon; he had to crane his neck to see her dark eyes. "How many times a week," he asked, "do people say, 'How's the weather up there'?"

"Not too often," she said. Stiff smile again. "I work mostly with medical wonks. They say, 'I hope you don't suffer from acrophobia.' That's a fear of heights, you know."

"I know," Simon said. "I myself suffer from arachibutyrophobia. That's a fear of peanut butter sticking to the roof of your mouth, you know."

This time her smile was wide and warm; it transfigured her features; she was suddenly attractive. "I must remember that," she said.

"Come along, darling," she added, holding out a long hand to Anthony. But the boy went to his mother instead. Zenobia promised they'd be back in a few hours and the three departed, Tony carrying his new wooden train. Brett double-locked the door behind them.

"What do you think?" he asked.

"Of Zoe?" Simon said. "A challenge. I'd love to dress her; she could be striking. Now she looks like a western omelet."

"Speaking of that, are you hungry?"

"Not for food, thank you. I lunched on the flight."

"You had airline swill? Are you mad?"

"Of course I didn't eat their fried Styrofoam with fuel oil gravy. I brown-bagged it. Made myself blini with crème fraiche and beluga. Super. I could eat only three and gave the fourth to the flight attendant. She ate it and gave me a look that said, 'Take me; I'm yours.' "

"And did you take her?"

"No, I asked for another iced vodka."

"Is that what you'd like now, sport?"

"I think not. Suggestions?"

"I have a chilled pinot grigio."

"Just right."

Brett went into the kitchen for the wine. Simon lighted a cigarette, relaxed in a tapestried armchair, looked around at the apartment he had designed, and was pleased with what he had created.

Visitors admired the furnishings and decoration and gained subliminal pleasure from the way Smithson had organized and used the space. The shiny tiled floors, high ceilings, and all windows overlooking the sea enclosed an aquarium of ambient light. Clever corners and blank walls charmed because, although everyone thought the apartment painted a flat white, he had used five hues of white, warm and cool, to provide subtle contrasts and give the illusion of an endless extent, a glowing cathedral.

Brett returned with their wine, handed Simon a glass, sat in a black enameled Shaker-style chair facing his guest. They both sipped, both nodded approvingly.

"Fruity," Folsby said.

"Like us," Smithson said. "Does the boy visit his grandparents often?"

"Every Sunday afternoon," Brett said. "They'd see him every day if they could. As you predicted four years ago, they're absolutely dotty about him."

"Which should help when the old man passes and the spoils are divided."

"It certainly has given me one up on my dear sister. Occasionally I notice her glancing at Anthony as if he's a puzzle, a problem she hasn't yet discovered how to solve."

"But she continues to push on the job?"

"Oh Lord, yes. And she has the luck of the devil. Her boss—our national advertising director—was absent a month having his prostate cut out. While he was gone Barbara took over his personal clients and almost doubled the ad linage."

"She's not sleeping her way to the top, is she?"

"I wish I could accuse her of it, but I honestly can't. She's just a dynamite salesman, saleswoman, salesperson—whatever. A real powerhouse. The old man is happy with her, of course. Sometimes I think I'm destined to play second banana at the Folsby Press and end up working for my kid sister."

"Not to worry. You've got a wife and heir on your side."

"Thank God for them. I do wish I had married a woman swifter and sharper than Zen."

"And bitchier?" Simon suggested.

"And bitchier," Brett agreed. "But do you want to hear something odd? Well, perhaps not odd but unexpected. I told you my parents are dotty about Tony. Believe it or not, I find I'm just as dotty. I never thought it would happen to me, but I love the boy more than I can tell you. He and I have some great times together. And I think he loves me as much as I love him. Sickening, isn't it?"

"It's natural. He's a beautiful lad."

"Handsome. And talking about looks, old buddy, yours disturb me. You seem pale and almost shrunken. Wan is the word. Are you okay?"

"More wine?" Simon suggested.

Brett went to the kitchen and brought back the bottle. He refilled their glasses and set the pinot grigio on the floor alongside his chair.

Smithson took a deep swallow and said, "I'm okay physically. I've had so many blood tests I'm afraid of becoming anemic. I've been lucky. So far. But New York is a charnel house. Brett, all the talent is dead or dying. Fun it ain't. And although I'm clean, it's killing me in another way. Not physically but mentally and emotionally. The nightmares are bad enough. What's worse is that I have them when I'm awake. Daymares. Last month I went to see *The Phantom of the Opera* and all I could think was that I'm becoming a phantom."

"What's the solution, Simon? Is there one?"

"I don't know. It's not only the plague, it's the city itself. Dirty and brutal. All sharp elbows and sewer talk. Manhattan is just not a nice place to live anymore. It depresses me, frightens me. It's killing me—or at least making me into someone I don't want to be."

"Get out," Folsby advised.

Smithson took a gulp of his wine and looked up hopefully. "I've been thinking of it. I've built up a good business in New York—but so what? If I did it once I can do it again. What would you think if I moved to South Florida, somewhere in Palm Beach or Martin counties? Buy a home, start an interior design shop down here."

Brett moved his head back and laughed. He slapped his knee. "Yes, yes, and yes!" he shouted. "Just the thing! Go for it! It would be your salvation and the answer to our problem of logistics. If you're in the neighborhood, life will become instantly sweeter. No more scary cruising for Daddy. What a joy!"

"You approve?"

"Do I ever! Definitely!"

"I'm going to love it," Smithson said happily. "You know the last time I was down here I went out early one day to buy a newspaper. And every stranger I met made eye contact and said, 'Good morning.' It's what I need in my life, sweetie: civility."

"Civility?" Brett laughed. "I thought servility was more to your taste."

Simon, grinning, said, "On occasion."

"I hope tonight is one of them. I have a plan. Let's go into the kitchen."

4

HOME FIRES BURNING...

It was a large, airy workshop with an overhead fan and exhaust. It had been equipped with state-of-the-art appliances: an enormous refrigerator-freezer, electric range with barbecue and eye-level oven, an under-the-shelf micro, granite countertop, and glass-doored cabinets.

Brett said he did most of the cooking. Zenobia was still a vegan although she accepted seafood and chicken occasionally. Her talents as a chef seemed limited to stir-fried vegetables. But Brett had devised a dozen variations of Caesar salad and was now trying meatless Thai dishes with some success.

"Is Zen still a teetotaler?" Simon asked.

"She is. But not her sister. Zoe has a yen for the sauce, but her capacity is quite limited. She can get swacked by sniffing a cork. I'm counting on it happening tonight."

Smithson looked at him, puzzled. "I don't get it."

"She drove her car over here, an old, beat-up Chevy."

Then Simon understood and smiled. "What a sly devil you are," he said.

"Just help me keep her glass filled," Brett said. "Because of this hellish weather I thought we'd eat lightly—just baked sea scallops and a salad. Does that set your salivary glands atwitter?"

"It does. How can I help?"

"You do the salad and I'll do the scallops. By the way, all the greens and veggies are organic. Zen insists everything we eat be organic."

"You too?"

"Me too," Brett said, and both men laughed.

They had dinner well under way and had finished the pinot grigio by the time Zenobia and Zoe returned with Anthony. The boy was now lugging his wooden train, a plastic fire engine, and a small stuffed lion which roared when its tail was pulled.

Brett groaned. "More presents from the folks?" he asked.

"They just won't stop," Zen said. "And Constance gave him a dollar for his piggy bank."

The two women took Anthony into the smallest bedroom, converted to a nursery with a high crib and a pirates' treasure chest of toys. Tony was bathed, fed, and tucked in, the stuffed lion placed on the blankets at his command.

The sisters returned to the dining room. Brett and Simon had the table set, candles lighted, and the first bottle of a dry California Riesling uncorked with a second bottle chilling in an ice bucket. But before the food was served Zoe and the men shared a shaker of dry-as-dust gin martinis.

"Is it strong?" Zenobia asked.

"A martini is a martini is a martini," Simon explained. "It can be neither strong nor weak. It just *is*. "

"Oh," Zen said.

Dinner was an instant success: food admirable, conversation sprightly and unflagging.

Zoe: "The salad dressing is wonderful. What's that unusual taste?"

Simon: "A secret ingredient."

Brett: "And its last name is Rathbone."

Simon: "What did Tony eat?"

Zoe: "Cheerios."

Brett: "During his first eighteen months he was breast-fed. While he was nursing I stood behind him crying, 'Next!' "

Zen: "This afternoon his grandmother asked him what he wanted for his birthday..."

Zoe: "And Tony said, 'A brother.' "

Brett: "It might be arranged."

Zen (blushing): "We must wait until he's older than four. We don't want two children in college at the same time."

Simon (laughing): "You do look ahead. More wine, Zoe? By the way, Zen, all the organic greens were loverly. Where did you find them?"

Zen: "Farmers' markets. I'd love to start a restaurant serving only organic food."

Brett: "Not a bad idea."

Simon: "I'll invest."

Zoe: "Include me. I'm thinking of starting a new career."

Brett (surprised): "Tired of the drug lab?"

Zoe: "The man I work for is supposed to be a genius. I think he's a dope."

Simon: "Most geniuses are. Me, for instance. More wine, Zoe?"

Zoe: "Sure."

Zen: "Take it easy, dear."

Zoe (tartly): "Why should I?"

Simon: "Why indeed? Brett, you score a ten on the scallops. Garlic?"

Brett: "Just a bit."

Simon: "Like being just a bit pregnant. Zen, motherhood has done wonders for your figure."

Zen: "Thank you. Brett hasn't noticed."

Brett: "Hah!"

Zen: "Well, you never said anything."

Brett: "I was too busy panting."

Zen: "Oh you!"

Brett: "Everyone ready for dessert? It's key lime pie."

Zoe: "I'll skip, thank you, and finish my wine."

Simon: "Me too."

Brett: "Zen?"

Zen: "Just a sliver."

Brett: "I'll join you. Then let's move out onto the balcony for a brandy."

Zen: "I don't think Zoe needs a brandy."

Zoe (muzzily): "Yes, I do. What should we call our organic restaurant?"

Simon: "How about 'Two Zs,' or maybe one word, 'Twosies.' "

Zoe: "Love it. Where's the brandy?"

The outside air was thick as a mousse. The night was black, a woolly blanket of clouds swaddling moon and stars. Zenobia and Brett stayed inside a few moments to clear the table and put leftovers away. Zoe and Simon carried snifters of cognac to the balcony and sat on wooden chaises said to be reproductions of the *Titanic*'s deck chairs.

Zoe took a gulp. "I hate men," she announced.

Smithson could hardly make out her face in the dim illumination coming from inside. Her features seemed pale and chiseled, almost marmoreal. She sprawled bonelessly, skirt hiked up above her knees to cool her bare legs.

"I can't say I blame you," Simon said. "For hating men. We're not a very admirable lot."

"Not all men," she amended. "Some are okay."

"I hope I'm included."

"You're a doll," she assured him. "A bald doll. But most men are dopes."

"An unhappy love affair?" he prompted.

"My own fault," she said numbly. "I kept hoping."

"We all do that," he told her. "It's not a criminal offense."

But she would not be comforted. "All my life," she mourned.

"How old are you, Zoe—if I may ask."

"Thirty-six."

"Then you still have a lot of living to do. You'll find someone."

She turned her head to stare at him. "Will I? Who? You?"

He tried to laugh. "I'm spoken for."

"Oh. Is she nice?"

"I think so," he said. "But I'm not absolutely certain. I'm hoping, y'see. Like you. Hoping is the name of the game."

She sat brooding. She had slipped limply down on the chaise, long legs thrust out. She suddenly roused, finished her cognac. She held the empty snifter out to him in a shaky hand. "Refill," she commanded.

Smithson took her glass and went back into the apartment. He found Zenobia and Brett coming from the nursery where they had been checking their sleeping son. The three stood in the hallway and conversed in low voices.

"Zoe wants another brandy," Simon reported. "She's rather smashed. Shall I bring it to her?"

Brett turned to his wife. "Darling, she's in no condition to drive home. I won't allow it. Can you convince her to stay the night—you two in the master bedroom? I'll bunk in with Simon."

"Yes, that would be best," Zenobia said worriedly. "Are you sure you don't mind?"

"Of course I don't," he said. "It's best. You agree, Simon?"

"Absolutely. Bring her a little more brandy, Zen, and I think she'll go along with you peaceably."

Zenobia left them, taking Zoe's glass. The two men smiled at each other.

"Bingo," Brett said softly. "We must be very quiet tonight. Not a sound."

"May I whimper?" Simon asked.

5

BUSINESS AS USUAL...

The Folsby Press Building on Corporate Boulevard in Boca Raton was a structure of no distinction whatsoever. Brett waggishly referred to it as "the bunker," a sobriquet which, unknown to the son, offended the father.

Emmet Folsby had envisioned the headquarters of his trade magazine empire as a factory and that was exactly what the architect delivered: a clunky edifice of white concrete with windows too narrow, ceilings too low, and the interior of the two floors laid out in a grid pattern. The furnishings, mostly gray steel, were designed for neither charm nor comfort.

The only chamber of any ease or corporate

glitz was the second-floor Conference Room. It was carpeted, pine-paneled, with a long table of burnished teak and comfortable arm-chairs upholstered in black leather. The walls held a collection of framed antique maps, and a splendid model of "Old Ironsides" was displayed in a glass case on a pedestal.

In this room early on Monday morning, August 7th, the national advertising executives had gathered for a final confab before their flight to New York. Their luggage had already been loaded into the silver stretch limousine in the driveway. It would convey the group to the Lauderdale airport, where the *Constance* was fueled and waiting.

Present at the meeting were Emmet Folsby; Harry Prentice, the national advertising director; his two deputies, Barbara Folsby and John Curry; and two advertising staffers who would accompany Emmet and Prentice to the West Coast and Curry to Chicago. Mrs. Blanche Singer, in her efficient, methodical way, had already distributed envelopes holding each traveler's itinerary, airline tickets from New York to their destinations and return, hotel and rental car reservations, and copies of flight insurance policies in their names.

Harry Prentice delivered the final briefing. He had lost a great deal of weight during his prostate surgery and convalescence. His collar was too loose, the double-breasted suit too large for his shrunken frame. He had not yet regained his strength; his voice lacked forcefulness and occasionally he paused to draw a deep breath. His listeners were shocked by his pallor.

When he finished his halting explanation of the new rate card discounts, Emmet asked if there were any questions. "Speak up now," he said with heavy good humor, "or forever hold your peace. No questions? Then let's be on our way."

Everyone rose and began to file from the room. But Barbara came around the table and put a hand on her father's arm to stop him.

"A few minutes, Em?" she asked. "Something I want to discuss."

"Can't it wait until we're on the plane?"

She shook her head. "This is private. It won't take long."

"All right," he said and sat down again at the head of the table.

Barbara was wearing a black linen pantsuit. The neckline of the jacket was cut quite low. She wore no blouse but had looped a fuchsia silk scarf about her neck and tucked into the jacket. Now she pulled an armchair close to Emmet, took off the scarf, leaned toward him. He became aware of her scent and thought it was probably Joy, her favorite.

He looked at her, thinking the passing years had not weathered her beauty; they had fined her features. Her face had not hardened but had taken on a more classic look, nose and cheekbones clearly defined. He had expected (hoped?) their carnal relationship would be cooled by time, their passion "settling down" and becoming more habit than need. It hadn't happened; she still stirred him as deeply as she had sixteen years ago in the stateroom of the *Folly*.

"You're going on to Boston tomorrow morning?" he asked, knowing full well she was.

She nodded. "Blanche got us all separate rooms at the Palace in New York." She stared at him a moment then said, "Well?"

"Yes," he said decisively.

She nodded again and hitched her chair closer. "Now let me talk; the others are waiting for us. On Friday night I went to a dinner for Oliver Pendragon. He's famous now. A celebrity in print and on TV."

"I know."

"You and Harry are going to Silicon Valley, aren't you? Computer and software clients. Oliver is director of this new genetic lab endowed by Dennis McCall. They'll need a big computer installation plus initial software and continual upgrades. Why don't you select a computer maker—one of our current advertisers or a holdout you want to convert—and sell them on the idea of equipping Pendragon's lab either as a charitable contribution or at a deep discount?"

"And what do they get for this largesse?"

"Publicity. Lots of free advertising. Oliver will plug their know-how in his print and TV interviews and in the articles and books he writes. He might even appear in their print ads and television commercials touting their products."

Folsby looked at her admiringly. "You should be in politics," he said.

"I am," Barbara said, and he smiled.

"Have you told Harry Prentice about this?" he asked.

"No."

"Why not? We do have a chain of command, you know. And he is your immediate superior."

"Em, look at the man; he can hardly stand up. Maybe eventually he'll be back to normal. Maybe. But right now he just can't cut the mustard. He hasn't the vigor or confidence to make the deal. You do. Em, you'll have to handle this personally—if you think it's a good idea."

"I think it's an excellent idea," he said. "But will Pendragon go for it?"

Barbara stood up, readjusted her scarf, smiled down at her father.

"Leave him to me," she said.

6

INFERNAL TRIANGLE...

At their first meeting they had a seriocomic discussion of how they were to address each other. Mr. Demijohn and Miss, or Ms., Johnson seemed pretentiously formal. Priscilla asked if he had a nickname, and Noah replied that during his football playing days in high school he was known as Scat for his ability to scramble quickly when the ball was snapped.

She laughed and said it might mean to scoot and was also a type of jazz singing in nonsense syllables, popularized by Louis Armstrong and Ella Fitzgerald. But in addition, scat meant fecal droppings of animals. In that case, he said, he would greatly appreciate it if she merely called him Noah. But, he asserted, he could not bring himself to address her as Priscilla or Pris.

"Too close to prissy," he explained, "and I judge you to be far from that. Will you settle for Cilla?"

She agreed and so they were Noah and Cilla to each other and to their friends. After they became intimate, he started calling her "honey," or "hon," in public. She made him stop.

"The next step may be 'Attila the hon,' " she said. "Just stick to Cilla." He obeyed.

Late on Tuesday evening, August 8th, they had dinner at a funky Italian restaurant in Cambridge, close to Noah's apartment. They ate linguine with white clam sauce and drank Soave. Noah would soon be twenty-six; Priscilla was a year younger.

He wore a lightweight navy blue blazer with khaki slacks. She was more formally dressed in coral silk trousers beneath a boat-necked tunic of the same fabric. Her shoes were black strap sandals; his were scuffed loafers.

"I called you this afternoon," she told him. "Twice. But you were gone all day. No one would tell me where you were."

"Company policy," he said easily. "Was it something important?"

"About my interview."

"How did it go?"

"Very encouraging. After I get my master's I'll be on their short list for that dig in south Turkey I told you about."

He stopped eating to look at her. "I'm happy for you but sad for me. If you go it'll be for a year, won't it?"

"At least. Two if their grant is renewed."

He shook his head dolefully. "Long time to be gone," he said.

"It's something I want to do," she said. "Good field experience. A great opportunity."

"But a year," he protested. "Maybe two. What will I do without you?" He sounded sincerely desolated.

"You'll live," she said. She toyed with her salad, not looking at him. "Where were you this afternoon?"

"I had a meeting with reps from the Legal Services Corporation," he said immediately. "They told me what they can do and what they can't do. I told them about the pro bono department we're setting up, and they were happy about that. They've got more on their plate than they can handle. We agreed to meet frequently to compare notes and avoid overlap."

"Men or women?"

He answered instantly. "Two men, one woman."

"All white?"

"No, one of the guys was black."

"Nice people?"

"Okay. Flaming liberals, all of them. They act as if representing indigents is doing God's work on earth."

"And you don't think so?"

"I think it's valuable. A worthy activity. But there's a political angle involved they don't seem aware of. Or if they are, they're not mentioning it. Maybe they figured trying to proselytize a member of a white-shoe law firm is hopeless."

She smiled. "Everything is political with you, isn't it, Noah?"

"It's becoming so. Espresso? Dessert?"

"No, thanks; I'm full."

"Should we take in a movie?"

"Too late. Let's go to your place and listen to Tony Bennett."

"You're in a romantic mood?"

"Why not?" Her smile was strained. "I may be gone a long time."

They rose and moved toward the door. She preceded him and he admired her posture. She had the small head and long neck of a Balanchine dancer and carried herself serenely, cool and somewhat aloof. Black hair was pulled back tightly from a high brow and cinched with a Navajo silver barrette set with a turquoise. Her skin was lighter than his, with a golden underglaze. He thought all her hippy, busty body had the deep glow of polished amber.

They walked back to his apartment hand in

hand. She was shorter than he, but her stride was almost as long. She jogged every morning and he had accompanied her, once, and had been amazed by her endurance. He complimented her and she replied cryptically, "I'm good at enduring."

As they strolled he related the news from Florida, learned during a phone call the previous evening...

His mother was well and doing ballet drills thrice a week at a barre installed in the exercise room. She hoped Priscilla and Noah would visit during the Labor Day weekend.

Judge Hampton, now eighty-three, had decided to ignore his doctor's warnings and had increased his daily alcoholic intake to one martini before dinner, one glass of wine during dinner, one cognac after dinner. He also smoked a cigar with his postprandial brandy.

Mrs. Constance was no better but considerably cheered by frequent visits from her daughter-in-law and grandson.

Anthony Scott Folsby was now walking and his vocabulary increased daily. He could now say, "Sar," which pleased Noah's mother mightily.

Mr. Emmet Folsby had forbidden his son to skipper the *Folly* again after Brett had taken the yacht up the Waterway with his family, sister-in-law, and a visiting friend, and had been involved in a minor collision. No one had been injured.

"And Barbara?" Priscilla inquired casually. "How is she?"

"Okay, I guess."

"Not getting married, is she?"

"I don't think so or Mother would have mentioned it."

His rented apartment was a temporary abode which would suffice until he was admitted to the Massachusetts bar and became a practicing and salaried attorney. Then he hoped to find a more impressive and comfortable home in Boston. Meanwhile he had a third-floor, one-bedroom shelter with slanted floors, scarred furniture, and a kitchenette the size of a closet.

There was no air conditioning and the apartment was hot and fusty when they entered. Noah tinkered with the rusted window fan, trying to get it started, while Priscilla wandered about, peering into the small bedroom and antiquated bathroom. She returned to the living room just as he finally got the fan working and rose from his knees, dusting his palms.

"It won't cool," he said, "but at least it will stir the soup." Then he noticed she was standing erect, head up, staring at him with an expression he could only interpret as a mix of rage and disdain. "What's wrong?" he asked.

"You," she said angrily. "You're wrong. All wrong."

He sighed. "Now what have I done, Cilla?"

"It's not what you've done, it's what you failed to do."

"Say what?"

"You very carefully replaced the sheets and

pillowcases although I know you usually change your bed linens on Friday nights. And you very carefully washed the bathroom sink and tub to make certain no blond hairs remain."

"Blond hairs? What on earth are you talking about?"

"What you neglected to do was use an air freshener—something strong to kill the scent of Joy. It's all over the place, even out here. Joy. It's Barbara Folsby's perfume, isn't it? I know she was using it when I met her in Florida. And I saw a big bottle in her bathroom when she was showing me her suite. Joy. Was the afternoon a joy?"

"I was at the..." He started but his voice trailed away. He drew a deep breath. "Can we sit down and talk about this, Cilla?"

"I prefer to stand," she said, voice tight with fury.

"Whatever you wish. But I'd like a chance to defend myself."

"Presumption of innocence?" she said bitingly. "Please don't get lawyerly with me."

"Well, there is reasonable doubt," he argued. "It may be true that I—"

"Oh, stop it!" she said and began to weep. "You've been bedding her for years and still are."

He was startled by tears from this calm woman and didn't know how to react. "What makes you suspect—"

"*Suspect?*" she said scornfully. "I *know*. Almost from day one. Your unexplained or too detailed explanations of your absences when she's in town. You're a lousy liar. And the way you looked at her when we were in Florida. And the smiles the two of you traded when the Folsbys' boat was mentioned. Do me a favor and don't insult my intelligence with denials."

"I'd like a drink," he said suddenly. "I have some plum brandy. Would you like a shot?"

Unexpectedly she nodded and he found the bottle under the sink and poured them each a small glass of slivovitz. They sipped but remained standing. She was rooted; he roamed about the room, glancing at floor, walls, ceiling. She stared at him.

He had put on weight, grown a heavy black mustache, and looked older than his years. He was not stout, but his solidity conveyed an impressive dignity. Mustache, bulk, handsome features—all created an image of importance, someone to be reckoned with.

To test his decision to admit his culpability or deny it, she asked, "Does your mother know? The Judge?"

"Of course not," he said at once. "How could they possibly know?"

Pleased by his reply, Priscilla said, almost softly, "She's a beautiful woman. I admit it."

He turned to face her. "Yes," he said, "but not as beautiful as you."

"Then what *is* it? She's white? A blonde? Is it race? A lollipop for your ego? Your revenge? Prejudice repaid?"

"Race?" he said disgustedly. "Do you know how bored I am with race? Endless talk about race. Endless writing about race. Newspapers, magazines, novels, plays, movies, radio, television. Race, race, race. And I'm bored, bored, bored! Give me a break! I will not let it dominate my life. I will not let it dictate how I live. I reject race. Completely and utterly."

"You can't," she told him.

"I can!" he cried. "I do and I shall continue. I have things to accomplish and I cannot waste time on race or let it influence my actions or my future. And that includes my relationship with Barbara Folsby."

"Are you in love with her?"

He came over to stand directly in front of her and look into her eyes.

"I don't know," he said, his voice muted now. "I tell her I am, but I honestly don't know. I've tried to analyze my feelings for her a hundred times and still haven't succeeded. Is it love? Affection? The sex? What then *is* it? I just don't know for sure. The closest I can come is calling it an obsession. Yes, she obsesses me. Is that love? I don't think so. It's like I'm haunted, possessed by a wraith."

"More likely a succubus," Priscilla said mordantly. She finished her drink, rinsed out the glass in the sink, set it upside down on the drainboard. She gathered up her shoulder bag and a straw hat she had carried all night. "I'm going now," she announced. "I don't think we should see each other again."

He was stricken. "Never?" he said desperately. "This is it?"

"Perhaps not never," she said. "But I'll be

227

going away for a year or two. Maybe when I return you'll no longer be obsessed."

"May I write you?" he asked humbly.

"Yes, you may if you like. I might even reply."

He moved to embrace her, but she slipped quickly aside. They stood a moment in awkward silence.

"Noah," she said finally, "one of these days she'll toss your black ass out. She'll get tired of you and find a younger stud: white, black, yellow, or purple."

Surprisingly he agreed. "She might do just that. She's a hard woman."

"Ruthless," Priscilla said.

"I don't think so—but she knows what she wants and goes after it hell for leather. She's singleminded."

"And you're the single."

"Nope, not me. It's the Folsby Press. She's even more ambitious than I am."

Priscilla strode to the door, paused, turned back.

"Noah, I have a story to tell you. I wasn't going to, but now I think I will. When I was being shown Barbara's bedroom down in Florida I saw a small statuette on her dresser. A carved wooden figure of a naked man wearing a little hat and standing on the back of a turtle. Barbara told me it was an antique voodoo doll from Haiti. You stuck pins in it while thinking of a person you wanted to hurt. Well, I examined it and it's not Haitian. It's from West Africa, probably Benin or

Togo. And it's not a talisman. Objects like Barbara's were made for women to use when their men were away at war or on hunts. Barbara's figurine is a dildo."

"You're kidding!"

"A dildo," Priscilla repeated firmly. "I didn't tell her of course. Because when I examined it I saw what appeared to be fresh holes. She's been sticking pins in while thinking of the man she wants to suffer. I thought you should know. Goodbye, Noah—and good luck."

7

UNCONQUERABLE SOUL...

Something wonderful was happening to Mrs. Constance Folsby...

Beginning when? Oh, it was born one day and just grew. New spirit, new faith. Why, now she was wheeling herself on slow trips up and down the long hall, Zenobia walking alongside and leaning over her to whisper secrets of the universe. New strength, new hope.

Oh, wait, before that... She awoke one morning with a marvelous revelation: She could conquer the pain, vanquish the weakness, end her dependence on others. It wasn't the *act* of suicide that exhilarated her, it was the *idea*. Not self-destruction, no, because Zen said the soul is indestructible. But the *idea* of suicide, sloughing off the decaying flesh—

an epiphany! It gave her control, you see, after years of being a suffering victim. The *idea* of suicide empowered her.

"Emmet, do you have a book of English poetry? The new magnifying glasses help and I'd like to read Keats again." Why was she already dissembling?

"I don't have Keats, dear, but I think Judge Hampton has an anthology we can borrow."

And there he was—not Keats but the poet she sought: William Ernest Henley. "I am the master of my fate/ I am the captain of my soul." It was a truth so invigorating she felt she could dance a jig. Of course! Of course! She could be master of her fate, captain of her soul. No one else. For the *idea* of suicide—not the act, mind you—gave her power to decide her destiny.

But her new concept had to be given credence. Suicide could not be just a fantasy; it had to be a choice in order to restore and vitalize the confidence and independence numbed by her illness. The planning was clear, well reasoned, and well executed. Not confused. She was certainly *not* confused at all but thinking logically and purposefully.

"Emmet, I want to change my will and leave everything I have to Anthony."

"Very generous, dear. Set up a trust fund. It will pay for Tony's education and get him started on whatever he wants to do. Who shall be trustee until the boy comes of age?"

"Brett, of course."

Emmet, knowing their son's extravagance

better than she, suggested he, the grandfather, serve as trustee. But Constance insisted Brett be named, and her husband, not willing to argue, acquiesced.

Determined, she succeeded in walking a few steps each day, unassisted, from bed to wheelchair. Everyone was delighted with her progress. Oh, if they only knew the reason for her renewed vigor!

The *how* of it required scheming and stealth.

"Emmet, I don't really need an aide from midnight to eight in the morning. I'm sleeping so well. It's an unnecessary expense. I can get along very well with Naomi and Sophie taking care of me during the day."

He was doubtful but agreed only if she let him install an alarm system: a red button on her nightstand which, when pressed, sounded a bell in his bedroom, Barbara's, and the housekeeper's. Push the button in case of need and someone would come running.

Now she was alone at night—a triumph!

Then, most important, a way to make her conception doable. Pills of course; that was the least messy way, and, for her, the easiest. She consulted an encyclopedia of prescription drugs—her bedside bible—and selected the medication she swallowed every day to alleviate her muscle spasms. The guide listed innumerable possible side effects and warned an overdose could cause depression of the central nervous system, difficulty in breathing, coma, and death. Just the thing!

Naomi and Sophie brought her pills to the

bedside in a tiny paper cup with a glass of water. They had been instructed to stand there a moment, observe, and make certain she swallowed the medication. But years of routine had dulled their caution. Now they brought the tablet at the time prescribed, dumped it into her palm, left fresh water, and went back to their romance novel or television screen.

She kept the unused muscle relaxants in a pouch of facial tissues concealed under the bed, tucked beneath the spring, overlooked when the bed linens were changed.

Sometimes her spasms were so severe she had to swallow the pill for temporary relief. But frequently, when she could endure the pain, she hid the little pink tablet under her pillow until night when she was alone and could add it to her horde unobserved.

And how her cache grew! A single pill, two, five, seven, twelve—and then she had to make a second bag of tissues to hold her jewels. Her treasure! It was power made tangible, proof she was indeed master of her fate, captain of her soul.

On Wednesday evening, August 8, Barbara, returned from Boston, sat with her mother awhile after dinner. They chatted of many things and Constance was pleased when asked if she thought Barbara should let her hair grow longer.

"Oliver thinks I look better with shoulder-length," she told her mother. "He likes long hair. What do you think?"

"You must please yourself, dear. But I do

believe it's a bit too short the way you're wearing it now. Almost mannish. But look what's happening to me! If this keeps up I'll soon be as bald as Simon Smithson."

She bent her head to show her daughter how the gray strands had thinned, white scalp showing in patches. Constance said it was probably due to all the medication she was taking. Whatever the cause, her hair was coming out in clumps and her comb and brush were tangles.

"I have the answer to that," Barbara said. She left the sickroom, ran upstairs, and returned a few moments later with four cloches: black velvet, red plaid, straw, and a deep green silk with a gold pom-pom on top. Mrs. Folsby tried them all with Barbara holding a hand mirror to show the result.

They agreed the green silk with pom-pom was the most attractive and did the best job of hiding Constance's scraggly locks. She tugged it down almost to her eyebrows and then tilted it to one side. It gave her a piquantly rakish look. Oh, how they laughed!

"Ah, Mom," Barbara said, and leaned forward to kiss her cheek. "It's so good to hear you laugh again."

"Why shouldn't I laugh?" Mrs. Folsby said. "I'm happy."

BOOK
5

1

EIGHT-THIRTY A.M....

"Hard aport!" Anthony Scott Folsby screamed in his treble voice. "Hard astarboard!" He turned from the control panel on the flying bridge of the moored Folly. "How was that, Grandpa?" he asked.

"Well done," Emmet said. "When you give commands you must speak up loudly and forcefully so your crew knows you aren't scared."

"I wouldn't be scared," Tony said.

"Of course you wouldn't. But you must prove it by speaking firmly. Now tell me: Which side is port and which side is starboard?"

The boy turned to face forward again. He held out his little hands and looked down at them. "Port is left," he pronounced, "and starboard is right."

"Very good," his grandfather said. "Now here's an arithmetic problem: I'm sixty-six. How many years older am I than you?"

"Can I have a pencil and paper?"

"Nope. Do it in your head."

Tony thought a moment. "Sixteen?" he said tentatively.

"No, you're subtracting from the first six. Subtract from the second six, the starboard one."

"Sixty-one?"

"Now you've got it."

"That's a lot of years."

Emmet laughed. "It sure is. What would you like to do now?"

"Can I shine the bell?"

"If you like. You know where the rags and polish are kept. Be careful and use the canvas gloves."

Emmet took his iced black coffee down to the foredeck and sat in a canvas chair. It was Saturday morning, the beginning of the 1992 Memorial Day weekend, and it promised to be a winner: hot sun, low humidity, pellucid sky, a gentle northerly breeze shirring the surface of the Waterway.

Anthony came up from below with the can of polish and a fistful of rags. He set to work shining the boat's brass bell. He was wearing a brimmed hat of white duck, sunglasses, T-shirt, and denim shorts. His arms and legs were tanned, his nose coated with sunblock.

Emmet watched him industriously rubbing away the tarnish and reflected the boy never lazed, never idled, never dawdled. He seemed entranced by all things mechanical, how they worked and how repaired when broken. He was a whiz at jigsaw puzzles and, for his next birthday, asked for a set of tools. At his age, Emmet recalled, Brett had been a scamp, a mischievous lad who loved to read or just lie on his back and watch the clouds drift by.

Emmet's love for his grandson was partly due, he knew, to the promise he gave of the family's

238

continuity. In a larger sense, it was the same reason people smiled when they saw a baby or toddler. The tot was evidence of humankind's immortality: a cause for rejoicing.

But more than that, Emmet loved the boy because he saw in him his own rude beginnings, his own interests, talents and, yes, his own passions, even in nascent form. He felt closer to grandson than son. Anthony may have inherited his father's golden hair, flashing smile, and roguish handsomeness, but they were two completely different and almost opposite personalities.

Emmet sat stolidly, sipped his coffee, and gazed at the yachts and launches plying the Intracoastal. He wondered what the future held for his grandson and remembered his own past.

Starting in boyhood he had impressed parents and friends with his practical, nuts-and-bolts approach to the business of living. He was a methodical young man, a firm believer in the carpenters' dictum: "Measure twice, cut once." In the early years of their marriage Constance had frequently referred to him as a "can-do man," for he could install a light fixture, replace a broken window, tile a floor, soundproof a ceiling, tune their car's engine.

Constance considered can-do meant a collection of useful skills. Emmet thought of can-do as an attitude, the belief you could accomplish almost anything if you put your mind to it. He frequently espoused that view in speeches to professional associations and in memoranda to his employees, many of whom were amused by his earnestness.

But that was his public philosophy. He had a private discipline so secret no one, not even his wife, was aware of it or knew how it dominated his life.

This doctrine was born after an unusual happening during his junior year at Purdue University.

For a brief time he was enormously attracted by a young woman two years younger than he. His interest in her was wholly sexual since he thought her a haughty woman of pinched intelligence. But despite her aloofness and her dowdiness of dress, her body had a loose sensuosity that inflamed him. He was bewitched, night and day, by the dream of possessing her.

He stated his desire forthrightly on their third date and was summarily rejected. He begged a long time to no avail and he finally left her, furious at his abject pleading and her refusal.

Less than a month later the unfortunate woman was assaulted and raped. Her assailant was captured almost immediately.

Emmet met her by chance a few weeks after the crime and stammered out, "I was sorry to hear of your trouble." He thought he was being sincerely sympathetic.

She looked at him coldly. "No, you weren't sorry," she said. "You were glad." And she stalked away, leaving him shaken.

He pondered a long time, deeply, on what she had said and eventually came to the shamed conclusion she was correct: He had felt an exultancy on first learning she had been forcibly and brutally taken. In a way he didn't wish to analyze, it was retribution for her rejection of him. But ugly as that realization was, the facile manner in which he had deceived himself seemed more shameful.

The incident taught him how easy it was to delude oneself. He vowed from that moment on he would be completely, even ruthlessly, honest with himself. No self-deception. No weaseling of motives. No denying his own frailties and failures.

He wished he might be as honest with others. It was impossible. Successful living demanded dissembling, pretense, subterfuge, and occasionally outright lying. But mendacity was not always for personal profit; it was sometimes needed to prevent unnecessary pain to others.

His sexual relationship with his daughter was a case in point. What could possibly be the benefit to anyone if it were known? In the public mind incest was invariably linked with abuse or even pedophilia. Emmet supposed such beastliness existed, but he thought it likely there were many situations similar to his: joyous and fulfilling, fed by consensual bliss.

He refused to deceive himself by claiming his physical intimacy with Barbara was engendered by his wife's illness. It was not true. Even if Constance were in perfect health, capable of and eager for intercourse, he would continue to betray her with their daughter. And search as he might, he found no guilt in it and could only conclude he was morally obtuse: an honest acknowledgment which never cost him a night's sleep.

At the same time he admitted his affair with Barbara was not due to an emotional or romantic love, greatly exceeding parental affection. If he frequently told her, "I love you," it was for her sake; it gave her pleasure and confidence—and helped disguise his rabid lust. But he knew. Ah, the games people play!

Anthony finished polishing the yacht's bell and Emmet congratulated him on a job well done.

"How about taking the *Folly* out this afternoon," he suggested. "See if the fish are biting."

"Just the two of us, Grandpa?"

"Well, Noah Demijohn is here on a visit and I bet he'd like to go. I'll ask him."

"And Dad?"

"We'll see what he has planned."

They crossed the highway hand-in-hand, happy the heavy traffic of the tourist season had dwindled. They found Brett on the terrace finishing a cup of coffee and a croissant. Emmet asked if he'd like to go fishing that afternoon.

"Can't make it," he said. "Zoe and Simon are coming over for a swim. You go ahead."

"Maybe Aunt Barbara wants to go," Tony piped up.

"Good idea," Emmet said. "I'll ask her."

Brett whisked off his son's white duck hat and ruffled his fine blond hair. "Hey, tiger," he said, "you're going to stay here tonight—the first time you've slept away from home. Think you can manage?"

"No problem," Anthony said seriously, and his father and grandfather laughed.

"Well, it used to be my bedroom and my bed," Brett told him. "Tonight it's all yours."

"And I'll be right down the hall if you want company," Emmet added.

"Can we play cards before I go to bed, Grandpa?"

"Sure we can. Your mother and father will be at a party and you and I will play cards in Grandma's room and have our own party."

"Can we build a house with the cards like you showed me how?"

"We can do that too," Emmet said and reached out to touch the lad's cheek.

He was there, alive and close, with his son and grandson. Three generations of Folsbys in the sunshine. He wanted to embrace them and be hugged in their embrace. Same name, same blood.

They were not separate; they were parts of one. He might be the eldest, the most experienced, the wisest. But being an honest man he thought himself the least worthy of esteem.

2

TEN A.M....

Judge Hampton had three tall mirrors installed in the exercise room. The panels were abutted to form a wall reflecting a polished maple barre at which Sarah Demijohn practiced ballet positions, not *en pointe* but in flat dance slippers.

She was now sixty-two, her body still robust and still remarkably limber. All her movements were nimble and if her legs and torso lacked the sparseness of a professional danseuse, she never appeared ponderous or exhibited anything but strong grace.

Noah and Judge Hampton, having finished their routines, sat on the padded bench and watched Sarah go through her workout. Her white leotard was already soaked with perspiration, her muscled legs gleamed. They marveled at her high kicks and the ease with which she did a series of deep kneebends. Then they resumed their conversation.

"Who do you think it will be?" the Judge asked.

"Bush of course," Noah said. "And Clinton, I'm guessing. He's young, handsome, articulate, and very, very ambitious. A lawyer, you know."

"I know," Hampton said. "What drives him?"

"Getting elected."

The Judge laughed. "He has the right priority."

"I was approached by one of his emissaries."

Hampton turned to look at him, astonished. "Were you really?"

"I was," Noah said. "A friendly dinner. We didn't get down to basics until dessert. By the way, they sent a black to convert me. I found it mildly offensive, but he was low-key enough."

"What did they want?"

"My support. I sent you clippings of the newspaper articles on our pro bono program. Apparently someone in Clinton's entourage read them and was impressed enough to make an initial contact."

"Were you promised anything?"

"Vaguely. Talk of a new administration. New faces needed. Especially attorneys. Especially minority attorneys. Perhaps in Justice, Housing, maybe even the White House staff. Nothing definite."

"What exactly do they want—just a statement of support?"

"I suspect they'd like me to play a more active role. Attend local meetings. Make speeches. Maybe even take part in TV debates."

"How do you feel about it, Noah?"

Sarah finished her exercises. She windmilled her arms a few times, breathing deeply, then came over to descend cross-legged to the floor before the two men. She looked up at them, gaze moving from one to the other as they conversed.

"Well, of course I was pleased, Judge. It was quite a compliment. Good for my ego."

Hampton grunted. "It proves you're beginning to get name recognition. That's all to the good. But how did you reply to the offer?"

"First let me tell you about a project I've been working on. I want to start a not-for-profit organization which will make small loans to wannabe entrepreneurs. Suppose a man wants to buy a newsstand, open a little convenience store, maybe even stock a pushcart. Or a woman wants to peddle cosmetics door-to-door, or start a home-cleaning service. Whatever. They're all would-be capitalists who dream of being self-employed. But they lack sufficient cash to get going. My fund would analyze their plan, check their credit rating, and, if they measure up, grant a small loan to help them make the move. No collateral required. Very low interest. And free advice from volunteer businessmen on how to make their dream a reality."

"I think it's a very good idea," Sarah said approvingly. "They would work for themselves, be their own boss."

"Exactly," Noah said. "My program would provide the venture capital."

"How large would the loans be?" the Judge asked.

"Probably a thousand dollars. I haven't made a final determination, but I'd guess a thousand would be the max. We certainly wouldn't attempt to compete with the Small Business Administration. This would be on a much more limited scale—a very personal loan program to create a new generation of small capitalists."

"And where would the money come from?"

"Corporations, banks, foundations, individual donations. I think I can structure the whole thing so contributions would be tax deductible."

"Have you spoken to your senior partners about this?"

"Yes, and they approve providing I do it on my own time and the firm isn't legally involved. I believe they see it as a way to win new clients from amongst the contributors."

"What are you going to call it, Noah?" his mother asked.

"Something else I haven't decided. Maybe 'First Start' or 'Bootstrap Enterprises' or anything which suggests the idea of taking the initial step toward financial independence. It is really a very conservative concept; its purpose is to further self-reliance and make the individual responsible for his or her success or failure. Judge?"

"Yes," Hampton said, "I think it's an excellent idea. It will require a great deal of hard work, but meanwhile you'll be developing managerial skills and making a number of important contacts who may prove to be of assistance in the future. Incidentally, you can count on me for a contribution when you get organized."

"Thank you, sir," Noah said. "My hope is that after the initial funding the organization may someday become self-supporting, making additional loans from the interest on loans previously granted. Anyway, with this project in the planning stage and requiring hours of work I decided now was not the time to get heavily involved in an election campaign. So I thanked the Clintonite politely and suggested he might check with me in four years if his man is elected."

Hampton smiled. "Good for you," he said. "You handled it wisely. And there is another factor involved. If you had agreed to his proposition and Clinton is elected, you may well have ended up in Washington where you would be a very small frog in a very large pond. Noah, as you well know, all politics is local, and the first thing you must do is establish a firm home base before you venture into the national jungle. Be patient. Get your fund up and running. Work on publicity and public relations. Create a favorable reputation and image. Meet all the movers and shakers. And I guarantee within four years the candidate himself, not a gofer, will personally ask for your support."

Noah rose. "I have you to thank for whatever good comes to me. I want you to know I am fully aware of how much I owe you, Judge. I don't plan to fail—and my success will be as much yours as mine."

"And me?" Sarah asked.

Her son laughed and swooped to kiss her cheek. "You come first," he said. "Always have, always will. You know that. Now I've got to go shower and change. I'm going fishing

248

with the Folsbys this afternoon. Emmet phoned and invited me."

"Just the two of you?" Hampton asked.

"No, little Anthony is coming along. And Barbara."

"I'm sure you'll have an enjoyable time," the Judge said.

Noah left the exercise room. Sarah and the Judge rose, stood facing, searched each other's eyes.

"When do you plan to speak to him?" he asked.

"After lunch," she said. "Before he goes to the Folsbys."

"I still think I should be part of it," he said fretfully.

But she was firm. "No," she said. "My way is best. If you are there he may lose his temper. Or you might. If hard things are said it would be the end of everything. Please, Sweet Daddy, let me handle it."

They moved toward the door, going slowly, the Judge leaning heavily on his cane.

"Whatever happens with Noah," he said, "it won't be the end of us. Never."

"Never," she agreed.

They lunched on the terrace: a shrimp salad with baked bagel slices, and pistachio ice cream for dessert. Noah carried the conversation, explaining how he intended to screen loan applicants to his mini-venture fund.

"No discrimination," he vowed. "Completely legal. All races, sexes, creeds, national origins. And age will not be a deterrent.

Everyone welcome. Everyone judged equally. All we want is a viable plan and ambition—lots and lots of ambition."

"And discipline," the Judge added, looking at him. "Self-discipline."

"Of course," Noah said. "That too. It's going to work, Judge; I just know it. It will make a significant difference locally, and nationally if the program is expanded."

"Social change," Hampton observed.

"No, no," Demijohn said quickly. "Well, yes, but social change isn't the main goal; it's secondary. I'm convinced economic improvement must come first. Improvements in education and the crime rate will follow. Don't expect morality from the hungry and impoverished. When the poor have economic clout and can use their money muscle, then we'll see social progress. My project is one small step in that direction. Hey, this is beginning to sound like a sales pitch. Pardon me. But I'm so high on this, I get carried away."

"Nothing wrong with enthusiasm," the Judge said. "Your plan will be dead in the water without it. And now, if you'll excuse me, I think I'll go upstairs for my nap. See you all at dinner."

They rose and watched him leave, walking slowly and haltingly. His shoulders were bowed, head lowered. They sat down again and Sarah poured them more iced tea.

"Getting old now," Noah remarked, "and it shows. How many years?"

"He's eighty-six," his mother said.

"His body may be withering but his mind still seems sharp. How's his memory?"

"He doesn't forget much," she said. "Not the important things."

"He's opened a lot of doors for me."

"I know. Don't slam them, Noah."

He straightened in his chair, looked at her. "What's that supposed to mean, Moms?"

She met his stare directly. "You're mixed up with Barbara Folsby, aren't you?"

He opened his mouth as if to shout a denial, paused, took a sip of tea instead, the glass shaking. She waited patiently.

"I should have known you'd see it," he said ruefully. "You've got the mojo."

"No," she said. "But I'm your mother. I gave birth to you. And I know you better than you know yourself."

"Maybe," he said, sighing. "Does the Judge know?"

"No."

"Good. Don't tell him. I don't know how he'd take it."

"Are you in love with the woman, Noah?"

"I don't think so. But she's got me, Moms. Like crack cocaine. I'm addicted and can't cut loose."

"Do you want to?"

"Wanting and doing are two different things. I think I'm clean, then she calls and I go running. She says, 'Jump!' and I say, 'How high?' Bondage? Oh yes. It's plantation time, folks."

"Does she love you?"

"Ask her that and she'd probably fall down laughing."

"Then what's got you hooked?"

He looked away. "Do I have to draw you a diagram?"

She put the tips of her forefingers together and the tips of her thumbs. She held the open oval before his eyes. "All for that?" she asked.

"Tell me about it," he said bitterly.

"You're moving up. College. Law school. Got a good job. Your picture in the papers. Now your project. This could hurt you bad."

"We're very careful."

"Careful?" she said scornfully. "I guessed. Other people will guess. Noah, you realize what you're risking?"

"Wait a minute," he said. "Suppose it does become known. I've got a white girlfriend. So what? There are plenty of interracial couples in politics and in the professions."

"Married?"

"Well, yeah," he admitted. "Most of them."

"You want to marry Barbara?"

"She'd never have me. I know better than to ask. I'm just her pet."

"And if it becomes known you're bedding a white woman, you think it won't hurt you with the partners of your law firm and with all the important people you're going to ask to contribute to your fund?"

He was silent.

"You'd be hurt," she insisted. "So would the Judge. And so would I. You know what would happen. Get people talking about you behind

252

your back, sniggering about you and your blond chick, you can forget about politicians asking for your support. You'd be bad news."

"If I had a black girlfriend," he said furiously, "no one would think anything of it. Race, race, race! It's not fair."

"Oh, talk sense, little boy," she said, giving him a disdainful look. "Since when has life been fair? What about a black girlfriend? What about Priscilla Johnson. She's back, isn't she?"

"Yes. She's in Cambridge, going for her doctorate."

"Do you see her?"

"Occasionally. Not often. Things have cooled between us."

"She knows about Barbara?"

He didn't reply.

"Well?" she demanded. "Answer me, boy. Does Priscilla know about Barbara or doesn't she?"

"Yes, she knows."

"And wants nothing to do with you. Good for her. Noah, I beg you, break off with Barbara."

"I can't," he said helplessly. "Moms, believe me, I know everything you say is true, but I just can't end it."

"You're one sad weakling—you know that?"

"I know. I have strength for other things. Got through college and Harvard Law. Good job. Appear in court. Plan a new project. Make my way up the ladder. But when it comes to Barbara I lose my will. I told you I was hooked. I know I should go cold turkey, but I know I'd never make it."

"It's going to go on and on?"

"Until she says stop. I know the day will come. She'll toss me out of her life. It will hurt. Oh lordy, will it hurt! But you know what? Deep down I'll be glad. Because when she says so long, buddy boy, I'll be free, clean. I'll kick the drug. Oh, she'll do it all right. She's got the power. I don't."

His mother stood up and turned her back to him. "I'd like to be angry and really scorch you," she said in a muffled voice, "but I can't. Because I was the same way with your father as you're acting now. I knew he was no good. I knew he was ruining my life, but I couldn't throw him out or leave him. Just *couldn't*. He was my habit. Then he just waltzed away. Like you said, it hurt but deep down I was glad because I was free."

He went to her, held her in his arms, kissed her tear-streaked face. But she pushed him away, gave him a crooked smile.

"I guess foolishness runs in the family," she said.

"I guess," he agreed.

3

TWELVE-FIFTEEN P.M....

Constance Folsby lay in her massive hospital bed, propped up on two plump pillows. She wore the green silk cloche cocked rakishly to one side. Her wasted body seemed lost beneath sheet and blanket. Zenobia sat alongside and held one of her mother-in-law's dry, skeletal hands.

Naomi, the aide, had taken advantage of the visitor's presence and had gone to the kitchen for lunch. Before leaving she had closed the drapes to block the noontime sunlight; the sickroom was pleasantly dim. The radio played softly. The Coles were singing "Unforgettable."

Brett, Zoe Plummer, and Simon Smithson had trooped down to the beach for a swim. Zen, wearing a terry coverup over her gray wool tanksuit, had tarried for what she dubbed a "nice gossip," giving the sick woman snippets of news and rumor. Constance listened with a benign smile, eyes dilated and bright.

"The party tonight is Simon's housewarming," Zenobia told her. "He bought this beautiful home on North County Road in Palm Beach."

"I know."

"I wish you could see how he decorated it. It's so—so *different*. He has such good taste."

"He gave me a music box," Constance said dreamily. "A lovely thing. It played 'Get Me to the Church on Time.' But I dropped it and it broke. I've been ashamed to tell him."

"He'll get you another," the younger woman assured her. "He has a lot of money and his interior design business is doing very well. He's decorating my new restaurant for free."

"How is it coming, dear?"

"Fine. It's being painted now. I hope to open in time for the tourist season."

"What are you going to call it?"

"Brett says we're spending so much money on it, it should be called *Le Pissoir.* He's only joking of course. We'll probably just call it Zen's. Simon is going to decorate it like a garden. Won't that be nice?"

"Your sister works for him, doesn't she?"

"Yes, and she loves it. Zoe didn't know much about interior decorating, but Simon is teaching her and he says she has a real talent." Zenobia leaned nearer and almost whispered, "And he changed her style of dressing completely. You should see her now."

"What does she wear?"

"Simon insists she looks best in tight pants or miniskirts with a wide leather belt and turtleneck sweaters or tank tops. All in black or all in white. And he wants her to use more eye makeup. Oh, she looks so elegant!"

"Do you think anything is going on there— between Zoe and Simon?"

"I don't think so. I asked her and she just laughed. I don't believe he's interested in her romantically. Maybe because she's taller than he is. But at least she's forgotten all about her crush on Oliver Pendragon. She never mentions him anymore. Barbara is seeing him, isn't she?"

"Yes. Frequently. She's known him a long time, you know—even before he became famous—but she's been seeing much more of him lately."

"Do you think they might get married?"

Constance considered. "Perhaps. Someday. I had a long talk with Barbara just yesterday, and I think she's getting to the point where she'd like to have a home of her own."

"And children?" Zenobia asked.

"Well, she's thirty-six so she better decide soon." She paused and pulled Zenobia closer. "I have a secret, but you mustn't tell anyone. I know he's a celebrity and all, but I don't much like Oliver Pendragon—do you?"

"No, I do not," Zen said definitely.

"He's become so self-important," Constance said. "So pompous. I really don't understand what Barbara sees in him."

"I think he's a stupid man," Zenobia said. "I met him at Simon's shop—he redecorated Oliver's apartment, you know—and Oliver asked me about the crystal I was wearing. I explained how it concentrates spiritual emanations and helps you achieve enlightenment and become part of the eternal spirit. And he said that was all hogwash. It's the exact word he used—hogwash."

"Well, I think he's full of hogwash," Mrs. Constance Folsby said, and both women laughed merrily.

Zenobia was happy the invalid was so cheerful.

4

ONE-TWENTY P.M....

Brett came in from the terrace to fetch a pitcher of sangria for his guests. He saw Barbara heading for the front door with her fishing gear. He called and she stopped and waited for him.

"Don't come into the house barefoot and without a coverup," she said sternly. "Emmet has told you a dozen times."

"So what?" he said. "Are you going to rat on me?"

"And I think your trunks are god-awful," she continued. "You're a little old for Mickey Mouse, aren't you?"

"What does Oliver the Twist wear?" he asked. "Disposable diapers? Listen, I want to talk to you about vacations. I don't think both of us should be away at the same time. Mother likes to have company. When are you taking your two weeks?"

"I don't know at the moment," she said. "I plan to request input from my staff and coordinate schedules so everyone isn't gone at the same time."

"Come on, cut the crap," he said roughly. "Now that you're advertising director, pick the weeks you want and let your peons figure out their vacation times."

"When are you taking off?"

"The two weeks after July Fourth. It's on a Saturday this year."

"All right," she said. "Maybe I'll take the two weeks before Labor Day. Where are you going?"

"Europe. With Zen and Tony. They've never been there. I figure London, Paris, and Rome—and wherever else we have time for. I've asked Simon Smithson and Zoe Plummer to join us."

She looked at him. "It'll cost a mint," she said.

"Who cares?" he said and laughed. "Too bad we don't have offices in Europe and then I could write off the whole trip as a business expense."

"Another thing," she said. "I think Anthony is too young to schlep all over Europe."

"Thank you, Dr. Spock," he said. "Who anointed you an authority on child care? And by the way, are you and Oliver the Twist coming to Simon's party tonight?"

"We may stop by for a short while."

"Will you, for God's sake, tell him to change his cologne. That gunk he wears makes my eyes water."

"Oliver doesn't—" she started angrily but Brett turned away, went back to the kitchen.

Barbara stood a moment, staring after him, thinking of something he had just said. In many ways he was intelligent; she had acknowledged it a long time ago. But when it came to the work ethic he was a nonstarter; she knew that too and wondered if it was because he simply didn't give a damn about business.

In any event, he had failed to recognize a

259

commercial idea with an exciting potential. She headed for the *Folly* again pondering on how best to profit from his denseness and her unexpected opportunity.

5

FOUR-TEN P.M....

The Folly headed back for the Hillsboro Inlet with Noah Demijohn and Anthony Folsby at the controls on the flying bridge. Noah was teaching the boy to pilot the yacht, placing his hands and correcting him gently when his movements were too abrupt or too tentative.

Barbara and Emmet slumped in canvas chairs on the short afterdeck and drank beer from chilled cans. A white tarp had been jury-rigged to shade them from the westering sun. Their fishing had been a cipher: not a nibble although they saw nearby boats hauling in a nice catch.

"Ah, well," Barbara said, "it's been a beautiful day."

"They're all beautiful," Emmet said, "if you can get up in the morning, look at the obituary page, and see you're not listed."

She smiled dutifully. Her father had expressed the same sentiment many times in exactly the same words. She stretched out her sleek legs and put her head back so her face was outside the tarp's shadow and she could get a deeper tan.

"Em," she said, "would it annoy you if we talked business for a while?"

He took a sip of his beer. "Business?" he said. "What business is that? I forget."

He was teasing her in his bluff, heavy manner, but she had learned to endure it. Disregard it, actually. She straightened in her chair and hitched it closer to his. She was wearing cutoffs and one of his old discarded dress shirts, the tails rolled up and tied under her bosom so her taut midriff was bare.

"You probably saw the rankings," she said. "We're still number five in total circulation, but our market share of advertising revenue is down."

"Not by much," he said. "We'll get it back."

"Doubtful. We haven't started a new magazine in two years."

"Any suggestions?" he asked. "Every industry is covered. Well covered."

"Want to hear a wild idea?"

"Only if you pop me a fresh brew."

She rose to bring him another beer from the plastic cooler. "You open it," she said. "I don't want to break a nail. I just had them done."

He opened the cold can. Before sitting down again she stepped to the rail and looked up to make certain Noah and Tony were still on the flying bridge. Then she moved her chair so she was facing him directly. She leaned forward, forearms pressing on her thighs.

"My wild idea is this," she said. "I want to

261

explore the possibility of the Folsby Press expanding overseas."

He was amused. "That *is* a wild idea."

"Sounds like it at first," she admitted. "But not when you analyze it. As you just said, every domestic industry is well covered. What about Europe, Latin America, even Africa? Do they have trade magazines?"

"I have no idea, but I imagine they do."

"Let me look into it, Em. If we don't grow the company we'll continue to lose market share."

He looked at her thoughtfully. "How would you handle it?"

"Start with Europe. Hire a research outfit to provide a rundown on all existing trade magazines: number of titles, industries, capitalization, circulation, annual advertising revenue. I'm not suggesting we start from scratch with our own books. But we might consider buying an existing foreign publisher or forming a partnership with one just to get our nose in the tent."

"Sounds like you've been giving this a lot of thought."

"I have," she said, looking at him steadily. "I can foresee Folsby Press offices in London, Paris, Rome—maybe even Moscow."

"Uh-huh," he said, sipping his beer. "And how do you plan to finance this expansion?"

"We have several options," she said. "Start slowly using our cash reserves. If that's not doable, negotiate a bank loan—a piece of cake considering our credit rating. Or third, go public and raise the necessary funds by selling equity in the company." She saw his grimace of distaste and immediately added, "I know you don't like the idea of going public. You think you'd lose control. But you wouldn't. Just retain an effective majority of shares or create a special class of stocks for yourself with, say, ten votes to every one vote of regular shares. I don't particularly care about going public either—but for a different reason. I can't see a great demand for shares in a publisher of trade magazines. No pizzazz. We could pay a nice safe dividend, but growth would be slow. It would be strictly an investment for widows and orphans."

"I agree," he said. "Let's forget about going public and stick to our own resources. Okay, you have a research outfit provide a list of trade magazine publishers in Europe. What's your next step?"

"Detective work," she said promptly. "Great Britain is no language problem. And I speak fluent French and passable Italian. I want to go over there, examine existing magazines, determine if any of the publishers want to sell out or are looking for an infusion of fresh capital."

He was silent, gazing beyond her at the crinkled sea and the far horizon. The *Folly* made a slow, wide turn to port, straightened, and entered the Inlet.

"When would you want to go?" he asked her.

"As soon as possible. I'm taking my vacation the two weeks before Labor Day. Brett is taking his right after July Fourth, so he and Zenobia and Anthony will be here to keep Mother company while we're gone."

He turned his head to look at her. "While *we're* gone?" he repeated. "*We?*"

"Of course," Barbara said firmly. "I wouldn't think of going without you. There may be important decisions to make. We'll do this business trip together."

He hesitated, mulling the pros and cons. Measure twice, cut once.

"You better go with me," she said saucily, "or I'll trade you in for a new model."

She laughed and reached to stroke his hand. She hadn't changed, he thought. First the bite and then the lick.

They stared at each other, expressionless at first, and finally smiling when both pictured old scenes reenacted in new surroundings. Feather beds and champagne breakfasts.

"All right," Emmet Folsby said. "We'll go."

6

SIX-FORTY P.M....

Zenobia and Brett consigned their son to the care of his grandparents and told him they'd return to retrieve him on Sunday morning.

"You're sure?" the boy said anxiously.

"Absolutely," his father said. "But only if you promise not to smoke a cigar."

"What?" Tony said, and Brett laughed and tousled his hair.

They had a new white Lexus and drove back to their Boca Raton apartment to dress for Simon Smithson's party.

"What are you wearing tonight?" Brett asked idly.

"My black velvet jumpsuit," Zenobia said. "And the wooden ankh you gave me—the one on the leather thong. What are you wearing?"

"White dinner jacket. I was going to sport those black tropical worsted Bermudas I had made, but I think I better stick with long pants. Simon would trump my formal shorts; he's wearing a kilt."

"No!"

"Truth. He's of vaguely Scottish ancestry, you know, and discovered there's a Smith tartan—which is close enough to Smithson. So he ordered a complete evening outfit from an Edinburgh tailor: pleated kilt, Prince Charlie coatee and matching vest—both with silver Celtic buttons—and kilt hose with scarlet flashes. Oh yes, and a black evening sporran made of rabbit fur. He should be quite a sight."

"He just loves wild clothes, doesn't he?"

"It's not an ego thing, Zen; it's a business decision. He claims when he and Zoe dress dramatically clients and potential clients interpret their eccentricity as a sign of artistic talent. It seems to be working; he has more decorating jobs than he can handle."

"It's certainly made a difference in my sister's looks. She is so striking! Like a high-fashion model. Brett, do you think there's anything going on between Zoe and Simon?"

"Could be," he said, and started talking about Anthony's liking for boats and the sea.

They were running late, so Zen took the master bathroom while Brett used the guest bedroom shower stall. The window of this bathroom faced the terrace; the glass was frosted to provide privacy.

He soaped and rinsed quickly, dried, and used Royal Copenhagen cologne. Before padding back to the master bedroom to dress, he stood a moment before the full-length mirror on the bathroom door and studied the reflection of his naked body.

It was not, he decided, an inspiring sight. He was only forty, but there was no denying the crispness of youth had vanished. His father's face had retained a hard ruggedness, but his had softened, slackened. He fancied he could even detect a nascent dewlap under his jaw.

The same melting seemed to be happening to shoulders, arms, torso, legs; gravity was taking its toll—and so were brandy alexanders and beef Wellington. It was not that he was becoming flabby, but there was a blurring of his flesh; he could no longer see rib cage or hip bones. His skeleton was being pillowed and hidden.

Even worse, the gloam coming through the

frosted glass window silvered his hair and gave his skin a pallid, grayish hue as if he were bloodless and devoid of vigor. But his flaccid image didn't dismay him as much as the thought of what the mirror might reveal in five, or ten, or twenty years.

He wondered if Simon was as conscious as he of the cruelty of aging. They had outgrown the flamboyance of their early love, but their attachment to each other was as strong as ever, their humor as bitchy, their physical passion as frantic. He had a sudden panicky fear they were fated to become old mascara'd poofs derided and rejected by a new generation of golden lads: the young and the beautiful.

He and Zenobia dressed rapidly and remembered to take along their housewarming gift: an antique Pierrot marionette. It would look charming perched on Simon's marble mantel.

As they headed for Palm Beach, Brett said, "I plan to drink too much so you must be the designated driver and get us home safely."

Zen asked, "Why do you plan on drinking too much?"

"Because I'm suffering from a severe case of weltschmerz."

"What is that?"

Brett laughed. "The sad realization life is a one-night stand."

7

SEVEN-FIFTY P.M....

Smithson had given a personal recipe to the caterer and asked the dish be prepared for his housewarming. He called it scampi piccata: shrimp dipped in seasoned bread crumbs and sautéed in butter, garlic, lemon juice, capers, and a bit of dry white wine. It was the hit of the buffet set out in his newly decorated dining room.

Brett Folsby had a few of the piquant scampi and rolled his eyes. "Too good for this rabble," he said, motioning toward the crowd eagerly filling cranberry-colored Spode dinner plates.

"You're in a peckish mood tonight," Simon observed. "Got the fantods?"

"More like langueurs. After I showered tonight I glanced at myself in the mirror. I was not impressed."

"At our age mirrors can be killers. I never look in one unless I'm fully dressed."

"Speaking of that, laddie, your kilt is splendid."

"Thank you. It has rattled a few cages."

"How many idiots have asked if you're wearing anything underneath?"

"Several. One old harridan actually groped me."

"No! What did you do?"

"Let her grope. And when she was shocked I said, 'What did you expect—profiteroles?' "

Brett clapped him on the shoulder. "Well

done. These people really are peasants, aren't they?"

"Wealthy peasants," Smithson said, and they moved to the nearest of three open bars to order fresh Stolis.

"Does it bother you?" Folsby asked. "Age, I mean. The big four-oh."

"It is not a subject on which I care to dwell. I keep thinking of Dorian Gray."

"What lies ahead? Cosmetic surgery?"

"If necessary. I'm game. Are you?"

"Not at the moment. But I'm afraid if I ask if you'll love me when I'm old and gray you'll say, 'I do, sport, I do.' "

Simon smiled. "You were an Adonis."

"I thank you. And you were a David."

"And as poorly endowed. How many years has it been for us?"

"Almost fifteen. You were wearing a fur necktie at the Four Seasons bar."

"And you were wearing a phallic tie clip. Fifteen years! Regrets?"

"None whatsoever," Brett said. "You?"

Smithson shook his head. "Not one. We were a lovely couple, weren't we?"

"Still are. But only to ourselves." They smiled at each other—smiles pinked with rue. Brett drained his vodka and ordered another. "I've already warned Zen and I better warn you: I intend to drink too much tonight."

"As much as you like," Smithson said. "Just don't upchuck on the velour. And now I must go play host. Stay late. Please. Drunk or sober, stay for a nightcap."

"Will do," Brett said and watched his lover move away, the pleated kilt flashing about his bony knees.

He carried his drink through the throng, nodding pleasantly at people he knew and at strangers. He wanted Simon's party to be a success, an occasion written about on the society pages, perhaps illustrated with photographs of the interior design.

Simon had described the decoration of his new home as "Mies van der Rohe meets Mario Buatta." "Or if you prefer," he said, "Frank Lloyd Wright meets Martha Stewart." He was not far off the mark. Who else but he would have the chutzpah to pair an ornate Louis XV desk with an Eames chair in black leather? Or set a simple laboratory beaker next to an elaborately decorated Murano glass ewer.

He had first essayed this mix of the austere and the rococo in Brett's Boca Raton apartment. And then, disbelieving less is more, he had exaggerated his "styleless style" in his own home. Many friends and acquaintances, comfortable with the pastel poshness of South Florida interior design, were puzzled and disturbed by Simon's nihilism. One was Emmet Folsby, who expressed his misgivings to Judge Hampton.

He said, "Smithson hates the idea that all the furnishings in one's home should match. I agree with him there, but they should reflect the owner's taste and preferences, even if they are the tastes and preferences of another age or another place. Victorian, for example,

270

or French Provincial. But Simon's work reflects nothing. It is simply a collection of disparate elements, a hodgepodge. It represents no particular culture or time."

"Perhaps it does," the Judge said. "It may quite possibly be ideally suited to the modern world."

"But there is no standard, no foundation, no tradition."

"Do those things exist today? All values have become relative. Low culture is deemed as valuable as high culture, bad taste as acceptable as good taste. There is no reality—only perceptions. Hype has replaced reputation and character has been invalidated by Freudianism. Ancient verities are not so much mocked as ignored."

"You're saying we live in moral chaos?"

"Exactly," Judge Hampton said.

"I don't want to live in a world like that!"

"Emmet, you surprise me. I know you for an intelligent, thoughtful man. But apparently you have not learned to accept change. And change is not always progress."

Another who found Smithson's ideas disquieting was Barbara Folsby. The design and decoration of Simon's new home made her feel inferior, as if they offered a message she could not grasp. She was a representationalist, unable to comprehend abstraction.

As she and Oliver Pendragon made their way through the jammed rooms they traded reactions to what Simon had wrought.

"It's a museum," Barbara said. "With all the

lived-in charm of a used furniture store. It's simply incoherent."

"No, no!" Pendragon said authoritatively. "He is designing for today. For tomorrow! I tell you the man has vision. He is saying one must—"

But then two couples came up, introduced themselves, and began praising Oliver's books and TV lectures. He responded like a stroked puppy and spoke volubly of current projects in his research center, hinting of sensational revelations soon to be announced.

Barbara plucked a glass of champagne from the tray of a passing waiter and moved a few steps away, bored by her escort's self-aggrandizement. She examined the over-dressed women about her and was content she had chosen to wear a double-breasted evening suit of deep purple cashmere. It was severely elegant, worn without blouse or jewelry. The long skirt had a thigh-high side slit, a feature which had caused Pendragon to snuffle with delight.

It suddenly seemed to Barbara all the women she saw were flashing wedding rings, from simple gold bands to sparkling rocks rivaling the Hope. She wondered if she might be the only single woman at the party. Not likely, but the possibility was enough to make her question her status and ponder on how marriage—even to Oliver, for instance—might affect her career.

Her life since college had by choice been spent in the Darwinian masculine world of business.

She had learned not only to survive but to flourish. Certainly being Emmet Folsby's daughter had helped. But she was convinced she would have succeeded in another profession, *any* profession, without his mentoring.

It had required arduous work, self-discipline, and determination as hard and unyielding as the diamonds worn like medals by the self-satisfied matrons she saw strutting about her. But for the first time she realized her business success had also demanded sacrifice: the willing surrender of what might have been a more deeply satisfying life.

Even with a lack of romantic attachment, the total absence of what she called the lovey-dovey syndrome, marriage offered certain advantages not to be scorned. Not the kind of marriage sought by Gracie McCall, who was now on her fourth husband. To Gracie, getting wed was a hobby. Barbara envisioned a profitable partnership, or perhaps a merger, which, although loveless, might enhance her position, give her the weighty importance, dignity, and authority a single woman was so often denied.

There were difficulties, she acknowledged, but none that could not be finessed. Her relationship with her father, the affair with Noah Demijohn, her executive rank at the Folsby Press—these were things almost certain to be affected by her marriage. But none seemed to her a danger or threat which could not be managed.

Emmet once said to her, "You think like a man." She knew he meant it as a compliment, but she thought him a fool to believe so. She considered masculine thinking blinkered, linear, lacking in subtlety and nuance. She was not yet ready to make a final decision but was convinced marriage was her choice to approve or reject; she refused to surrender to the will of a suitor or the fickle power of circumstance.

She saw Oliver still lecturing, his audience now two youngish women who seemed mesmerized by their proximity to a famous personage. Barbara, aware of and amused by the aphrodisiac effect of celebrity, returned to take his arm possessively. "Come along, dear," she said. "We must thank the host."

"What?" he said. "Oh, yes, so we should."

She tugged him away from his rapt listeners and they moved toward a room where a tuxedoed septet was playing old show tunes.

"I have no desire to thank the host," she told him. "But you looked as if you needed rescue from those two groupies."

"Actually," he said in his pontifical manner, "they were asking very cogent questions regarding the genetic origin of phobias. Listen to the music! Would you care to dance?"

"Not this minute," Barbara said, resisting the temptation to add, "Or at any minute," since she had once endured his lumbering efforts to rumba. "Why don't we try the buffet?"

"Good idea," he said, brightening as she knew

274

he would, for he was not only a gourmand but had a special fondness for *free* food and drink. He was not, she admitted, a penurious man but definitely frugal despite his hefty income.

As they moved around the buffet table and she saw him heaping his plate she thought of the many things about him she found offensive, off-putting, or ridiculous—like his bunglesome love-making. She questioned why she or any other woman would consider marrying this man or any man with as many undesirable traits.

The answer was so obvious to her she almost laughed aloud. A woman might deliberately marry an inferior man (for financial security perhaps) because she would suffer no hesitation or qualms in being unfaithful.

They were seated at a small bistro table enjoying scampi piccata and other delicacies when Simon Smithson stopped briefly to exchange greetings. He was accompanied by Zoe Plummer, who wore a silvery Lurex tank top with silk harem trousers in a harlequin pattern. She gave Oliver a frigid nod.

"The shrimp are excellent," Barbara said politely. "Lovely party."

"Thank you," Simon said. "And do try the lobster ravioli."

"Hey," Pendragon said, "you wearing anything under the kilt?" And he actually winked at Barbara.

"Seek and ye shall find," Smithson said lightly, and he and Zoe smiled and moved away.

"How *could* you?" Barbara said.

"How could I what?" the bewildered Oliver said.

"It was such a gauche thing to say."

"Gauche?" he said, much aggrieved. "I thought it was funny."

She was about to scathe him but caught herself. "It was rather funny, Oliver," she said meekly.

Zoe and Simon wandered through the diminishing press of guests, stopping occasionally to chat or answer questions about some of the furniture and bric-a-brac.

"Let's go upstairs for a few minutes," Smithson said to his assistant. "I need to rest my face after three hours of non-stop smiling."

They paused at the nearest bar for glasses of chilled Chablis. Rather than use the wide front stairway where people were seated on the marble steps, they carried their wine to the back of the hallway. There, behind a closed door, a cast-iron spiral staircase led to the second floor. It had been designed for use by the staff, but Simon had found it useful when he wished to avoid unwanted visitors.

They went directly to the master bedroom—really a suite with sitting room, dressing room, walk-in closet, and large bathroom. Smithson had done everything in pure white: walls, carpeting, drapes, curtains, upholstery. But in the center of the sleeping area was an enormous Chinese sleigh bed in crimson and gold, intricately carved with colored glass inset as eyes of writhing dragons.

They sat on a Le Corbusier chaise covered with white sheeting and sipped their Chablis. They were directly over the room where guests were dancing and faintly they heard the band playing "Falling in Love Again."

"Beautiful song," Zoe Plummer said.

"Yes," Simon said. "She just died you know."

"Who just died?"

"Marlene Dietrich. It was *her* song. And Sylvia Sims died. All the good ones are going."

"Like Lawrence Welk," she said.

"Thank you. Did you ever hear the definition of a gentleman? It's a man who can play the accordion but doesn't."

"Oh, you," she said.

"Do you like the band?" he asked.

"Very much."

"I told the agent what I wanted: musicians who could play old jazz and pop tunes. Danceable and hummable. He said he had no band like that but could put together a group of ancient freelancers who could play the cabaret music I wanted. I feared the worst, but these guys are gems. I don't think one of them is under seventy, and their shiny tuxedos are almost as old. But they know the songs and have a real nineteen thirties sound. The clarinet and sax are particularly good. And did you hear the cornet solo on 'I Can't Give You Anything But Love'? Marvelous!"

"You live in the past, Simon," she said, laughing. "In some ways. And in some ways you're more modern than tomorrow."

She had been working for him about a month when one day, during lunch at a small cafe on the Waterway, she suddenly said, "You're gay, aren't you?"

"I am," he said promptly. "Are you offended?"

"Of course not," she said. "It makes things easier."

He thought that was funny. "For whom?" he asked.

"I just mean I don't have to worry about you hitting on me."

"What if I did?" he said, teasing her.

"I'd probably say yes," she admitted. "I love my job. Simon, what should I say if people ask if you're gay?"

"Give them the traditional American response: 'He's as queer as a three-dollar bill.' "

"You don't care what people think of you?"

"Of course not—as long as their checks don't bounce."

That was the only time they discussed the subject. And she had been right: Things did become easier for both, closer, more intimate. Now he picked up her hand, kissed the knuckles. She drew her hand away to caress his bald pate.

"My very own cue ball," she murmured.

"I think the party is going well," he said. "Don't you, dear?"

"Very well, luv. Everyone seems to be having a good time, eating and drinking up a storm."

"But no fights," he fretted. "A party's not a success without at least one good fight."

"You're really a social creature, aren't you, Simon? I mean, you like company."

"I do. Even animals. When I lived in New York I had these two fat Persian cats, Hotsy and Totsy. They were wonderful company."

"What happened to them?"

"They both went to the Great Litter Box in the Sky before I moved to Florida. Totsy died of kidney failure and Hotsy passed away within six months—of a broken heart, I'm sure."

"Why don't you get another cat down here? Or two."

"Oh, I couldn't. It would betray my love of Hotsy and Totsy."

"That's crazy."

"I guess. But I have a better idea than getting cats. Zoe, this house is too big for just me. Even with a live-in staff I feel like I'm rattling around in a railroad station. There are two big empty bedrooms. Would you like to move into one?"

She looked at him. "Are you serious, boss?"

"Absolutely. Get out of the rattrap West Palm condo you have. Take whichever bedroom you like. Decorate it as you please. Use the garage. Come and go as you wish. No rent. No utilities to pay."

"And no sex," she said, smiling.

"Right—no sex. Just love. Do you want to think it over?"

"I just did," she said, "and the answer is yes,

yes, and yes. It'll be a strange kind of arrangement, won't it? Hardly conventional."

"Oh, Zoe," he said, "convention doesn't exist anymore. Unmarried couples live together all over the place. Gays live with gays, lesbians with lesbians, and sometimes gays with lesbians. I know four people who live together in a big Manhattan apartment. Four people, four different sexes. It's a whole new world. There are no longer rules of conduct and behavior. Do your own thing—whatever. The only no-no is hurting someone else. Now I think we better go downstairs and start making like host and hostess again."

"When can I move in?" she asked eagerly.

"As soon as you like."

"We'll plan meals and go food shopping together," she said happily. "I'll make sure you take your vitamins every day and you'll remind me to get to the foot doctor once a month for my plantar wart. We'll both complain about muscle aches when the weather changes and agree tomatoes have no taste anymore. We'll be like an old married couple."

"I prefer to think of you as my fairy godmother," he said, and she thought that was hilarious.

They walked arm in arm to the front of the house and descended to the dwindling party via the wide marble stairway.

Simon told the dance band to take a break and grab some food and drinks before the caterer closed up shop. He also offered each of the group a President Grant if they would play an extra hour beyond midnight, the contracted end of their performance. They readily agreed and the host suggested a few tunes he'd like to hear, including "Muskrat Ramble."

Then he and Zoe stood at the front door and bade farewell to departing guests. Most of them—even the sober—swore it was the best party of the year and Simon's new home was a smash. Air kisses were exchanged, a few slumbering drunks were roused and gently ejected. Meanwhile the catering staff had been cleaning up, carting away all the uneaten food, soiled plates, cutlery, all the equipment they had supplied. Unopened bottles of liquor were left for Smithson's future use as arranged—and paid for.

By midnight the rooms were quiet and empty, exhaust fans were whirring to expel cigarette smoke, food odors, perfume. Only the band remained, glasses of whiskey on the floor within easy reach, making soft music of ache and longing.

Zenobia and Brett Folsby hadn't departed and joined Simon and Zoe. A chilled bottle of champagne was found, opened, and poured into plastic cups. Even Zen agreed to take a sip. Then the four moved outside to the tiled terrace. The band was playing "Just One of Those Things."

The moon was out of sight, but the night sky had a pearly glow. A cool northerly kept the humidity low; the air smelled as if it had been washed and hung up to dry. There was a salting of stars. Fronds of tall palms cast moving shadows on glistening tiles. The world seemed to move, contracting and billowing.

Brett raised his champagne to heaven. "Thank you, God," he said.

"I thought you were going to get sloshed," Simon said.

"He tried," Zenobia said.

"Did I ever!" Brett said. "But it didn't work."

"The night is young," Simon said. "We need more bubbly."

"I'll get it," Zoe said and went back into the house. When she returned with another bottle the band was playing "You Do Something to Me" and Brett and Zen were dancing slowly across the terrace.

Simon poured their glasses full, and he and Zoe began dancing together—but really just embracing each other tenderly and swaying in time to the music. Then the four paused to drink more champagne.

"Let's live forever," Brett said.

"Good idea," Simon said. "If anyone deserves immortality we do."

The band was playing "Night and Day."

"Our spirits will live forever," Zenobia said.

"Can't miss," Zoe said. "Simon asked me to move in with him and I'm going to do it."

"That's nice," her sister said.

Brett approached Simon and bowed deeply. "May I have the pleasure of this dance?" he asked.

"*Enchanté*," Simon said.

Brett held him closely and away they went, twirling and dipping as the band segued into "A Fine Romance" and Simon's kilt swirled.

The women laughed, clapped their hands, then came together to dance. The two couples circled about each other, gliding dreamily under the luminous vault and listening to old men playing "Someday I'll Find You."

8

THREE A.M....

Mrs. Constance Folsby lay wide-eyed and smiling in the dim stillness. She tried to define how she felt. It was, she decided, more than joy; it was ecstasy. And yet ecstasy was usually linked to physical or spiritual rapture. Her bliss sprang from an intellectual insight less than a week old. It had brightened her life.

She found herself speaking softly aloud, describing her epiphany to the world. It was important.

"You see," she whispered, "I suddenly realized it was not sufficient to declare myself master of my fate, captain of my soul. Masters and captains are not submissive and spiritless, nor do they shilly-shally. Masters and captains *act* through conviction and determination. They deny the false and embrace the true. They right the wrong. They are not content merely to suffer and endure."

There. She had spelled out the divine logic

of what she was about to do. It would be an assertion of her will, an affirmation of her wholeness.

Oh, how slowly she pushed blanket and sheet aside. She moved her legs sideways, out of bed. She took a deep breath and lurched upright. She wavered a moment, found her balance, sat firmly. Her feet, now flat on the floor, were clad in cotton bootees. She wore a thin linen nightgown, bodice trimmed with lace. Covering her scanty hair was Barbara's green silk cloche, tilted askew.

"Water," Constance murmured and glanced at the nightstand. Sophie had left a filled glass fitted with a jointed straw. The thermos alongside held more. Plenty of water.

"Pills," she said, bent awkwardly, and drew from under the bed her four pouches of facial tissue, each holding a small cache.

She put them on the bed, unfolded them carefully. Her hands were trembling. She picked out the tablets and piled them in her cupped left palm. They made a little white mountain.

"Enough," she said, happy with her treasure. "Surely enough."

She twisted from the waist to reach for the water glass. Her left hand spasmed and spread. The pills spilled to the floor. Just a few remained stuck to her palm.

She watched the white tablets bounce, skid, roll away. Then they all came to rest and she stared at her scattered deliverance, impossible to retrieve. She sat motionless for several moments, wondering if the confetti of pills was a Sign.

"Not a Sign," Mrs. Folsby uttered gently. "It is a Test."

And she knew exactly what she must do.

She pushed herself from the bed, stood erect. She swayed and stayed in one position until the tremors in her legs ceased. She moved slowly to the wheelchair, taking short steps, sliding her feet to avoid stepping on the sprinkled pills. She lowered herself into the chair, used hands and arms to lift her legs onto the steel rests.

Then she sat back, exultant at her initial success, knowing she had the strength and resolve to complete her task.

She did not start the motor but wheeled herself quietly to the door. It had been left slightly ajar and she pushed through easily. Then she was in the long hall. It was illuminated with faint night-lights. Constance turned her chair to face the terrace doors at the far end. The shadowed corridor, gleaming dully, was her road.

She stared at the deserted passage, motionless. Memories came unbidden—of parties and dances, tears and laughter, triumphs and tragedies, Emmet's stern rumble of command and the shrill piping of little Anthony.

"The years!" she breathed. "The years!"

It had all passed so swiftly, life melting in the Florida sunshine. The world was there and then it was gone. But Zenobia had said another universe awaited. She believed it.

She began wheeling herself slowly toward the glass doors leading to escape. As she rolled she looked up fondly at the watercolors she and Emmet had collected and placed on the walls of their home. All those clipper ships—so graceful! She paused a minute to gaze at her favorite. Not because of its hull shape or spread of sail but the name—the *Flying Cloud*. Wasn't that lovely!

She continued her journey, moving with no creak or scuff. The glass door to the terrace unlocked and slid back smoothly. Everything in their home worked easily and efficiently. Emmet, the can-do man, saw to it.

Then she was on the open terrace and halted to look hard at the vanishing world. A north wind had freshened and chilled. The sea had risen and a black book of water turned white pages endlessly onto the strand. The moon was not visible but she fancied its glow lingered.

It had been years—*years!*—since she had last been outdoors at night. "Hello, sky," she called. "Hello, stars. Hello, flying clouds. I love you all."

She wheeled herself to the concrete ramp leading downward. She held the rims as firmly as she could, but when she began the descent the strength in her hands faded, her grip slackened. The chair moved swiftly down the incline, across the concrete platform. The small front wheels rolled off into the sand, the chair was tipped suddenly forward. Constance was thrown facedown to the beach.

She lay a moment, breath rasping. Then she

stirred, turned on her side. She looked for a support to help her rise. But the chair leaned tipsily; it would not serve. She raised her head, looked about. The beach was empty. Even the ocean was blank; no lights of fishing boats or passing ships.

Never did her resolution falter. She had always been a woman of mettle and self-pride. To act the craven now would nullify her brief existence. "I have not winced nor cried aloud..."

She was able to get to her knees. She began to crawl toward the churning sea. The wind caught her cloche and whipped it away. Her nightgown tangled, she paused to tug it high on her shrunken thighs. Then she continued the slow, laborious drag across cool sand. She ignored the pain when palms and knees pressed on bits of broken shells. Her cotton booties were rubbed off, bare toes dug shallow furrows.

She felt her energy ebbing but then she was on firm, wet sand and the ocean's crash was louder. A little farther and hands and knees were in foamy water as the waves came dancing in. She laughed with delight, knowing she had truly been master of her fate and would now be captain of her soul—to join all those gone before to the eternal oneness.

It required little more effort, for the sea rushed to assist her. She crawled on and the waters embraced her, lifted her, dragged her deeper and tumbled her about, sporting.

She gave herself willingly, opening her arms wide, accepting all: the pain, the glory, a light that blinded and set her free.

BOOK
6

1

THE CAN'T-DO MAN...

After the suicide of his wife everyone expected Emmet Folsby to be grief-stricken, depressed, melancholy—and so he was. But as weeks, months, years flew by his sorrow was blunted. What remained sharp was a grim testiness he strove to keep hidden. Perhaps only Barbara was aware of it and guessed (wrongly) its cause.

Shortly after his wife's death Emmet and his daughter attempted to resume their physical relationship. The endeavor in his bedroom was an awkward, embarrassing failure.

"Too soon," Emmet said.

"Of course," Barbara said. "We'll wait awhile."

A few months later they tried again with the same frustrating result: Emmet was incapable of making love.

"Perhaps it's being here," Barbara said. "In our home. Her home."

"Yes," Emmet said, "that could be. Let's take the *Folly* out tomorrow."

But even on the bunk in the master stateroom, the yacht anchored in a calm sea, his impotence persisted.

"Guilt?" Barbara asked.

"Of course not," he said angrily.

But she was not convinced. "It's odd," she said. "You didn't reproach yourself when

Mother was alive, but now that she's gone you feel guilty."

He made no reply.

Trying to be completely honest with himself he gave much thought to the reason for his inability to give her pleasure. He believed he discovered why he, always a lusty man, now found himself powerless with a beautiful sex partner.

To test his theory he made an appointment with an expensive prostitute he had visited occasionally in the past. She was a svelte, attractive woman, a divorcée in her late thirties, an accomplished harlot. She owned a home on Bayview in Fort Lauderdale and had a son at a military academy in Virginia.

He found he was as unable to be sexually intimate with her as he had been with his daughter.

"Don't worry, honey," she said to him. "It happens."

"Perhaps I'll have better luck next time," he said, paying her.

"Sure you will," she said—but he knew he wouldn't.

He could go to a physician, but he was certain they'd find him in excellent health. He could then consult psychologist, psychotherapist, or psychiatrist—and knew if he confessed his incestuous affair with his daughter they would declare, as Barbara had, his inability to copulate was due to a repressed feeling of culpability for the wrongs inflicted on both wife and daughter.

Emmet firmly believed they would be wrong.

His impotence was caused not by his past behavior; it was the result of a sensory memory that haunted him and did not fade with the passing years.

He had been awakened by the frantic housekeeper, blanched and trembling. Listened to her stutter. Dressed hastily in shorts and singlet. Went running on bare feet. Saw open terrace door and spilled wheelchair.

"Gone?" he said wonderingly aloud.

And down at the water's edge was a circle of early beachwalkers, heads lowered, staring. Except one woman who had turned away, face in her hands. A bloated sun was rising, reddening the sea. Far out, a line of black rain squalls moved slowly southward. Emmet heard the wail of an approaching siren.

He flopped to his knees beside his wife. Her body was twisted, half-buried in sand. Tatters of nightgown clung, not hiding her bony nakedness. Her mouth was filled with sand and coins of sand closed her eyes. White skin had been sliced by shells, coral, stones. One arm was broken, bending back from the elbow. How small she looked, how drained and flattened, as if she had been pasted to the earth.

When the rescue crew arrived Emmet would not allow them to exhume the corpse of his wife. But still kneeling he brushed the sand away with his fingers, slowly, carefully, tenderly. He cleaned sand from her eyes, tried to cleanse her mouth, dug about to free her body from the shallow grave. He straightened her limbs. He moved scraps of linen to hide her nudity.

He leaned down to kiss her cool, limp lips—and tasted salt.

Then he stood and stumbled back to the house, not wanting to see Constance Louise Folsby slid into a plastic bag.

Three years later he still tasted the salt—and it unmanned him.

On the Monday morning of March 13, 1995, a meeting of the Executive Committee was held in the conference room of the Folsby Press Building. The topic under discussion was whether or not to organize a subsidiary company to be called Folsby Press International to handle the growing foreign investments and ventures of the parent corporation.

The gathering was officially chaired by Emmet, who sat at the head of the long table. But the debate was dominated by Barbara Folsby, who had been relentless in pushing Folsby's overseas expansion. She had made several trips to Europe, usually accompanied by the general counsel or Chief Financial Officer. Emmet had made no trips abroad with his daughter. Their original foray had been canceled following the death of Constance Folsby.

Barbara's presentation was detailed and forceful. Speaking without notes she rattled off the costs, revenues, and profits of Folsby investments in Great Britain, France, and Italy. She recommended investigation of publishing opportunities in the formerly Communist nations of East Europe. She suggested the Far

East as another potentially profitable market for Folsby's trade magazines.

"All these activities require an independent and dedicated staff," she argued. "We need a separate international publishing and advertising organization. Globalization is a fact of life, and if we neglect it we are condemning ourselves to the status of also-rans in world commerce. We increase market share or we are marginalized. 'Expand or perish' must be our watchword. Only profitable expansion abroad will ensure steady growth in revenues and profits."

She concluded and the assembled executives looked to Emmet Folsby for his reaction. To their surprise he seemed to rouse from a doze. He glanced at his watch.

"Thank you, Barbara," he said. "A very perceptive analysis. And now, if you will excuse me, I have an important appointment I cannot delay. Please continue to discuss the subject. I am willing to abide by your decision, whatever it may be."

He rose and strode determinedly from the room, leaving them all astonished and wondering what appointment could be more important to him than deciding the future of the business he had created.

Emmet stopped at his office to tell Mrs. Blanche Singer he'd be gone for the remainder of the day.

"Not sick are you, Mr. Folsby?" she asked anxiously.

"No, I'm fine. Why do you ask?"

She had been his executive assistant long enough to speak frankly. "I've been worried about you. You've seemed so withdrawn and—and distant. Is anything wrong?"

"A lot on my mind."

"Problems?"

"Nothing I can't handle," he told her. "See you tomorrow morning."

"Have a nice day," she said faintly.

He drove his black Cadillac directly to the Henry Simpson Boatyard in Pompano Beach. It was the marine center where the *Folly* had been refitted, had its annual overhaul, and where upgraded electronic gear was installed when needed. Emmet paused a moment to look around the bustling marina. Artisans were working on everything from a battered dinghy to a sleek oceangoing yacht twice the length of the *Folly*. It was, he reflected, a pleasure to watch can-do men at work.

He climbed the outside staircase of a two-story shop to the shipyard office, which appeared to be constructed entirely of unfinished plywood. The owner was half-hidden behind a desk piled high with blueprints, navigational charts, a slew of boating magazines. He looked up when Emmet entered, rose creakily to his feet, held out a bony hand.

"Mr. Folsby," he said. "A pleasure. How is your health, sir?"

"Very well, Mr. Simpson. And yours?"

"Nothing wrong that a new hull wouldn't cure. Take a load off your feet."

He fell back into his chair. Emmet perched on a stool alongside the cluttered desk.

Simpson was pushing eighty. He habitually wore a shiny three-piece suit and white shirt with a starched Herbert Hoover collar. Neatly centered below his prominent Adam's apple was a small black leather bow, pre-tied.

"Is this a social visit?" he asked. "Or you having problems with the *Folly*?"

"Half and half," Emmet said.

"Then let's have the social half first," Simpson said. He opened a desk drawer, brought out a bottle of Jack Daniel's and a stack of paper cups.

"A little early in the day for me," Folsby protested.

"It's never too early," Simpson said. He filled two cups, handed one to Emmet with a steady hand. "Your health, sir."

"And yours, Mr. Simpson."

They both sipped. "Ahh," the owner said. "Mother's milk. Now what's the problem?"

"More questions than a problem. Occasionally I've taken the *Folly* out by myself. Short trips on the Waterway. Once or twice through the Inlet. Never had any trouble."

"A sweet hull. They don't make them like that anymore."

"Now I want to take a long cruise. By myself."

"How long?"

"Around the world," Emmet said.

Simpson's expression didn't change. He had been in the business long enough to know the term "eccentric yachtsman" was a redundancy.

"I expect to be gone at least a year," Emmet continued. "Maybe two or three. It depends. I'm in no hurry; I'm not out to set any records. I'll probably be doing island hopping when I can, but I know I'll have some long stretches. To the Azores, for example."

Simpson finished his cup of whiskey and poured himself another. "The Pacific is the killer," he said sagely. "A lot of open water out there."

"I know. Can we increase the *Folly*'s range?"

Simpson stood up stiffly, went to an old wooden file cabinet. He searched and finally found the folder holding the *Folly*'s hull and deck plans plus a record of all the alterations made. He brought the material back to his desk, sat down heavily, began to flip through documents. He wasn't wearing spectacles, but occasionally he used a big magnifying glass.

"Just you?" he asked Emmet.

"Correct."

"We could pull out the two smaller staterooms and use the space for storage. Fuel, fresh water, provisions."

"Will it affect the trim?"

"We'll make sure it doesn't."

"What about navigation and conning. Will I be able to handle both alone?"

"You won't have to," Simpson said. "When you figuring on taking off?"

"This year. After the hurricane season."

"Good. By then we'll have some new state-

of-the-art gadgets. One will pick up a satel-
lite signal. It gives your position within spit-
ting distance. You can connect it to an
on-board computer wired to the controls.
Punch in your course and the signal and computer keep you steady on."

"An autopilot?"

"Something like that. At least you'll be
able to sleep nights without worrying about
drift. But when it comes to squalls, storms,
waterspouts, hurricanes, cyclones, and such,
you'll be on your own. Same holds true if
you find yourself in a crowded shipping
channel."

"I understand."

"You got guns aboard?" Simpson demanded.

"A thirty rifle and thirty-eight revolver."

"Better add a heavy shotgun."

"Pirates?" Emmet asked.

"Not so much as going into strange harbors
on foreign islands."

They spent more than an hour going over
in detail the alterations and additions *Folsby's
Folly* would require for a circumnavigation.
Simpson promised a cost estimate within a
week. Then he loaded Emmet with literature
and manuals on the new electronic gear and
said he would be able to provide the charts
needed. He also handed over a thick catalogue
from the chandler he recommended.

Emmet finished his drink and thanked the
yard owner for his assistance. "One more
thing," he said. "I want to change the name
of my boat."

"Oh? To what?"

"Folsby's Spirit."

Mr. Simpson looked at him. "Whatever you say."

Emmet drove home and asked the cook to prepare a seafood salad for lunch.

"With a bottle of beer," he added. "Please bring it up to my study when it's ready. I'll eat up there."

He was seated at his desk, just starting the salad, when his private phone rang. The caller was Judge Seth Hampton.

"Emmet, are you all right?" he asked.

"Fine, thank you."

"I was a bit concerned. I called you at your office and Mrs. Singer said you were gone."

"Decided to take the day off."

"Good for you. It's time you started relaxing. You're past retirement age, you know."

"Yes," Emmet said, "I'm well aware of it."

"Sarah and I were hoping you'd join us for dinner tonight."

"It's very kind of you, but I have a great deal of personal business needing attention. Can't make dinner, but I would like to come over later. I have something to tell you. Would it be possible?"

"Of course! We'll be delighted to see you. Around nine or so?"

"I'll be there," Emmet said.

He hung up and continued his lunch. As he ate he studied the chandler's thick catalogue, amazed at the variety of provisions offered: fresh foods, frozen, canned, dried. Four pages were devoted to liquors, wines, beers, and soft drinks. Formulas were given to help estimate how much liquid (including fresh water) and food should be provided per person per day. There was also a section listing sundries, including mousetraps, wax candles, and toilet paper.

It was strange but flipping through the catalogue of needed supplies made him realize for the first time the magnitude of what he planned. It was as if Robinson Crusoe had been given the opportunity to provision his island. That was how Emmet saw his projected journey: a voyage on a floating desert island. With no desire to find a Friday.

Barbara had a dinner date with Oliver Pendragon that evening so Emmet ate alone in the dining room, which now seemed to him to be too large, too empty, too silent. But he had never been guilty of self-pity and didn't propose to start now. Alongside his plate of lamb chops with garlic mashed potatoes he placed a yellow legal pad and as he dined he made notes of what he proposed to do and how it might best be managed. His lone and lengthy cruise aboard the *Spirit* was only part of his plans.

He returned to his study after dinner and phoned Brett's home. He had short conversations with his son and daughter-in-law and was happy to learn Zenobia's restaurant was doing wonderfully. Then he had a long talk with Anthony—really the reason for Emmet's nightly calls. Tony, now eight years old, told him of all his school activities and how a girl in his class had invited him to her birthday party.

"Are you going?" his grandfather asked.

"Mom says I have to," the boy said and added disgustedly, "And I gotta bring her a present. Listen, Grandpa, when can we go fishing again?"

Emmet knew he'd soon have to leave the boat at Simpson's for its makeover. He said, "How about Saturday if the weather holds?"

"Cool!" Anthony said. "I want to do more casting like you showed me. Maybe I'll catch something."

"Sure you will. Get a good night's sleep, Tony, and I love you."

"Me too," the boy said, giggled, and hung up.

Emmet showered and changed to casual clothes. Shortly before nine o'clock he set out for Judge Hampton's home. He walked the short distance along the verge of the highway. Since his wife's suicide he had avoided the beach.

They sat in the Judge's study and Sarah poured snifters of cognac. Upon reaching his present age of eighty-nine, Hampton had declared, "The hell with my heart and liver. I'm ahead of the game. I'm going to drink and smoke as much as I wish. And I'll still live to see the new century."

"Of course you will, dear," Sarah assured him. "You're too mean to die."

He liked that and repeated it frequently.

Sarah offered the men a humidor of Havana cigars. She was still obtaining them illicitly from a source the Judge didn't wish to question. He and Folsby lighted up, puffed, sat back contentedly.

"Well, Emmet," Hampton said, "you mentioned you had something to tell us."

"I do," he said, and related his plan to sail alone around the world and how he was having the *Folly* altered and equipped to make the voyage possible. Sarah and the Judge looked at him, looked at each other, looked at him again.

"My God, have you thought this over carefully?" Hampton asked, leaning forward.

Emmet nodded. "For a long time. Months. Years."

"Since Constance passed?" Sarah said softly.

He bowed his head. "Yes," he said in a low voice.

The Judge stirred. He seemed irritated by Emmet's news. "How long will you be gone?" he inquired.

"A year. Two. Three. Perhaps more. It's unlimited. Open-ended."

"You may never return?"

"It's a possibility."

The Judge made a sound, almost a snort of scorn. Sarah sensed a tension between the two men she did not understand. "Is it safe?" she asked Emmet.

"Not a hundred percent," he said, shrugging. "What is?"

Hampton sipped his brandy and said what was riling him. "Is this an escape?" he demanded.

Emmet raised his chin. "No," he said. "It's a search."

His answer mollified the Judge. "What will happen to the Folsby Press while you're gone?" he asked in a calmer voice.

"You reminded me I'm past retirement age. Well, I'm going to. I intend to give the company to my son and daughter. I'm going to have the attorneys and accountants start on it tomorrow. Naturally I'd like to minimize the tax consequences."

The Judge sighed. "You're certain you want to do this, Emmet?"

"No doubts at all. I have sufficient investment income to live comfortably without taking another dime from the Folsby Press. Even if I return I have no desire to resume control."

"What do you mean *even* if you return?" Sarah said, shocked. "You *are* coming back, aren't you?"

"Probably. But many unexpected things can happen. No use trying to predict the future. Judge, when I receive opinions from the lawyers on the gift of the Folsby Press stock to my children I hope you'll be willing to vet their plans and give me your reactions to its effectiveness and legality. Perhaps you'll have suggestions on how the transfer might be bettered."

"Of course, Emmet. I'll be happy to provide what advice I can. I'd like to start by persuading you to forget the whole idea and remain owner and CEO of your own company. I know how much it means to you and how hard you've worked to grow it. You might opt for semi-retirement, you know. Retain ownership but let Brett and Barbara manage the Press. You would still receive income—even as a consultant—and your shares could become part of your estate."

"No," Emmet said decisively. "I've given it a great deal of thought and I have decided a clean break is best for all concerned."

"What will happen to your beautiful home?" Sarah asked—almost a wail.

"It will be given to Barbara and Brett. If one wants to sell out to the other, it's their business. I really don't wish to retain ownership."

Sarah rose to refill their snifters. They talked a long time of the other problems Emmet would have. The disposal of his car, for instance, and his personal belongings: clothes, books, tools, jewelry—all the mementos of his life, including family photos, souvenirs, old correspondence.

"You could put everything in storage," Sarah suggested.

"Yes," Emmet said, "that's a possibility."

"A question," Hampton said. "You say you plan to convey your shares of stock in the Folsby Press to Barbara and Brett. Do you intend to divide them equally? Each to get half?"

"Difficult decision," Emmet said shortly. "Haven't made up my mind."

The Judge didn't believe him, but his voice

and manner were so testy Hampton thought it best to change the subject. "Have you told your children what you are planning?"

"Not yet, but I will tomorrow or the day after. There's no point in trying to keep the matter confidential. In fact, it would be impossible after the company's attorneys and accountants start working on the mechanics of the transfer."

Then they were all silent, their gathering suddenly seeming like a leave-taking, a farewell ceremony.

"When are you going, Emmet?" Sarah asked.

"I'd like to leave in November," he said. "After the hurricane season. I still haven't plotted my course—whether to go through the Panama Canal or around the Cape of Good Hope. So you see I have a lot of work to do before I shove off, and I better get started on it tonight. Thank you for the refreshment and for listening to me babble."

He rose and leaned across the desk to shake Hampton's frail hand. The Judge held on to his fingers a few moments longer than normal. "We'll see you frequently before you leave?" he said. It was a plea.

"Of course you shall," Emmet said.

Sarah accompanied him downstairs to the front door. There she came close and gripped his upper arms.

"I'm worried about you, Emmet," she said, and he thought he saw the glimmer of tears. "To sail so far away by yourself—it is dangerous."

"I'll be fine," he reassured her. "A walk in the park. And I promise to send you a post-card from every port I hit."

"I'll worry until you return safely," she said.

"I forgot to tell you," he said. "I'm changing the name of my boat to *Folsby's Spirit.*"

Her smile was ecstatic. "Now I feel better," she said.

He strolled slowly homeward. Nice night. Clear, cool, crisp. He hoped he'd have many such nights on his voyage.

The Judge had asked if it was an escape and Emmet had said no, it was a search. But that, he now admitted, was a misnomer. He had used it deliberately to avoid giving his long, lonely cruise an explanation he feared Hampton and Sarah would think fanciful and foolish.

For most of his adult years Emmet Richard Folsby had mused on how similar were living and business. Just as you did in operating a commercial enterprise, in your personal life you strove to maximize profits (happiness) and keep liabilities (disappointments and sorrows) to a minimum. You stretched the law and regulations for your benefit when the possibility of exposure and punishment were unlikely enough to justify the risk.

As business did, living demanded growth. You sought to increase your market share of pleasure, avoid woes, and plan a happy future. And like business success, success in living sometimes required chicanery and double-dealing. You had to recognize that living, in the manner of business, was conducted in a competitive world. Frequently your desire for happiness was impeded or thwarted by the desires of others.

And when your private life failed, you were faced with bankruptcy. But under Chapter 11, rehabilitation and reorganization were possible; your life might be redesigned to function profitably. You could start anew, hopefully wiser and more alert to the dangers of speculation and the limits of self-interest.

Rehabilitation and reorganization: those were the motives for the actions Folsby proposed. He was not too old, he told himself, to create a new life. On his lonely voyage, unencumbered by the debts and responsibilities of his past, he would fashion the form and substance of a fresh existence.

2

GREAT EXPECTATIONS...

They lay naked in the Chinese sleigh bed, passing a black olive back and forth between their wet lips. But then Folsby crunched down and swallowed.

"Swine!" Simon said.

Brett laughed and slapped the other's haunch lightly. "April Fool!" he said. "Remember?"

"Every day is April Fools' Day," Smithson said. "Be a good boy and open another merlot."

Brett slid out of bed and padded over to the bar. It was a huge 1920s steamer trunk converted to a cellarette and swung open. He began to uncork the bottle.

"Heavens to Betsy," Simon called, "I do believe the lad is getting paunchy. I'd complain bitterly if I wasn't getting paunchier."

Brett brought the wine back to the bed and filled their glasses. "It's hell becoming a golden oldie," he said. "And don't get sloshed, old buddy. We have to pick up the ladies at nine."

"Zoe says the restaurant is doing great."

"Gangbusters. If business continues after the season is over Zen wants to open another place in Palm Beach."

"You have the gelt to swing it?"

"Not at the moment," Folsby said. "But I will have if my sister decides to buy my half of the Hillsboro house."

"You don't want it?"

"Hell no! Too big. Too old. And crossing A1A during the season is murder. I'm a condo-type chap. I don't want the aggravations of landscaping, plumbing, repairs, and similar duties. Let Barbara have the pleasure."

"Will your father be angry if you sell out?"

"He says no. He doesn't care what we do with it."

"Tony is with him now?" Simon asked.

"Yep. Spending a happy weekend with Gramps. No fishing because the *Folly* is in the shipyard being readied for the cockamamie around-the-world cruise the old man is taking.

He and Tony are building a model of the *Flying Cloud,* an old clipper ship. Emmet bought a kit and he and the boy are putting it together."

"Your father is a strange man, Brett."

"Not so strange. Just stodgy and hidebound. My God, he still reads newspapers and wears wingtips."

"But you can't fault his generosity."

"Right you are," Brett said. "And I'm going to exploit it. When I own half the Folsby Press I'll insist on being named editorial director of all our domestic and foreign magazines."

"You think Barbara will agree to that?"

"Oh, I'm sure we'll have plenty of screaming arguments, but if I let her have a free hand with the advertising side she can't object to my managing editorial. To tell you the honest truth, chum, she knows more about business than I do. I mean, all the gobbledygook about revenue, net profits, return on equity, cash flow, and so forth. Barbara loves numbers. They bore me."

"And talk bores me," Smithson said. "Especially on these occasions when actions speak louder than words."

Brett laughed and put his wine glass aside. The two men twined. Each knew the other's body as well as he knew his own. If the wild fervor of youth was gone, the slow, tempered love of advancing years was an equal, perhaps superior, replacement.

Simon pulled away a moment. "Darling, have you ever seriously considered stepping out of the infamous closet?"

"Of course not," Brett said. "Why on earth should I? I happen to enjoy the closet with all those old galoshes and fur coats smelling of mothballs."

"Do moths really have them?"

"Besides," Folsby went on, "I'm married. It may not be blissful wedlock, but it suffices and I am content. And, of course, I have a son I adore. No, I shall remain happily behind a triple-locked and barred door."

"Also," Smithson said, "if you confessed your predilection your father might be so horrified as to hand the Folsby Press in toto to your dear sister."

"Heaven forfend!" Brett cried. "Please, God, let my old man go to the ends of the earth in ignorance of my frailty—although I suspect he'd consider it a depravity. O what fools these mortals be!"

Simon leaned to nibble him. "Oh what foods these morsels be," he murmured.

3

GREAT EXPECTATIONS (CONT'D.)...

They lay naked in Pendragon's rumpled bed as a steady June rain hissed outside and streamed the windows. Oliver played with her, making a constant "Mmmmmm" sound she assumed was a drone of gratification.

Barbara had always enjoyed sex but was

not obsessed with it, considering the desire for physical pleasure as natural and healthy as eating and sleeping. But sex with Oliver was more task than pleasure, requiring a conscious act of will. She endured his fumbling and blather by divorcing thoughts from body, conquering her repugnance by musing on her past, the present, and how her future might be affected by her father's intended gifts.

"Beautiful," Oliver breathed. "Just beautiful."

The man was so soft, so pudgy. He lacked the hard strength of her other lovers. Emmet was lost to her, but she still had Noah Demijohn's raw, elemental passion. Her carnal relationship with him was suddenly important, a reason she could even consider marriage to this walking pillow.

"I love you, Barbara," he crooned. "So very, very much."

She had grand plans and being Mrs. Barbara Pendragon would be more help than hindrance. It would give her status, the respect and deference due the wife of a famous scientist. There was talk of Pendragon being selected to head a Presidential commission created to recommend how federal research funds should be allocated. A visit to the White House as Oliver's wife was an attractive prospect.

"You know what I like," he whispered. "Please let me."

But her own ambitions took precedence over his. During the years at the Folsby Press she had made many discoveries of how the world worked and had formed many opinions widely divergent from the views she once held and espoused in her valedictory speech at her graduation. She had been an innocent then, an optimistic idealist. Reality had not so much hardened her as given her a sharper, more pragmatic approach to achieving her aims.

"Oh, yes," he said, almost sobbing. "So nice, so nice."

She still considered herself a feminist but now disagreed completely with the strategy and tactics of the movement's theorists and leaders. Their goals were chiefly concerned with sexual, social, and political hegemony. Barbara believed their efforts misdirected and should be wholly devoted to women's economic progress. Only when females won a greatly enlarged role in the marketplace would the desired changes occur.

"I'm the world's luckiest man!" Oliver cried.

It infuriated her that so many women were financially illiterate. They were adept at shopping for discounts and using 2-for-1 coupons, but few had a working knowledge of how money was used to make more money, how risks and benefits were evaluated, how to distinguish between investing and speculation, how to provide for their own financial security.

"You know I want you forever," he pleaded. "You know it."

It might be crass but nevertheless true: Money ruled. Systems of government, family values, gender equality, social advances—all were dependent on economic well-being, i.e., on money. It not only made the world go 'round, it *was* the world. And women could never hope to control their lives and enjoy independence until they had the wherewithal.

Barbara was not a mammonist. She did not worship money. But she knew the power it bought. Owning half the Folsby Press would expand her life, provide opportunities much more exciting and satisfying than an evening of grappling with this sweaty lump.

They were dressing when she looked around his cluttered condo with distaste and said, "Oliver, you really need more room. This place is so cramped."

"Yes, yes," he said eagerly. "I quite agree. I need a house, a big house with many rooms, a place where I can entertain and hold press conferences. I must contact a real estate agent as soon as I have time."

"No," Barbara said, "don't do that. Wait a few months. I have something in mind."

"Oh? What?"

"It's a secret," she said, despising her coyness.

"If I get a house," he said, "a real home, will you come live with me? As my wife," he added hastily.

"I've learned never to say never," Barbara lied and let him kiss her.

4

A TANGLED WEB...

On Sunday afternoon, August 20, 1995, Emmet Folsby hosted a champagne and caviar brunch at his Hillsboro home. He considered it something of a farewell party—although he would not depart for three months—and invited only old and close friends of the family.

The party was catered and a strolling guitarist hired to provide elevator music. Despite Emmet's approaching solo voyage it was a festive occasion, the liveliness not at all diminished by the presence of several guests using canes, walkers, and wheelchairs. All attending had known one another when they ran the beach, swam in a choppy sea, played tennis and golf, and danced at the Club. There were many "Remember whens..." and the wry laughter of the Medicare generation.

By six o'clock the guests had left with embraces, kisses, prolonged handshakes, tears. The guitarist was gone. The catering staff had cleaned up the party's debris, packed their equipment, and disappeared. Only Sarah Demijohn and Judge Seth Hampton remained, at Emmet's request. The three sat at one end of the bare table in the dining room and sipped chilled framboise from liqueur glasses.

"It was a lovely party, Emmet," Sarah said.

"Thank you. I think everyone had a good

315

time. They should have; we went through more than thirty bottles of champagne! I asked you to stay because I have something to tell you. Judge, have you had a chance to review those documents conveying the ownership of the Folsby Press to my son and daughter?"

"I have indeed," Hampton said. "I saw no obvious red flags. The use of your estate tax exclusion should certainly reduce or eliminate gift taxes. The only thing that concerns me is the dollar valuation of the company and the corresponding fair market value of your ten thousand shares. I thought it surprisingly low."

Emmet smiled. "It *is* low," he admitted. "And the tax attorney says we're sure to get an audit. But he claims a clash with the IRS will eventually result in a compromise and the agreed-upon value will still be less than the true value. I hope he's right. In any event, I'll be far away at sea when the audit is made and it'll be Barbara's and Brett's problem, not mine."

"Which brings up another question," the Judge said. "I know the transfer document you gave me to read was a preliminary draft, but the number of shares to be given to each of your children is nowhere stated. I presume each will receive five thousand shares representing a half-interest in the Folsby Press."

"It's what I wanted to tell you," Emmet said.

He rose and began to pace, circling the empty table. His head was lowered, hands thrust into his trouser pockets. He was silent a long time. They waited patiently.

The sun was long gone from the south windows. A silvery twilight filled the room, making Emmet's wispy hair appear thin and white. With the dusk had come a muffled quiet. His footsteps on the marble-tiled floor were reduced to a soft shuffle, his voice took on the sibilance of a whisper.

"You'll probably think me a fool," he finally started, "but I've always thought of my company as much a creation as a symphony or sculpture. I know it is just a money-making commercial enterprise, but it has been my life's work. My wife's and mine," he hastily amended. "It is only a business, but we created it."

"You provided careers and jobs for a lot of people," the Judge observed.

"Yes," Folsby agreed, "and the Press would not have succeeded without them. Which is why tomorrow morning I intend to fly the *Constance* on a tour of all our offices to thank our employees personally. Some have been with the company more than forty years. Their lifetime! I'm trying to tell you how important the Folsby Press is to me. Perhaps it will help you understand what I plan to do."

He returned to his place and took a sip of his drink, although he remained standing. Sarah and the Judge were seated close together and Emmet looked down at them directly.

"I have given the matter a great deal of serious thought," he said stiffly and repeated,

317

"A great deal. I have come to the conclusion the Folsby Press cannot be effectively managed and continue to flourish under divided control. It simply wouldn't work. A ship at sea can't have two captains in command. A successful business needs a single chief executive, someone capable of exercising power and willing to accept responsibility."

"I think you're right, Emmet," Hampton agreed. "It's been my experience that equal partnerships are never as efficient as enterprises ruled by one man."

Folsby gave them a bleak smile. "But in this case it will be one woman. I intend to give sixty percent of my shares to Barbara and forty percent to Brett. My daughter will, in effect, become boss of the Folsby Press."

Sarah and the Judge cried, "Emmet—!" simultaneously, but he held up a palm to silence them.

"The most difficult decision I've ever made in my life," he said solemnly. "And I'm convinced it's the right one. I know I am not indispensable to the continued success of the Folsby Press. But I want to appoint a successor I can trust. I want to be certain what has been created with so much sweat equity will keep on growing."

"Why Barbara?" asked Sarah almost timidly. "Why not Brett?"

Emmet resumed his pacing. His voice was louder now, his stride more confident.

"Sarah, I love my son," he declared. "He is handsome, personable, very intelligent. And he has blessed me with a grandson who has brightened my life and helped me endure the loss of Constance. But I realized a long time ago my son is not a serious man. He has a marvelous sense of humor, but being lighthearted is one thing, being superficial is another. And his best friend, Simon Smithson, the interior designer, may be talented but I find him frivolous and his close friendship with Brett disturbs me.

"As for Barbara, she is far superior to her brother in those qualities and skills required of an executive. She is beautiful, can be charming when she wishes, and has an intuitive grasp of business practices. She is still learning but never makes the same mistake twice. I admit she occasionally is capable of unnecessary ruthlessness. But she is still a young woman, and I believe experience as majority owner of the Folsby Press will soften the way she deals with others and teach her a less combative response to the opinions of her associates."

He stopped speaking, and Sarah and the Judge looked at each other.

"It was your decision to make, Emmet," Hampton said at last. "And I'm sure you found it painful."

"Have you told them yet?" Sarah asked gently.

"No," Folsby said, "and I'm not looking forward to it, as you can imagine. Right now Brett is on vacation in Hawaii with Zenobia and Anthony. They won't return until Labor

Day. I'll tell him and Barbara soon after that. I debated whether or not to tell them separately and decided it would be best if the three of us met to discuss the future of the company. I know how disappointed Brett will be, but I hope he will accept the inevitable and continue to contribute to the success of our magazines. Meanwhile I trust both of you will hold what I have just told you in the strictest confidence. After Labor Day it will become a matter of public knowledge and the attorneys will complete the transfer documents."

They assured him of their discretion and shortly afterward made their departure. Sarah hugged Emmet and kissed him on both cheeks. The Judge shook his hand firmly and wished him the best of good fortune. Folsby slumped at the table and poured himself another raspberry brandy. He did not offer to see them to their car. They left him alone, huddled over his drink in the fading light.

Hampton's mansion was a short distance away, but he had such trouble walking they had driven to the party in the Judge's '94 white and tan Corniche convertible. Sarah helped him climb awkwardly into the open car. He sat slouched, gripping his silver-headed cane.

They didn't speak on the brief drive home and when they arrived and parked on the brick driveway they sat a moment before alighting.

"Emmet explained his decision very convincingly," the Judge commented. "But I can't help thinking he had an additional reason he chose not to mention."

"There is something else," Sarah said. "Bad blood between Barbara and Brett."

"Oh? How do you know that?"

"Noah told me. He said Barbara is always saying hard things about her brother, cutting him down."

"Did she tell Noah the reason for their hostility?"

"No," Sarah said, "and he didn't ask."

"Sibling rivalry, I suppose," the Judge said. "Competing for their parents' love. Or perhaps there's another more personal reason we'll never know. You think Emmet is aware how his children feel about each other?"

"How could he not know?"

"Yes, you're right. And realized giving them equal shares of the Folsby Press might result in open warfare that could wreck the company."

"Poor Emmet," Sarah said sorrowfully. "He's giving up the business he and Constance worked so hard to build and now he must tell his children his decision, knowing it will drive them even farther apart."

Hampton turned his head to look at her. "What a perspicacious lady you are, dear Sarah," he said admiringly. "Yes, poor Emmet. But you must realize that despite his brains and experience he is a man who finds it difficult to cope with change. It confuses him, makes him uncertain. I don't waste my time fretting about change. I'm too busy figuring out how to profit from it."

She was puzzled. "I don't understand."

He told her what he proposed to do and she stared at him, shocked.

"You're not!"

"I am," he said defiantly. "A devious plot but with a good chance of success."

She shook her head. "You're a mean man, Sweet Daddy."

"I know," he said, smiling. "You told me. Too mean to die."

5

A DONE DEAL...

Hampton waited until two o'clock Monday afternoon before phoning the Folsby Building and asking to speak to Emmet. He was told by Mrs. Blanche Singer that Mr. Folsby had already departed aboard the *Constance* to visit his offices in other cities and was not scheduled to return until Friday. Satisfied the man was safely out of town, the Judge asked his call be transferred to Barbara Folsby.

"Judge!" she caroled. "How nice to hear from you. How are you and Sarah?"

"Frisky as teenagers," he said. "Barbara, I haven't had a chance to congratulate you and Brett on your upcoming ownership of the Folsby Press. What a wonderful opportunity for you!"

"Isn't it?" she agreed. "Of course we were saddened to learn Daddy is giving up the company—it means so much to him, you know—but we're excited at the prospect of managing such a vital business and helping it grow. It's an awesome responsibility."

"It certainly is," Hampton said warmly. "And I'd like to talk to you about it."

Brief pause. "To me?" she asked. "Or Brett and me?"

"Just you," he said. "Is there any chance of your visiting me tonight at my home?"

"Judge, is there anything specific you want to discuss?"

"A matter of some importance," he said dryly. "Your future."

She tried to conceal her surprise with a light laugh. "My favorite subject," she said. "I have a dinner date tonight and then I'll have to go home and change. Will ten o'clock be too late for you?"

"Not at all," he assured her. "Ten is fine. See you then."

The Judge spent the remainder of the day planning the meeting. He instructed Sarah to greet Barbara at the outside door but then send her up to Hampton's study by herself.

"Tell her you're busy working on your accounts," he suggested, "or give her some other excuse. She must understand her talk with me will be private. No one will be a witness to what we say and what is promised."

"Do you really think this is going to work?" Sarah asked anxiously.

"I'm certain of it," he said. "Deals are easy to make when both parties believe they are benefiting. Barbara is a very intelligent, shrewd woman with a good head for business and a keen sense of her own self-interest. But I doubt if it will occur to her to question my probity. I'm counting on her believing I am an honorable man incapable of deceit—a dangerous assumption several people in my past have had cause to regret."

Hampton then selected his wardrobe for the evening's performance. He decided on a three-piece suit of black tropical worsted, white shirt, subdued maroon cravat, white pocket handkerchief. It was a conservative costume calculated to impress Barbara with his gravitas. All he lacked, he thought mordantly, was a judge's robe.

He also spent time mentally rehearsing his arguments. He knew what he wanted to say; the sequence of his speech was just as important as the content. It was crucial to grasp and hold Barbara's attention from the start. He would then endeavor to keep her unsettled and on edge until the final decision. First the picador, then the matador going in for the kill.

He waited, sitting impassively behind his desk until shortly after ten o'clock when there was a brisk rap at the study door. "Come in," he called and rose to his feet with the aid of his cane. Barbara Folsby entered and paused to close the door behind her.

Then she hurried to his side, squeezed his free hand, gave him a melting smile, put her cheek next to his.

"So good to see you again, Judge," she said. "It's been a long time."

"Too long," he agreed. "My, don't you look marvelous!"

She was wearing brief blue denim cutoffs with a thin pink jersey tank top. Bare legs, shoulders, and arms were honey-tanned. Naked flesh looked warm and firm, skin smooth and unwrinkled, breasts and thighs as tight as a girl's.

The Judge had no doubt she had dressed as calculatingly as he. She used her beauty as a weapon just as he used his age. And he admitted to himself his advanced years were not a complete defense against her ripe physicality.

He had her sit in the armchair alongside his desk rather than the couch across the room. He asked if she'd care for a drink, but she politely declined.

"Barbara," he said, "this meeting will be between just the two of us. No witnesses. No tape recordings. I ask you to treat it as an intimate and confidential dialogue of no concern to anyone else."

"Of course," she said, impressed by his solemnity.

"I'll try to be brief. Since your mother's death your father and I have become close friends, much closer than before Constance's passing. I provided what solace I could and he has consulted me frequently, especially after he decided on his solo voyage around the world and his surrendering the ownership of the Folsby Press."

"Did you try to talk him out of it?" she asked curiously.

"I did not," Hampton said. "Surely you know when Emmet sets his mind on a course of action it is difficult if not impossible to dissuade him."

"Yes, that's true," she said, and he thought he detected a note of relief in her voice. "You're right."

"A few weeks ago he gave me the first draft of a legal document conveying the ownership of the Folsby Press to you and Brett. He asked me to review it for legality and make any suggestions for changes I thought might be useful. Here it is..."

Hampton opened his top desk drawer and withdrew a thick legal document bound in a blue cover. He displayed it to Barbara for a moment before replacing it in the drawer.

"I thought the conveyance was suitable and needed no revisions. My only objection was that nowhere was it stated what portion of Emmet's shares was to go to you and what portion to Brett. I presume you and your brother reckon you will each receive half."

She stared at him, perplexed. He thought the years had treated her kindly. Her features had fined down but retained a classic beauty. How old was she now? Thirty-nine? Perhaps she had become more handsome than pretty, but her attractiveness was increased thereby.

"Yes," she said, her voice faltering. "Brett and I thought we'd each receive five thousand shares."

"I assumed the same thing," the Judge said. "We were all mistaken. In a long conversation just last night Emmet declared his intention not, repeat *not,* to divide ownership of the Folsby Press equally between you and your brother. One of you shall be given a majority of the shares, making the recipient the de facto owner of the company with all the powers an owner possesses and may exercise at his or her discretion."

"But *why?*" Barbara cried wildly. "Why is he doing this?"

"He presented very cogent reasons for his decision," the Judge went on. "Obviously he had pondered the matter a long time, and I was unable to refute him. First of all, he feels divided ownership would result in differences of opinion between you and your brother and squabbles which would have a damaging effect on the prosperity and growth of the Folsby Press. Emmet is a man who believes in a strong hand at the helm, of a boat and a business. There cannot be, he says, a clash of wills, which might result in the endangerment or loss of boat or business. He believes divided ownership simply would not work."

"We could make it work," she said desperately. "We could—"

Hampton held up a hand to stop her. "Your father is also aware of the animosity between you and your brother. It only compounds his

327

fears of divided ownership and the harm it might do to the company. Barbara, forgive an old man's curiosity, but what is the reason for the hostility between you and Brett?"

She shrugged. "No reason. No sibling rivalry or a traumatic event when we were kids. It just *is.*"

Hampton sighed. "It sometimes happens. Unfathomable. And a pity."

She drew a deep breath and lifted her chin. She looked at him steadily. "So Brett is to become my boss," she said flatly. "Is that what you want to tell me?"

"Not at all," the Judge said smoothly. "Emmet, having made the decision to avoid an ownership equally shared between you and your brother, is now faced with the quandary of deciding which of his children should receive a majority of his shares and so take control of the Folsby Press."

She made no attempt to hide her shock. "You mean he has not yet decided?"

"He has not. He presented to me arguments why each of you should be favored. Brett is the senior, a married man who has provided Emmet with a delightful grandson he dearly loves. But you, Emmet believes, are superior to your brother in business skills and knowledge of how the company works. His choice will be an extremely painful one, no matter which way it goes, and he has asked me for my advice and recommendation, hoping my opinion will help him decide."

"You mean he's leaving it up to you?"

"Of course not! Barbara, you know your father better than that. No one can dictate to him what he should or should not do. But he is eager to learn my views, and I honestly believe they will be the deciding factor."

She looked at him a long time with narrowed eyes. Her lips were pressed tight, her jaw hardened. Hampton understood then what her father had meant when he referred to her occasional ruthlessness.

"And what is your opinion, Judge?" she asked in a voice which grated slightly.

"It depends," he said.

"On what?"

"Not on what but on whom. And the whom is you. Let me explain. It concerns Noah Demijohn."

Her expression didn't change, and he wondered if she played poker. If so she'd be a formidable opponent.

He delivered a short synopsis of Noah's career and what he, Hampton, had done to further it: Harvard, law school, a job with a prestigious legal firm, and introduction to the Massachusetts power elite.

"Noah has performed brilliantly," he told Barbara. "He now has statewide name recognition and will soon be known nationally when his project for small, low-interest loans to hopeful entrepreneurs becomes a countrywide program. He has won an enthusiastic following of both whites and blacks.

The political parties are courting him. There is talk of his running for public office. I truly believe he is destined for success."

"Judge, I've been aware for some time of what you've just told me. But what does Noah's career have to do with your decision on control of the Folsby Press?"

He drummed his fingertips a moment on the desktop, then drew a deep breath. "There is one thing which could seriously damage or perhaps derail his progress. It would happen if it becomes generally known he has a white mistress. You."

She did not scream "How dare you!" She did not demand "How did you find out?" She did not waste time on tearful denials. She went immediately to the question most important to her—and the Judge admired her pragmatism.

"Does my father know?" she asked.

"Not to my knowledge," Hampton said.

"I think I'll have that drink now," Barbara Folsby said. "If I may."

"Of course. There's cognac on the sideboard. Please pour drinks for both of us."

When they were resettled, had raised glasses to each other in a silent toast and sipped, she said, "Judge, why are you so concerned about Noah's career and his political future?"

"I saw his potential when he first came here to live and I resolved to do all I could to help him, to open for him doors which would not ordinarily be unlocked for a poor black boy.

But I would be less than honest if I claimed altruism as my sole motive. What I have done and will continue to do for Noah is partly for my private aggrandizement. It has kept me active in my old age and given me the illusion of power. I have never, *never* attempted to take credit for Noah's success or even let it be known publicly how much I contributed to it. But his triumph is my triumph. Up to this moment only his mother and I have known it."

"And now you're afraid I'll destroy all your work?" she said.

"All my hopes and dreams," he corrected.

"Judge, I really don't feel the relationship I have with Noah is all that awful. We are, after all, two mature consenting adults."

Her comments angered him. He made a brushing away gesture of his hand. "Let's not get into the morality of the situation," he said, his voice tight. "Morality is irrelevant. If he were a garage mechanic, movie actor, or even corporate attorney, no one would give a tinker's damn if he kept a harem of white women. But Noah is a politician intending to run for elective office and if his affair with you were made public via tabloid journalism the fallout would be horrendous. I'd guess he'd lose most of the blacks—and particularly black women—and alienate many white voters who are now sympathetic to his goals. Barbara, I assure you the American electorate is not yet ready to accept interracial marriages or liaisons amongst their political leaders. Don't bother telling me it's a racial, hypocritical attitude. Of course it is. But it exists, and any political hopeful who ignores it is a fool."

Barbara was silent a long time, staring down at her brandy glass and turning it slowly in her long, graceful fingers. Finally she looked up at the Judge.

"So what you're about to suggest," she said, "is that I end my affair with Noah. In return you will promise to do your best to convince my father to give me the lion's share of the Folsby Press."

Hampton smiled. "Exactly! Barbara, you are one of the most intelligent women—no, one of the most intelligent individuals—I have ever met. Not only are you well educated, but you have a very profound and practical knowledge of how the world works. I would be completely honest in telling your father he need have no fear for the company's continuing prosperity under your control. You really are remarkably astute."

(The Judge believed flattery must be excessive to be successful. Moderate flattery was no flattery at all.)

"And if I reject your suggestion?" Barbara asked, ignoring Hampton's praise.

His smile lost its warmth. "Then I will make no recommendation to Emmet either way, and you must gamble he will select you rather than your brother as his successor."

She hesitated and he knew she was fearful he might not remain neutral if she spurned his offer.

"All right," she said suddenly, "I'll break off with Noah. But I should warn you, Judge, if I do not receive a majority of Emmet's shares and find myself working for my brother, I shall probably take up with Noah again. And believe me, I am capable of doing exactly that."

"I wouldn't doubt it for a moment. You drive a hard bargain."

"I've learned how."

"Your reaction to my failure would be understandable."

"And acceptable?"

"Would I have a choice?" he asked and she laughed. "Barbara, how soon will you be able to speak to Noah?"

Her reply came swiftly. "And hand him his Dear John? I can fake a business meeting in Boston and fly up there tomorrow or Wednesday. I like to get unpleasant things over with as soon as I can."

"May I ask you a personal question? Was there ever any possibility of your marrying Noah?"

"None whatsoever," she said and finished her drink.

She rose to leave and he marveled at the silky way she moved, not crudely seductive but sensuality incarnate.

At the door she paused to shake his hand vigorously. "It's been a pleasure doing business with you, Judge," she said with a brilliant smile.

When she was gone, the door closed behind

her, Seth Parnell Hampton cast his eyes upward.

"Thank you, God," he said piously.

6

SUCH SWEET SORROW...

A few years previously Noah Demijohn had written to Judge Hampton as follows:

"You'll recall some time ago we had a discussion as to whether politics should be called a science, art or craft. I now believe it should be termed a technology!"

Noah then went on to list and describe some of the methods and techniques used in modern electioneering: polling by phone, focus and dial groups; advertising; radio and TV commercials; the Internet; telemarketing; radio and TV talk shows; negative advertising; spin control; press conferences and one-on-one interviews; and of course the arcane practices of fund-raising.

"Whatever happened to torchlight parades?" he lamented.

He admitted to the Judge the purpose of this increasingly complex and expensive methodology was to create a public persona with a better chance of being elected than the actual candidate.

"The image is everything," Noah wrote. "It is the age of perception politics, and if you wish to win public office you must learn to dress and speak in an inoffensive manner and espouse only those views favored by the voters. Politicians follow; statesmen lead."

Noah confessed he himself had surrendered to the power of hype. He had wanted to leave his cramped Cambridge apartment and move to a new, luxurious co-op "within bragging distance of Beacon Hill." He could easily afford it but feared how the description of such a lush dwelling would resonate in an interview during which he pleaded the cause of the needy. It would help his image, he decided, if the media could report on the modest walk-up flat he presently rented. And so he didn't move.

"Not that I live in squalor," he assured the Judge. "I have had the place painted and carpeted. An air conditioner has been installed. Plain and simple furniture has been purchased from Crate & Barrel. It is really quite comfortable, adequate for my needs, and still qualifying as 'modest' in newspaper articles."

It was in this refurbished apartment that Noah Demijohn and Barbara Folsby met in the late afternoon of August 23, 1995. She had phoned the previous day and told him she was flying to Boston on Wednesday for a business meeting. She would be unable to have dinner with him but hoped to see him, even briefly. They agreed to meet in Cambridge at five o'clock.

"I won't be able to stay," she informed him. "I must get back to Florida tomorrow night. But we'll have time for a talk."

He assumed she meant it would be a sexless assignation, but he was not completely disheartened. They had trysts in the past planned to be "talks," which had evolved into quick and fervid mini-orgies. So he chilled a bottle of sparkling wine and when she arrived he greeted her with a hungry embrace from which she extricated herself with some difficulty.

"Ah," he said, "we're in an aloof mood, are we?"

"Aloof?" she said. "I don't think so. Just thoughtful and perhaps a little nervous."

"How about a glass of wine to calm your nerves?"

"No, thank you. Noah, I'm on edge because I have something important to tell you and I'm hoping I can depend on your goodwill and understanding. I'm getting married."

He froze, staring at her. "I think *I* need a drink," he said. He swigged directly from the bottle and some of the wine spilled down his chin. He wiped it away with the back of his hand.

"I didn't want to write," Barbara continued, "or use the phone. This is not easy, but I had to tell you personally. I owed you that."

"You don't owe me anything," he said thickly. "Getting married, huh? To whom?"

"Oliver Pendragon."

"Pendragon? That racist!"

"Noah, how can you say such a thing? Oliver hasn't a racist bone in his body. He's never uttered or written a word which could be interpreted as racist."

"Of course he hasn't. Because he knows what a controversy it would cause and how he'd be criticized. It would mean the end of his grants from the government and private foundations. But all his work and opinions imply racism. He says everything is genetically determined. That includes intelligence, doesn't it? Of course it does. And it's just one small step away from trying to prove blacks are genetically inferior mentally. The man's a charlatan!"

"My God, Noah, since when have you had a ghetto complex?"

"I don't, but I can recognize racism, overt or hidden. You're making a terrible mistake, Barbara."

"I think not," she said evenly. "Oliver has many fine qualities. And we share many interests."

"Like those porn videos you told me he watches?"

"Don't be gross. Noah, I had hoped you'd be happy for me and wish me well."

"I am and I do. I just don't like your choice. Do you plan to be faithful to him?"

"What a ridiculous question! Of course I'll be faithful. It's part of being married, isn't it?"

He gave her a lupine grin. "Not always. So what it comes down to is you're giving me the broom—right?"

"I told you it's not easy," she said in a low voice. "We had some wonderful times together."

"We did," he agreed. "And you're certain you want them to end, married or not?"

"I'm certain."

He took another gulp from the wine bottle. "I knew it would happen, knew from the start that someday you'd dump me."

"It's not the end of the world, you know. You still have Patricia, don't you?"

"Priscilla. And I don't *have* her. She's her own woman."

"But you do see her?"

"Occasionally."

"Marry her, Noah. Be happy and forget me."

He looked at her searchingly. "I *will* forget you. It may take time, but eventually you'll be gone."

"Not much of a compliment."

"I told you it may take time. You'll forget me the minute you walk out the door. You're a hard woman, Barbara."

"Only as hard as I must be."

"Must be? Why?"

"To be my own woman. Like your Priscilla. I think I better go now; I have a plane to catch. Noah, I'm going to follow your career with great interest. I wish you the best of luck."

He was silent.

"Aren't you going to wish me luck?" she said.

"No," he said. "I'm going to wish Oliver Pendragon luck. You've got something better."

"What?" she said.

"Balls," he told her, and she whirled and left him alone and laughing. He didn't begin weeping until the door was shut.

She had hired a chauffeured limo at the airport. It was now parked in front of Noah's tenement. The driver, a tall, mournful Asian, climbed out and opened the door for her. She instructed him to drive back to Logan.

There was a small typewritten note taped to the back of the driver's seat: "Thank you for not smoking."

"Do you have a cigarette?" she asked the chauffeur.

"No, ma'am," he said, "I do not."

She didn't smoke, had never smoked in her life. But if he had given her a cigarette and a light she would have tried it—all because of the smarmy notice. Sometimes her own behavior puzzled her.

She took out her Filofax but didn't open it. Instead she thought about her parting from Noah and decided it had gone well. She had not expected physical violence, but she had anticipated a messy and emotional confrontation.

He had accepted unquestioningly her lie about an impending marriage. Other than accusing Oliver of racism, his objections to his dismissal seemed tepid to her. She was surprised and not a little chagrined by his mild reaction. She wondered if in his professional career he had the fire and drive to achieve the destiny Judge Hampton had envisioned for him.

She had time for a grasshopper before boarding the shuttle. The drink enlivened her and she began to imagine what she might accomplish when she became honcho of the

Folsby Press. Consumer magazines had always interested her, and she thought it possible she might dare an entry into that competitive field.

On the flight back to New York she was seated next to a man she judged to be in his middle forties. He wore a wedding band and carried a laptop computer. He was dressed casually in snug chinos and a blue golf jacket. His hair was a warm brown but his neatly trimmed beard was grizzled.

When the plane was aloft he turned to Barbara and said, "Joy."

She was about to say, "I beg your pardon," then caught his meaning and laughed. "Yes," she said, "I am wearing Joy. Not many men can identify perfumes."

"My wife's in the business," he explained. "Designs perfume departments for stores, recommends brands, trains the salesclerks. She's always bringing work home, which is how I learned to tell Chanel No. 5 from Arpege. My name is William Leverett and I prefer Will to Bill."

"I'm Barbara Folsby," she said, "and I prefer anything to Barbie."

"Understandable," he said, and after a few moments of chitchat they exchanged business cards.

"I know the Folsby Press of course," he said. "We get your magazine on teleconferencing hardware."

"And what exactly is Technodot?" she asked, scanning his card.

"Consultants on the purchase and installation of computer and communication systems. We design original networks or make recommendations on upgrading."

"We've got a horse-and-buggy setup," she confessed. "Eleven scattered offices, domestic and overseas, and we still write letters or use the phone and fax. There has to be a better way."

"There is," he assured her. "Instant communication throughout your organization with state-of-the-art security."

"Would you be willing to send someone down to Boca Raton, examine our equipment, and make suggestions? We'd pay for an evaluation and proposal of course."

"I won't send someone down to Boca Raton," he said, grinning, "I'll come myself. I've never been to Florida."

"You'll like it," she told him. "Providing a hurricane doesn't intrude. How soon can you come?"

"Let me check the schedule at the office and call you tomorrow. May I do that?"

"Of course. The sooner the better."

"That's the way I feel about it," Will Leverett said, looking at her.

In the terminal he asked if he might buy her a drink, but she told him she had to catch a flight to Palm Beach. They shook hands and he vowed again to phone her the next day. He gave her a wide smile and walked away. His chinos, she noted, were obviously and rousingly tight.

"Mr. Buns," she said to herself, laughed, and decided at that instant she really would marry Oliver Pendragon. Then she enplaned and flew southward to what she was certain would be a wondrous future.

7

FAMILY VALUES...

After his wife's death Emmet Folsby had the sickroom emptied out. Everything went to charities: hospital bed, radio, TV set, furniture, area rug, even the curtains and drapes. Even Constance's clothing. All vanished.

The sickroom was left stripped and desolate. Since he was giving the house to his children Emmet felt no need to redecorate; let them use the chamber as they wished. Meanwhile the windows were dulled by salt-laden winds, the parquet floor lost its luster, the air itself seemed tarnished.

It was in this barren room that father, son, and daughter assembled on the evening of Friday, September 8. Emmet had selected it for their meeting simply because there were no chairs; he hoped standing would help shorten a family gathering he feared might become rancorous.

It had rained fitfully during the day. The showers had ceased but the night sky remained overcast, muffled with billowy clouds occasionally brightened by flashes of distant lightning. Within the lifeless room the only illumination came from a small crystal chandelier in need of dusting. The three stood directly beneath this antique fixture. They formed an isosceles triangle with Emmet at its head.

He reiterated his intention of giving them ten thousand shares of Folsby Press stock. He told them the legal documents had been completed; the conveyance would take effect on November 24, the day following Thanksgiving. Similarly, ownership of his home would then be transferred to them, to be shared equally. It was also the date on which he planned to leave on his voyage.

As his children listened in expressionless silence Emmet said his initial resolve had been to divide the ownership of the Folsby Press equally between the two of them. But long and difficult reflection had caused him to revise that plan.

"I'm not sure," he went on, "you fully understand how much the company means to me. Your mother and I worked very hard, made many sacrifices, took horrendous financial risks to build the Folsby Press into the successful business enterprise it is today. Although I am relinquishing ownership, the future of the company is important to me. I want it to flourish and remain profitable. I am not surrendering control to see it wither and fail."

To avoid that, he continued, he had concluded equally divided ownership was impractical. The Folsby Press required a single firm hand at the helm. Every successful business did. Divided responsibilities, duties, and powers were a recipe for squabbling and failure.

When both Barbara and Brett seemed about to speak, their father held up a palm to stop them.

He also, he informed them, knew of the ill will existing between them, a hostility dating from their childhood.

"I don't know the reason for it," he said sorrowfully, "and don't wish to know. Your mother sought to deny it, but she was as conscious of your enmity as I. It was a cause of sadness for both of us. Now your antagonism becomes another factor in my deciding equally divided ownership wouldn't work."

He then repeated the praise of each he had expressed to Judge Hampton. He assured them both of his undying love and asked them to put aside their animosity and to devote all their energies to the continued prosperity of the company.

He then announced he was giving six thousand shares to Barbara, four thousand to Brett.

"My decision is final," he said.

"Thank you, Father," Barbara said primly.

"What?" Brett shouted, not believing. "What? Why? Why are you doing this?"

"For reasons I have already stated," Emmet said tonelessly. "Barbara is more knowledgeable about the business than you. She is better qualified to oversee the progress of the company."

"It's not fair!" his son cried, face stuffed with rage. "I've worked as hard as she. I've—"

"I'm fully aware of the contributions you've made to the success of the Folsby Press," his father said. "And I hope you will continue to contribute for many years to come. But I must do what I think is best for the business."

"It's not best!" Brett almost screamed. "A woman can't boss a company as big as ours. She'll be laughed at, disobeyed, or just ignored while everyone does as they please. And the competition will clobber her!"

"I don't think so," Barbara said evenly. "No one is going to clobber me."

"It's not right!" Brett yelled at Emmet. "I'm not even sure it's legal. I'll soon find out."

"Are you threatening me?" Emmet asked quietly.

"No, I'm not threatening you. But I think you're making a horrible mistake."

"I'm doing what I think best," Emmet repeated. "I'm sorry you feel injured. The company comes first."

"Oh, screw the company!" Brett said wrathfully.

His father looked at him steadily. "You have just confirmed the wisdom of my choice," he said. "I had hoped we all might have a rational discussion of the future of the Folsby Press, but obviously this is not the time or place."

He stalked out of the room, leaving his son and daughter facing each other.

"Bitch!" Brett snarled at her.

"I'm sorry," she said.

"No, you're not."

"No," she agreed, "I'm not."

"I refuse to work for you," he grated. "I won't do it—ever."

"Resign?" she said. "What will you do? How will you live?"

"Why should you care?"

"Of course I care. I'm not a monster, you know."

"You could have fooled me," he said.

She stared at him thoughtfully. "There is a solution," she said. "After Father leaves on his trip, let me buy you out. Out of the company and out of this house. We can work a deal. It'll put money in your pocket and perhaps guarantee you an annual income for X number of years."

"God bless the queen," he said. "You'll have it all."

She shrugged. "Think about it, Brett. It might be best for both of us."

"But better for you."

"Take the money and run," she advised. "You said you'll be unhappy with me in charge. This way you'll be independent."

He moved to the door. "I'll think about it, Barbie," he said. "Right now I'm going to get bombed."

"Naturally," she said.

Seething with bitterness and resentment he fled to Simon Smithson. She went to her bedroom, savoring her triumph. Meanwhile,

Emmet Folsby had retired to his study and was trying to disremember the nasty scene with his children by selecting those books from his library he intended to take with him on his voyage.

But he found he could not concentrate on whether to choose *Tom Jones* or *Roderick Random*—or both. Instead, his thoughts locked onto his own actions and motives in the division of his estate.

It was true, as he had said, Barbara was better qualified than Brett to lead the Folsby Press into the twenty-first century. But were management skills the only reason he had favored her over her brother?

He strove, as always, to be absolutely honest with himself. And the fear lurked he might have rewarded Barbara partly or wholly in gratitude for the many years of physical pleasure she had provided.

Was he logically appointing the more eligible of his offspring to head the business or was he deluding himself and actually, as an honorable man, repaying a sexual debt?

He despaired of finding a quick and neat answer to that conundrum. He could only hope he would learn more about himself during his lonely quest at sea.

8

THE ARGONAUT'S
FAREWELL...

"Do you really like the cap, Grandpa?" asked Anthony Scott Folsby.

"Of course I do," Emmet said. "It's a most excellent cap."

"I bought it with my own money."

"I know you did, and I thank you for it."

"I picked it out because it says Captain on the front and it's got gold braid."

"It's very handsome," Emmet said, adjusting the brim, "and a perfect fit."

"It looks okay," Tony said. "How long will you be gone, Grandpa?"

"I don't know exactly."

"You won't get killed, will you?"

"I don't know that either."

"I wish I was going with you."

Emmet leaned and took the boy into his arms. "I wish you were too."

"Will you write me letters?"

"I will if you promise to do everything your parents tell you, study hard, and grow up big and strong."

"It's a deal," Anthony said.

Emmet laughed and stroked the lad's fine golden hair. "Now let's go ashore," he said. "I've got to say goodbye to everyone and get under way. I want to catch the tide."

He kissed Tony's cheek before loosening his

embrace. Then the two jumped down onto the dock. They had come aboard the yacht to start the engines gargling quietly. Now they joined the people on the swath of lawn between dock and highway.

It was a braw day. A few marshmallow clouds sailed across a periwinkle sky. A mild breeze scarcely ruffled the sea. The titian sun was strong, but the air remained cool enough for sweaters and jackets. Fishing boats were out in force and someone said the blues were running.

"I don't think he'll come back," Brett said to his wife.

"Why do you say that?" Zenobia asked.

"Just a feeling I have."

"If he doesn't return, Tony will be heartbroken."

"He's young," Brett said. "He'll forget. I won't."

"You've got to get over it," she told him. "You love your father; you know you do."

He looked at her. "I don't have that much love," he said. "And what I have belongs to you, Anthony, Simon, and Zoe. I have none left for my father or sister."

"Love is inexhaustible," she said sententiously.

"Garbage," Brett said. "When are we seeing the bank about the Palm Beach restaurant?"

"Monday afternoon."

"We'll stall them until my deal with Barbara is finalized. We may not need a loan."

"That would be nice," Zenobia said.

A few neighbors wandered up and Emmet

349

chatted with them awhile, shaking hands with the men, kissing the women's cheeks. He received a few going-away gifts: a bottle of brandy, a volume of Kipling's verse, a package of Dramamine, which made everyone laugh.

"I don't see why you can't tell him," Oliver Pendragon said crossly to Barbara.

"I've told you, Ollie," she said, hiding her exasperation. "He'd insist on postponing his trip to be here for the wedding. I can't let him do that. We'll announce it and have the ceremony while he's gone."

"It doesn't seem right," he said fretfully. "Who will give you away—your brother?"

"He'd love to give me away," Barbara said.

Emmet kissed Sarah and leaned down to hug Judge Hampton, who was sitting on a small folding stool.

"Goodbye, old friends," Emmet said. "Stay well. I hope to see you again someday."

"Make it soon," Hampton said. "Don't take foolish risks and write when you have the opportunity."

Emmet left them and Sarah said, "He's not coming back."

"How do you know?"

"He doesn't *want* to come back," she said. "He wants a new life."

"He'll never escape the old," the Judge said. "Hello, Barbara. Come to bid the sailor farewell?"

"Judge," she said, "I haven't had the chance to thank you personally for your efforts on my behalf."

"I did all I could," he said modestly. "I'm happy our deal ended successfully for you."

Sarah looked at him with admiration, thinking Sweet Daddy was really a piece of work.

"And for Noah, too," Barbara said, glancing to where he stood talking to Priscilla Johnson.

"They came down for the Thanksgiving weekend," the Judge said. "A delightful couple."

"Do you think they'll marry?"

"I hope so," Sarah said. "Noah needs a good woman."

Barbara smiled serenely and moved back to Oliver, taking his arm.

"When can we inspect the house?" he asked. "After your father leaves?"

"Can't," she said. "I've got to get back to the office this afternoon. We have a computer expert down from New York checking out the new hardware he installed. I want to make certain there are no glitches."

"Why are you smiling?" Pendragon said.

"Thinking of the computer consultant. He's a funny man. Always telling jokes."

It was true; Mr. Buns *was* amusing. He had also proved to be an ardent and imaginative lover when Barbara spent quality time in his motel suite.

"We'll have dinner tonight," she told Oliver, "and then go over the house and decide what changes we want to make."

"We'll be so happy," he said, sighing. "I can't believe it's happening to me."

"You deserve it," she said, patting his hand.

Emmet wanted to embrace his son, but Brett stood so stiffly his father had to be content with a brief, cold handshake. But Zenobia hugged him tightly, her tears wetting his cheek.

"Take care of yourself," she said in a choky voice. "And come back to us soon."

"Be well," Emmet said as lightly as he could. "And don't let Anthony forget me. I'll write—to you and the boy."

"Yes. Please. As often as you can. I'll pray for you."

"Thank you," he said.

Then he and Barbara stood close, gripping each other's arms.

"You come back," she whispered, "and we'll take up where we left off."

He tried to smile. "It's a deal," he said. "Goodbye, darling. Be happy."

"I intend to," she said. " 'Thank you' doesn't cut it, Em. I owe you everything."

"No, you don't," he said. "You did it all. By yourself."

Tears came to her eyes. She kissed him and turned away.

He waved—a wide gesture encompassing them all. He jumped aboard the yacht and climbed to the flying bridge. Barbara went to the forward bollard, Brett and Anthony to the aft.

"Cast off!" Emmet shouted down.

They freed the lines and tossed them to the main deck. The boat was heading northward. Emmet made a wide turn toward the Inlet. They all saw *Folsby's Spirit* painted clearly on the transom.

Shrill cries—"Goodbye! Goodbye! Goodbye!"—echoed across the Waterway and many waved as the *Spirit* moved slowly toward the wide ocean and beyond. Emmet tipped his cap gravely to family, friends, neighbors.

Then he was gone and they all dispersed, returned to their homes, and got on with the business of living.